The Eternal Gateway:

Requiem

By SB Jones

This is a work of fiction. All the characters and events portrayed in this book are either the products of the author's imagination or are used fictitiously.

The Eternal Gateway: Requiem

Copyright 2011 by SBJones Publishing

Published by SBJones Publishing

Cover by: Van Noy Studios, Tay the Model

Edited by: Carolyn Johnson, Elizabeth Elison

ISBN: 978-0-9836818-2-3

www.TheEternalGateway.com

Prologue

"Duke Falconcrest, your request to leave the Mage Council has been denied," boomed a robed figure among many in a circle surrounding him. The council chamber was brightly lit by both magical and mechanical sources of light. Duke stood center as the council announced its decision to the young mage's request to leave the service of the mage council and army. "Your actions, leadership and bravery during the War of Antiquities have not gone unnoticed by this council."

"Then I choose exile," replied Duke Falconcrest.

"An impossible request. No mage of your power can leave the watch of this council. Your abilities as a mage have not been seen for millennia," echoed throughout the chamber.

"I have created a mark of silence, which will allow the council to free its mind of any responsibilities it would have over a rogue mage. Once placed, it will bind all magic from the user. I have also placed binding runes as well so that only members of this council can remove the mark. Thus anyone the binding is placed upon will be unable to wield magic," declared Duke. A low murmuring grew in parts of the chamber. A magical binding would be both a curse and a blessing for the Council. No longer would rogue mages who have little magical powers be required to stay in the Council's keep. Criminal mages could safely be kept away with no risk of their powers harming the innocent. However, a binding this powerful could also incapacitate leaders and members of the council.

"The council hereby reserves the right to revoke your exile at any time it sees fit. The mark of silence will be placed upon you." As Duke Falconcrest places his hands on the dais in front of him, the remaining council members start the ceremony. Runes are wrapped around Duke's wrists and neck. The multi-colored runes of power flare and seal the mark of silence in place. Slowly the runes fade and vanish from view. Some of the council members leave, others stay and giving parting words of fortune and luck on the future Duke has chosen for himself.

Chapter 1

Xavier Ross stood on top of the tallest building bordering between the upper class area, the transport loading docks near the river and massive train systems that stretched between the great cities. The night sky was obscured by thick low clouds that would be tomorrow's fog when the temperature cooled. The light from the oil powered city lamps lit the bottom of the clouds and cast a faint glow across the cityscape. Xavier paced from one corner of the roof to the other. Things were bad in the world. The largest city state to the north had its government overthrown and replaced, rumor had, by Therion of the disbanded Mage Council. The clockwork factories there were creating new weapons of war as fast as materials could be fed into them.

Technology had been eroding away at the aristocratic rule of the magic users. Steam power, alchemy and clockwork creations allowed anyone to travel quickly, light up the dark, and even fly. A person did not require a magical lineage and years of study to create fire at their fingertips. A little coin to grease the wheels and anyone could get their hands on one of the new inventions of the alchemists.

The whipping sounds of the wind alerted Xavier to the arrival of the person he had been waiting for. Standing quickly from one knee was a woman unlike any other in the world. Her dark red hair, pale white skin and almond shaped eyes had not been seen for a thousand years. An extinct race: the Keratins. An off shoot of man? Possibly, but they had been hunted, killed in great wars, even bred out of existence. Only legends remained now and her method of arrival confirmed that Keratins had the ability to fly. It wasn't magic or technology. It was born to them. As easy to them as it was for Xavier to run or jump. Things were bad in the world indeed, if legends from forgotten times walked again.

"You are here, exactly as the Time Walker said you would be" stated the woman.

The Time Walker was another legend returned. He was the Guardian of the Eternal Gateway, stepping in and out of history at random.

"Of course I am. You must be Angela Atagi," retorted Xavier. "You're more than what I expected," eyeing the woman up and down with a smirk.

"I'm not here for your pleasure Xavier. What have you found out so far?"

Xavier shakes off a fake shiver. "Sassy too, I like that." As he takes a step closer, reaching into a pocket to find a match and cigarette. Xavier strikes the match. Angela's eyes take in the marred face of the man. Burn scars run from most of his scalp down the side of his face. The hand holding the lit cigarette to his mouth is textured like red wax. "What, am I not pretty enough for you?" as he mock tosses a clump of hair behind his ear.

"We are going to kill him," Angela whispers, "and many more along the way."

"War is dangerous now isn't it. Can't make an omelet without breaking some eggs!" Xavier shakes his head. "Aw, did the Guardian fill your head with stories of being chosen. That you're going to help save the world." The mocking tone ends. "Well snap out of it!" he shouted. "You were handpicked by The Guardian from a world that no longer exists. You're here to play some part in this mess, a tool and nothing more!" Xavier's scolding is cut short by Angela with a backhand across his scarred face.

"Speak to me like that again, and your first flying lesson starts here off this rooftop."

Smiling, Xavier wipes a drop of blood from the corner of his mouth. "Fine, our world's savior, the Chosen One, might live in a small village a day's travel to the east. That's as much as I have been able to find out so far." Xavier moves to the edge of the building to sit down for another cigarette as the last one was lost. "After the Mage Council was disbanded, most of the archives were sealed and few witnesses are still alive today that would even know what went on then."

"What about Therion?"

"Therion is now in control of the largest city on the planet to the north. With control of Courduff he now has a large enough power base to start conquering the neighboring cities and then the rest of the world." Xavier lifted his chin a bit and looked in the direction of the taken city. "However,

3

there is enough resistance from the larger, more independent city states that he will most likely start to tackle them from the inside. Promise people places of power in return to weaken or overthrow their own city and ally with him." Xavier finished by waving his hand across the view of the city below them.

"I do not like being here. The flying machines unsettle me." Angela points across the city at the different airships and dirigibles moving about the horizon. "Do you have the items the Time Walker promised?"

"Nothing but business for the Keratin, I see," said Xavier as he moved to retrieve a large case from the darker corner of the rooftop. Placing the case in better light he popped it open and spun it to face Angela. "Two Keratin war blades. The hilts had to be replaced and the blades have had indestructible runes placed on them so they will never need to be sharpened and they should never break."

Angela withdrew the blades from the case in front of her for closer inspection. The blades were most likely from a time earlier than Angela herself. The replaced hilts had balanced the blades to near perfection and the runes to keep them forever sharp were etched down both sides. "And the bow?"

Xavier turned away again and returned with a simple short bow. "I expected more, but it's what you requested. There are arrows for it under the blades." He watched as she strapped the blades across her lower back and slung the bow to a secure fit.

The explosion lifted both Xavier and Angela into the air. Stunned and rolling onto her back, Angela watched as the dark low clouds swirled out of the way as the airship descended. The explosion left a ringing in her ears that deafened the sound of the giant fan blades that maneuvered the airship over the building. Ropes dropped down and with them men. Bright lights from underneath the vessel lit up the rooftop. Shielding her eyes, Angela couldn't see Xavier Ross anywhere. He was not her concern any more. She had the items that would help her survive and find the Chosen One. They would also help keep her alive here in a moment, as four men dropped to the rooftop.

Shaking off the last bit of the static in her head, Angela got to her feet. Her hearing had a while to go before the ringing would stop. She caught a glimpse of Xavier going over the far side of the building down a fire escape. *Leave it to the burned rat to survive,* she thought.

The first man was dead before his feet landed on the rooftop, an arrow through the neck and out the other side. A second arrow was already in flight when a ball of bright energy shot down from the vessel above. The energy ball flashed out of existence and the arrow found its mark in a second man's chest.

"Well, well." Standing where the energy ball had landed was a short dark-skinned female. The new comer watched as her second man fell to his knees and died. "This simply will not do." With a wave of her hand the remaining two men ran to where Angela had seen Xavier disappear. "Alive if you can." Three more arrows flew from Angela's bow at the new comer as she sprinted to a bit of cover on the rooftop.

The dark-skinned lady spun and dodged to the side as the first arrow flew through the air where she previously stood. The second missed as well as she leaned away from its path and the third ricocheted off into the night as it hit an invisible barrier inches away from the her hand.   "This is going to be so much fun," the lady sung with delight. Blue energy flew from her outstretched hand and destroyed a good amount of cover Angela hid behind.

Angela scrambled to put more distance as well as anything solid between her and the mage. Magic users were not unknown to Angela and she had fought them in the past. But here in this new time who knew what they might be capable of after another thousand or more years of study and practice. "Come out, come out my pretty friend," cooed the woman. "We only want to talk to you."

Hearing the woman come around the side of the cover as she called out, Angela took one last glance at the rooftop and the airship above. Steeling herself she pressed hard and ran for the edge of the rooftop. The dark-skinned lady saw Angela as she emerged from the darkness sprinting to the edge of the building. Another beam of energy flew from the woman's hand. The rooftop burned and exploded behind Angela as the energy beam chased her. Angela could see the dark-skinned woman paralleling her to the edge of the rooftop while maintaining the magical energy that threatened to end her existence in a heartbeat. The new mage's idea of talk was clearly intended to be a one sided conversation.

Bastiana watched with wonder as she chased the red headed beauty to the edge of the rooftop. She stopped her magic just short of cutting Angela in half. Her prey dove over the edge of the building with bits of flame and shrapnel. She stopped at the edge of the roof to watch as Angela fell towards the ground far below. Her eyes shone with envy as she saw Angela's fall turn to flight as she sped up and away from the building. "Fly my little angel. Fly."

Angela could feel the heat from the mage's attack as she dived off of the building. The ground rushed towards her, but she held off as long as she could before controlling her fall to put as much distance between herself and the insanely powerful mage that wanted to kill her. Pulling her fall back to the sky and away from the rooftop, Angela rotated to look back at the flames and the dark-skinned woman standing on the roof's edge. It looked like the mage's eyes were filled with lust as Angela pressed hard to fly away from the scene. "The world here is crazy," Angela muttered to herself.

Bastiana stood a few more moments on the rooftop as she watched Angela fly further away into the city proper.

Her hand had found its way to her face and she lightly bit down on her finger to contain the ecstasy that flowed through her after the encounter with the Keratin. Stepping back, Bastiana concentrated and the ball of energy from before emerged from her center as she teleported herself back to the airship above. Flashing back into existence on the bridge of the airship a deep voice asked, "How did it go my dear?"

Turning to the center of the bridge where the voice came from. "I want it," replied Bastiana. She strode to the front view port of the Colossus and pointed out to where the Keratin was about to fly out of sight. "Will you get it for me?" she teased looking back.

Chapter 2

Xavier beat out the small bits of fire that dotted his clothing from the explosion as he raced as fast as he could down the fire escape. From the noise above it sounded like the Keratin had her hands full and if he didn't hurry his ass, they would bring the building down on top of him. Blood dripped from his nose as well as from cuts and scrapes on his hands and face. The explosion had tossed him like a kid throwing a doll across the room. Bright flecks of light still dotted his vision as he made his way to the street below in a controlled stumble.

Pausing to catch his breath and taking one last glance at the rooftop, an explosion casts light to the street below. The shock causes two men racing down the same fire escape to miss a step and Xavier sees his pursuers.

Spitting blood, "That stupid woman," Xavier cursed. "Can't do anyone a favor anymore, I hope she gets herself killed."

Xavier knew how to survive; he didn't pick this building as the meeting point without a backup plan. Running as fast as he could to a rubbish bin he pulled back a cloth to reveal a pair of clockwork bombs. Putting one into his pocket, he wound the timer of the second and set it back in the trash. Adrenalin helped clear his head as he ran to the end of the block as his pursuers reached the street floor. Moments later an explosion filled the street where Xavier had exited. Smoke and dust billowed out around the building as he ran. Slowing to a walk about a block and a half away from where the bomb went off, Xavier pulls out a bent cigarette and lights it.

Frustrated he kicks at some trash in the street and sends it scattering along with the rat that was cowering underneath it. "Damn it! This isn't how it's supposed to happen." Swinging his arms around and muttering like a madman he happens to look back in the direction he came. The two men after him step out of the smoke filled street and begin running towards him. Xavier paused mid-tantrum "Oh crap," and starts running.

Returning to the center command chair of the Colossus, Vincent gave the command to pursue Angela. Control engineers called into voice relay tubes to the engine rooms below. Workers moving fast pulled levers and applied breaks to the various systems of cables running throughout the massive airship that supplied power to the drive fans and navigation rudders. At the heart of the Colossus was a giant rune etched furnace. Inside contained a green fire that burned hot enough to melt iron. Long ago furnaces like this were used by master smiths with the aid of the Mage Council to forge weapons that would never break, or armor that was as light as cloth, but stronger than steel. Today only a small handful of rune furnaces exist, and even fewer who knew how to make them work.

Bastiana stood at the front of the bridge. Her eyes were unfocused as she called out to the crew behind her where Angela was flying. "She is staying low between the buildings," her arm pointed off to the east, "crossing the rail system and entering the business district." Divination was one of the rarest forms of magic. Bastiana had a gift for the Divining art, a skill that had not gone unnoticed by Vincent when he found the girl years ago. Her ability to locate his enemies had allowed him to build a powerful criminal empire. Once word reached Vincent of anyone trying to establish their own territory or enterprise that interfered with his, they met a swift end. The same end the Keratin they were chasing was about to receive.

"Increase altitude and cut her off," instructed Vincent. "Bastiana, my dear, take a couple of men and go to the forward deck. You will have your new toy shortly."

Focus returned to Bastiana's eyes as she sprinted to the lower decks to emerge on the front observation deck of the Colossus. The wind blew her short hair as light from the airship and city made it look like dancing dark flames. *A fitting look,* thought Vincent. It matches her youthful temper and the darker desires to have her own way, regardless of the cost.

Angela flew as fast as she could. Keeping low between the buildings made putting any significant distance between her and the insane mage difficult. Few streets in the city ran straight for any distance, however those same streets provided little cover from above and she knew she would be easily spotted by the airship. Staying to the back streets and alleys while changing directions every few blocks meant she would not be leaving the city anytime soon.

Passing over the river to the docks was going to be difficult she knew. Losing the cover of the buildings would leave her exposed to the airship she could hear behind her. However, if she kept low to the water, she might be able to sneak past. Taking a moment to fly to the tops of the buildings to see where her pursuers were was a mistake. The Colossus was less than two blocks away and headed right for her. "Damn, they can track me," cursed Angela. A spotlight from the airship swept across the building top where Angela had just been.

Angela flew towards the ground as fast as she could, letting gravity help her gain speed for her sprint across the wide slow river. The loading docks and massive train system there should allow for her to throw off any pursuers. The rail system has been charmed by mages to allow for fast safe travel to the various city states. They were also protected to make sure their cargo reached its destination. Many of the cars were also employed to ensure privacy. Large trade consortiums mandated these private rail cars to transport their alchemists and their inventions in secrecy to avoid espionage.

The air changed instantly as Angela crossed out of the city and over the water. Gone was the stale smell and the heat of the city, it was replaced with the cool crisp air that blew over the river. A beam of hot blinding light cut across her path and caused the river to protest violently as it erupted in flash boiled steam. Hot spray and the threat of being cut in half forced her to turn parallel to the river. A deep pair of thuds could be heard from the sky above and again the water in front of her exploded as the shells fired from the Colossus hit the water. Abandoning her attempt to cross the river, Angela flew back to the nearby shore to find cover amongst the buildings again.

Sitting in a passenger car as the train crossed a bridge to the dock, Xavier watched through the window at the battle over the river area. "Oh, nice," he approved as the magic cut into the river creating a wall of steam behind it. "She deserves it." Few others were on the train to witness the fighting. One man had clearly missed his stop and was asleep in his seat. Xavier had a new set of cigarettes and pair of gloves courtesy of him. The rest of the confrontation passed from view as the train made its way to the dock station.

"She's pulled back into the buildings there," pointed Bastiana.

"Bring us down and around. Let us see where she is hiding," ordered Vincent. The Colossus moved and hovered above the river. Deck men scanned the area with their spotlights and crew kept their eyes out ready to fire the cannons when ordered. One spotlight goes dark, its operator dead on the deck with an arrow embedded in his chest.

"There she is," delighted Bastiana. Her smile replaced with outrage as two more of the deck crew fell to Angela's deadly aim. "Enough games pretty girl." Blue orbs of magical energy begin to engulf her hands. "This will fetch you from your hidey hole." Twin orbs of light fly from her hands and spiral into the darkness of the buildings where the arrows were fired. The spell casts off sparks of energy that lick and burn the buildings as they pass. Explosions detonate where some of the larger bolts connect with building material. The spell has the desired effect Bastiana was looking for but not the results.

Angela did not want to be here. The Colossus had cut off her escape route the Time Walker told her to use if she ever got into trouble. The alley had dead ended and that left going forward through the Colossus or up over the buildings to be cut down by the crazy magic user as the only escape options. Her mission already failed before it even started. "If it is my fate to kill this mage for the Chosen One, then so be it." Drawing the Keratin war blades she sprints a few steps and launches towards the airship as magic orbs begin destroying the alley.

Angela in full flight shot out of the smoke and dust blasted up by the last spell. The twin war blades casting off sparks absorbed from some of the spell. Her clothing is torn in several places and burnt welts could be seen where some of the spell had connected. Several tiny cuts seep blood all along her left side from the shrapnel caused by the final explosion, and her entire right arm is bright red from the earlier vaporized water.

Her condition stuns Bastiana, "I'm so sorry."

Angela connected with a soldier stationed near the deck cannon. His body hit the deck sliced clean through the middle by the speed and force of the war blades. The rest of her momentum slammed into a soldier on the far side of the deck sending him into the darkness and water below.

Seeing five of his crew die in the last minute Vincent's jaw tightens with frustration. "Helm bring us higher. There is going to be a lot of destruction and I want to minimize the collateral damage if I can. Bribes are expensive."

Angela turns to face Bastiana. The wind from the Colossus's turbines blows her red hair around. Death radiates from her eyes as she moves to square off with the mage. The windows and floors of the nearby buildings rush by as the airship gains altitude. They soon pass in the distance below. Angela charges. Bastiana hesitates still shocked at the beauty she has damaged, but the fiery haired death rushing at her kicks in her survival instincts. A flash and Bastiana's hands are filled with a long staff etched with runes and steel banded ends. The advancing blades move with precision and ferocity. The only direction to move is backwards as Bastiana spins and parries the flurry of blows. Sparks fly where the twin blades connect with the staff. Light sprays from a rune on the staff when Bastiana fails to knock away a thrust to her stomach. The staff's magic absorbs the deadly blow leaving a burn mark where the rune had been on the staff. A matching rune is scarred onto her skin where the blade should have pierced.

"I will kill you for that," Bastiana screams in outrage.

The Colossus ascends into the cloudbank. "This is high enough helm," ordered Vincent. The light from the rune staff causes concern. "Hold here until I return. It seems I may have to put a stop to this before she gets herself hurt." Vincent leaves the captain's chair and makes his way below to the front deck.

Angela eyes the result of her assault and the protection the staff provided Bastiana. Rage fills Bastiana's face and as her magical force pushes Angela back. Bastiana twirls the staff above her head and advances on her. Loud cracks echo where the rune staff collides with the war blades. Bastiana's assault quickly begins to overpower Angela. The magic enhanced blows from the rune staff push her back across the deck. The weight of the night's events are piling up to the point where her muscles and adrenalin just can't overcome them. Pushing past the fatigue Angela matches Bastiana blow for blow, neither one giving up ground. Flashes of light from the fight light up the insides of the clouds like lightning. Stabbing the staff into the deck of the airship Bastiana blasts Angela to the far side of the Colossus. Angela hits the rail hard and slumps to the deck. Sharp pains hint at wounds on the inside with each heavy breath. *One broken rib at least, maybe more*.

Seeing Angela broken against the rail of the airship Bastiana lets up. Rage forces tears to run down her cheeks. "Why do you make me do these things?" Clenching her fists she lets out a long scream at Angela.

Angela sees Vincent step onto the deck and walk towards the screaming mage. Loose items and debris from the fight begin to vibrate and hover off the deck. The power building up in the mage is uncontrolled. Sparks of electricity begin to arch away from her and begin to damage parts of the airship. Seeing this as the only chance she has Angela rolls under the railing and falls into the clouds below.

Chapter 3

A background hint of livestock and dung hung lightly in the air, behind the rest of the sights and sounds of the midweek market. Arguments over the price of food can be heard at almost every market stand. The distant clang from the blacksmith shop could be heard as they pound out the orders for horse shoes, pins, and other items requested. Children with various amounts of dirt on their cloths dart amongst the crowd to keep themselves entertained while their parents shop or sell at the market. Groups of people shift around gossiping about everything from who they saw go to the doctor's office to the amount of rain that's fallen so far this year, just another typical boring day.

A long sigh escapes Kail's mouth. "You know the next harvest is still two months out. Soft turnips and produce is all there is Mrs. Wilson. The price hasn't changed all summer, and it won't change when the new stuff gets in. It's one coin per turnip."

"Robbery young man, robbery."

With a forced smile and a mocking nod, Kail hands the old lady a bag with turnips. With a grump Mrs. Wilson grabs the bag and slaps down four coins and gives the produce cart a hard kick that causes a couple of items to roll off and fall to the ground as she storms off into the crowd.

"Are you kidding me?"

"I see Mrs. Wilson stopped by."

"Yeah," muttered Kail picking up the items from the ground, and wiping the dirt off placing them back on the cart. "It's weird; she does this every week and never seems to remember."

"Don't worry about her too much. At least she buys every week. More than I can say for most of the folks in this town." Doing a quick inventory in his head of the remaining stock he says. "Looks like we're still selling less each week."

Arranging the rest of the produce as best he could for display, Kail sighed. "I'm sorry Royce, but you know it gets harder and harder to push the same stuff that was picked over the week before, and the week before that."

"Don't worry about it son, we make more than most with our harvests, and it's not like we're going to starve. We have piles of it to eat if no one else buys," chuckles Royce. His gaze covered the rest of the midweek market. "Will you be fine here? I need to check on the order for some new cart wheels for the coming season."

"Yeah, no problem. I don't see a rush of people lining up to by soft roots," his voice full of sarcasm.

"Ok, I'll be back before market close to help pack everything in," Royce called over his shoulder as he maneuvered through the crowd and made his way towards the inn and tavern house, the opposite direction from the hammering of the blacksmith's forge.

Not surprised by the direction his uncle moved, Kail shakes his head with a smile. The tavern was a worse pit of gossip than when old ladies gathered to cackle at each other. All problems in the world have been solved by old men over ale, if they were in charge. The mood in the market had been changing slowly the last few months. Fewer people stayed to chat as a rush had seeped into many peoples' step.

Aldervale is a small city to the east of Courduff. The market was one of the larger around with all the farmland reaching out. It also had a large rail stop before heading into the large city state capital of Courduff. There really were not a lot of people who lived in Aldervale, but it would swell on the market day when everyone came in to sell their wares or stock up for a while. Royce Kelly was one such farmer. Having inherited the family farm a while back, he was quite successful. Having the estate only an hour ride from the market helped. He had married his childhood sweetheart shortly before inheriting the farm. Jessica Kelly, Kail's aunt had her life suddenly upturned. Marrying young and suddenly finding herself the matron of a large estate was not expected. Neither was the day that Kail had been placed in their care. Fifteen years ago a boy of four had been delivered to the Kelly doorstep. He could only remember bits of that night, but the men who dropped him off would not talk to him, nor would they explain anything other than it was for his own good. He could not remember his real parents anymore other than the impression that they moved around a lot. He didn't have any strong memories of any particular place or another. Whenever he asked his uncle about them, he always got the same story. Royce's brother ran off when they were still kids and he never heard from him again until Kail arrived. He guessed that his brother had joined up with the army in Courduff. There was a lot of warring back then, and he assumed his brother had been killed. Why else would they have brought Kail here?

"Still selling dirt as food Kail?" a girl's voice called out.

"Hello Sarah, kind hearted as usual. Hi Ari," replied Kail to the two Ebonmore sisters that seemed to make it their personal mission in life to both annoy and tease him as much as they could. "How are things going at the inn?"

"None of your concern Kail, we've been reduced to fetching food for that wretch of a woman that got dropped off. She's been here for weeks, talks funny and looks at you like she's planning the best way to send you to the next world," complained Sarah.

"She's not that bad. But she is rather pretty when she's not looking at you," countered Ari the younger of the two sisters. "She doesn't come out much anyway, and I don't blame her."

"Is this one of the people that was attacked by robbers a few weeks back on the way to the market?"

"Yes, she and a big man came in together. He had to carry her in, and I heard she got beat up pretty badly in the assault," explained Ari. "He paid for the room and left coins for food and care if she needed it, but hasn't been back as far as I know, but some ugly vile man has been to see her a couple of times. He smells of smoke and is all scarred up."

"Vile is too kind of a word. The other day I caught him leering at me after he visited. I bet they owe him money, and the man that left her here has run off," Sarah spat while filling a basket with food from the cart.

"Well the capital has sent some soldiers at least to investigate. At least someone is doing something about it. The old government never seemed to care what happened outside the city," Kail said.

"I know, it's great isn't it," Sarah's eyes lit up. "Some of them are staying at our inn, too."

"They are nice and very polite," smiled Ari.

"You know they have been talking and looking for people who are interested in joining them," Sarah said. "You should go sign up, or would you rather sell dirt food your whole life?"

"Yes ma'am, right away ma'am," responded Kail with a mock salute.

With a disgusted humph, Sarah slapped down a handful of coins and gave the cart a hard kick causing several items to crash to the ground. Flashes of Mrs. Wilson earlier but now with Sarah's face invaded his mind. "Are you kidding me!" The Ebonmore sisters walked away. Sarah with her nose turned up, and Ari right behind her but who turned and gave him a shy smile and a wave. The rest of the day passed without incident. A few of the soldiers from Courduff milled about and talked to people. Some asked questions, others went about the same as anyone else browsing the market.

Royce never showed up when the market began to pack up for the week. Some of the people who had farther to travel to their homes were already gone. Kail decided to pack up a little early as well. Knowing that he would have to come back to get his uncle when Aunt Jessica found out.

Arriving home with enough daylight to at least get back to Aldervale, Kail quickly unhitched the cart and switched the tack and harness of the horse for a ride back. Running around the barn and past the side of the house he slows down. Three horses were tied up front next to the porch. The markings on the saddle bags have the insignia of Courduff on them, and voices can be heard coming from the open doorway.

"Aunt Jessica?" he called questioningly passing into the house.

"That sounds like Kail," he could hear his aunt's voice from the other room addressing someone. "Come in to the kitchen Kail, we have guests." Entering the kitchen, Kail could see three soldiers standing around the table. Empty plates and the smell of cooked food lingered in the air. One of the soldiers stood straighter than the rest and by the markings and decorations he wore placed him as an officer of some sort.

"Evening young sir," greeted the officer.

"Kail, this is Lieutenant Wilhelm Bailon," offered his aunt. "He and his men stopped by to chat, and I offered to feed them up."

"Hello, Lieutenant."

"We were just ready to depart your hospitality Mrs. Kelly, if we go now, we should be back at the Ebonmore Inn by dark," nodded the lieutenant. The soldiers gave their thanks and left to ready the groups' horses.

"Did your uncle come home with you?"

"No Aunt Jessica, but I have the horse ready to go," explained Kail.

"Well, if you hurry, I'm sure the Lieutenant and his men won't mind if you ride back to Aldervale with them," Jessica pre-invited to the officer.

"That won't be a problem ma'am, we would be happy to escort your nephew back to town. We're all headed that direction anyway," offered Lieutenant Bailon as he made his way to the porch where his men were waiting with the horses. "Grab your horse and catch up, we will meet you at the end of the property."

"Alright," Kail nodded. Grabbing a sack and filling it with some bread and cheese from the kitchen. *Royce would probably need something too if he never made it out of the tavern*, thought Kail, going back to double the amount of food in the sack. "Be back after dark Aunt Jessica," he called out running down the porch steps and to the barn. The soldiers were already nearing the edge of the Kelly farm. Jumping on his horse, Kail kicked it into a gallop to catch up with the soldiers waiting on the road to Aldervale.

The soldiers nod when Kail caught up. "Good to have you with us," greeted Lieutenant Bailon. As the four riders made their way back to Aldervale, the conversation covered many topics. Kail explained some of the local happenings, from Mrs. Wilson's strange behavior to how Sarah Ebonmore did the same thing not an hour later. Chuckles of how the mind's of women work to the quality of their drinking water made the rounds. Midway to Aldervale the topic of the soldiers from Courduff's presence came up. "True we have been talking to local boys and men to see if they had considered a life with the army."

"As you've seen, a uniform makes the ladies hot," laughed one soldier.

"It's a soldier's duty to aid a lady in distress," barked the other.

"Yes, yes," conceded the Lieutenant. "There are a lot of… unadvertised benefits when you join the army. But one of the more relevant reasons is that the new ruler of Courduff, Therion, is looking to have an airship base built here in Aldervale. You have seen the increased traffic from the trains. The amount of materials that are passing through here are getting to the point where security is starting to become a concern."

"An airship field?"

"Yes, we have been making inquires to buy the land out past the rail stop to have it built. We prefer to have a more local presence with the men that would be stationed there. It makes people more comfortable to see familiar faces than a large group of armed strangers they suddenly find themselves living near."

"I can see how that might make things easier. Tell me more about the new ruler, this Therion guy. I've heard grumblings around town, but I've never been to Courduff or met many people from there to know," queried Kail.

"It's a very volatile subject in Courduff right now. But as you know, the city has been ruled by the Mage Council for as long as anyone can remember. Therion for the last twenty or more years has been the leader of the council and there have been fewer and fewer mages to fill the voids left by the ones that have died. The War of Antiquities thirty years ago saw many of them lost. Their power base weakened and allowed the inventors and alchemists to sway political power into their favor. Therion being one of the youngest mages left ceded to the consortiums to disband the majority of the council's power, but remains the ruler to appease the old families that have their power base built around the mages."

"Sounds awfully complicated to me," pondered Kail.

"Indeed, many people's entire lives are lived in the political arena. It's not a life I would choose to walk," agreed Bailon.

"Don't forget about the zealots running about either," piped up one of the soldiers. "When the Mage Council is broken, the world will fall to darkness."

"I prefer to leave such worries to the hands of the clergy," retorted the Lieutenant. "A man should have his path and do the best he can to help others when he can. Filling your days with doom and hoping for a Chosen One to save you is a waste of time in my book. Waiting for a prophecy to make your life better isn't going to happen; you have to do it yourself."

That ended the subject rather quickly and the timing wasn't bad either. The party had arrived at Aldervale. "Thank you for the escort Lieutenant"

"You're welcome Kail. Give our thanks again to your aunt for the food and I'm sure we will see you around," Lieutenant Bailon waved as the soldiers headed off to the inn. Kail made his way to the tavern and could hear that everyone inside had once again solved all the problems of the world and he had no doubts that he would hear them all from his uncle on the way back home.

Chapter 4

Kail and his Uncle Royce were setting up the cart for the midweek market. A week had passed since he had ridden with the Lieutenant. Old man Leonard MacDonnell had quickly sold his land by the rail stop and rumor had it that he moved to the capital and left everything behind. Money does strange things to people they say, and as far as Kail could tell, it was true. With that it didn't take long before a train full of soldiers and other workers from Courduff arrived and quickly started to work on clearing the land for the airstrip. A lot of local men hired on to help with the construction as well. It was quite the sight to watch, and the workers drew a crowd of onlookers every day, to watch with awe at the speed that they could get things done. Most of the trees had been cleared away and the ground surveyed out. Stacks of building materials were being delivered everyday by train and only a day ago an airship had spent half of the day above Aldervale before returning to the capital city.

The market place was busier than usual. More than half of the early customers were strangers. Most of them were from Courduff: soldiers, officers and workers for the new airstrip being built. But there were a lot of other new faces as well. Contractors looked to build housing for the influx of people as well as merchants looking to set up shop in Aldervale to sell to the Courduff military. There were also the families that started to show up. Aldervale was starting to grow rapidly and the local town council was busy everyday with meetings and scrambling with issues that were never a concern before. The issue that had most of the locals grumbling was the riff-raff and vagrants. There had not been any unusual crime reported, but complaints of beggars and unease about the general safety of the town, especially at night were increasing.

None of the merchant or shop owners were complaining though. The inn was completely filled and Ebonmore was in negotiations with some of the contractors and military regarding expanding the inn as well. The tavern had never seen so many patrons pass through its doors, but there had been more than one wife who was upset at the state her husband had come home in, when the companion women started to arrive, that was the last straw for some. "Interesting how much has changed in so little a time," commented Royce to Kail eyeing the change in the market crowd.

"Yeah, it will take some getting used to that's for sure. At least we manage to sell all the soft turnips. It's amazing when someone else wants to buy it they don't seem to complain when they know it might not be there anymore."

"Just make sure you save a handful for Mrs. Wilson," joked Royce. "Will you be fine for the rest of the day? I have to meet up with some of the officer types at the inn. They are interested in contracting the next harvest to feed the soldiers that will be stationed at the airstrip."

"Sure, it shouldn't be a problem," Kail had been managing the marketplace mostly on his own for quite a while now.

"Good, if you sell out early, you can go back to the farm and get more or take the rest of the day and do whatever. I'm sure the Ebonmore girls would like to see you."

"Yeah, I'll jump right on that," rolling his eyes. "Actually that sounds like a good idea. I might go talk to the Lieutenant."

"Ok, but don't go signing your life away without talking to your aunt and me first. Sarah isn't going to wait years for you to wander back to town in a uniform and sweep her off her feet."

"Yeah, whatever, now go sell the next harvest so I won't have to suffer standing here next year waiting for Mrs. Wilson to kick the cart each week."

The morning passed quickly and the market stayed busy into the afternoon. It was easy to sell the produce with so many people, and it did not take long before the last item left in the hands of some creepy guy Kail had not seen before. He was glad to see him leave and would have just given the guy the food for free just to get him to go away. The guy's face was all burned up on one side and his hand the same. But the worst was the amount of hate the guy seemed to hold for him. He was pretty sure that if there had not been a market full of people and soldiers, the man would have tried to throttle him right then and there.

Packing up the cart Kail headed back to the farm. He contemplated his uncle's words from earlier. Seeing the soldiers from Courduff come to town and how they all seemed to go about their business intrigued him. Also it brought up that there was an entire world out there that had remained completely hidden from him here in Aldervale. Also the idea of trying to find out more about his parents was flittering in his mind as well. The Courduff army would have all kinds of resources available that might help him find information. He was sure even his aunt and uncle wouldn't mind knowing as well. Things were never going to go back to the way they were and he wasn't sure if that was a good thing, or a bad thing. So many questions, Kail was beginning to understand why some of the townspeople were grumbling.

"I'm done early Aunt Jessica," Kail called out as he stowed the cart and re-saddled the horse.

"Wow, it's been a long time since we have sold out at the marketplace."

"Yeah, with all the new people in town, it's not too hard. I'm going to take a sack of food and stop by Mrs. Wilson's place. We were out of food before she normally arrives."

"That's very kind of you Kail."

"Also, I think I'm going to go to the inn as well. See if I run into the Lieutenant and talk to him. If he's there, great, if not, well I'm sure I can tease Ari and Sarah."

"Alright, I know your uncle has already talked to you about that. Be careful, if you stay out too late," replied Kail's aunt with concern.

Thoughts of what the conversation might be like between himself and Lieutenant Bailon filled Kail's head for most of the ride back to Aldervale. He was definitely going to ask him about the airships. They were something that interested Kail. Arriving at town, Kail made his way to Mrs. Wilson's home. A group of four soldiers were leaving as Kail approached. He could see Mrs. Wilson standing on her porch with a scowl. He hoped she hadn't kicked one. "Hello Mrs. Wilson. I brought you some of our produce. We sold everything before you normally arrive."

"Humph, you here to rob me too young man?"

"Uh, no Mrs. Wilson, in fact this week's food won't cost you anything. We only charged you before to cover the damages to the cart every time you kicked it each week," smirked Kail.

"So we're a funny man now. I don't like funny men. You won't think it's funny when it's your turn," Mrs. Wilson emphasized with a finger jab to Kail's chest.

"What's that supposed to mean? The soldiers already came by our farm last week."

Mrs. Wilson's eyes took on a new ferocity and her pupils dilated quickly so much that the color was completely lost, "Follow the flame. The crest of the falcon will return. Finish what has not been started," and just as quickly her eyes returned to normal as Mrs. Wilson kicked Kail hard in the shin. "And that's for staring open mouthed like a fool!" and slammed the door in his face.

Caught off guard by the whole encounter the only thing that came to Kail's mind was to shout, "Are you kidding me!" through the closed door. "Old people," he muttered as he made his way back to the street. Kail was nearly knocked to the ground as he rounded the street corner to the inn and collided head long into someone.

"Watch where you're going boy," a man's voice barked.

"Sorry," Kail replied as he dusted himself off. "Maybe..." but the rest of his sentence failed as he stood looking at the face of a very angry man. A man with a scarred face and a balled scarred fist, it was the man from the market earlier today. Kail wouldn't be forgetting that face anytime soon.

"Maybe what boy?"

"Is there a problem here gentlemen?" a third voice said.

"Out of my way boy," the scarred man pushed past Kail and made his way around the street corner without acknowledging the voice. Lieutenant Bailon stepped up to where Kail stood and watched the man leave.

"Unpleasant fellow, I have yet to question him. How are you doing young master Kail?"

"Um, yeah, I'm fine. Hey, I was just coming to the inn to see if you were here and maybe talk a bit."

"Sure, let's go inside where it's more pleasant, but I warn you, things have been busy of late so we may be interrupted," the Lieutenant explained as they made their way inside the inn. Kail had been inside the Ebonmore Inn several times growing up in Aldervale. It was often used to host parties and other community functions, but it was completely different now. The large open lobby was completely filled with tables, chairs, and people. Most of the tables were occupied by soldiers that Kail could only guess were officers of sorts. Many seemed to be busy with various sorts of work that made the army function. Other tables had a mix of soldiers and locals drinking, laughing, playing card games, and even dice. Apparently Ebonmore had installed a bar along one wall and several patrons were gathered near. One table near the entrance had a small line of three people standing in front of it.

"What's that?" Kail asked pointing at the line of people.

"Recruitment information," replied Bailon. "Let's sit over here. We shouldn't be bothered as much, and it's a good spot to see the room." The pair made their way through the crowd to one of the tables along the wall. "Can I get you something to drink?"

"Water is fine," answered Kail.

"How old are you now Kail?"

"I'm nineteen, why?"

"It's after hours. I think the topic of the evening will require something more stout than water," commented Lieutenant Bailon as he left Kail at the table to go get drinks. Kail could see the shift in the atmosphere. The formality the soldiers held themselves to began to fade and he could see how much like normal people they were. Tired eyes were rubbed and the smiles became more genuine as the day's duties came to an end. The volume in the inn also increased as more people arrived. In the center of the room a large round table was completely surrounded by people sitting with half again as many more standing. A card game was being played and judging by amount of people and money on the table, it was quite popular. Sitting next to one of the soldiers was Sarah Ebonmore. She caught Kail looking at her and gave him a disgusted smirk turning back to the soldier she had been hanging on next to her. He must have been someone important because he had more decorations on his uniform than Lieutenant Bailon. He could hear her peel of laughter from across the room; apparently the officer had won that round.

Shifting his gaze away from the snotty Ebonmore girl, Kail did not see her sister Ari anywhere. Ari was a lot nicer and shyer compared to her sister. He imagined that she probably did not like the large crowd of people at the inn now. He didn't blame her; it would take some getting used to. Kail could see the Lieutenant talking to the barman and he shuddered at what he was going to be drinking soon. A couple of other soldiers were there as well ordering drinks and talking to the Lieutenant. A large empty spot further down the bar had only one person standing there. She was unlike anything Kail had ever seen before. Her skin was very pale as if she only went outdoors on the cloudiest days and her hair was red like fire, not the kind you see in the fireplace, but the raging fires you see in the distance when forests are ablaze and the sun sets behind the smoke. Her choice of dress stood out as much as she did. It did little to hide her legs and shoulders, but it was the eyes that he couldn't keep from staring at. Their almond shape took in the whole room. More than once a soldier would head towards her, and her eyes would dart at them like a weapon so they would quickly abort their approach and head to another destination.

"You might want to close your mouth when you stare at a woman, least she think you are a fool or simpleton of some sort," chuckled Lieutenant Bailon sitting at the table and passing a drink to Kail.

"What? No... I wasn't," stammered Kail with the heat rising to his face as he blushed at being caught staring at the woman.

"She is quite something to look at though. But not very friendly. I've had the chance to talk to her a couple of times."

"Who is she? I've never seen anyone who looks like her before in my life."

"That's the woman who was attacked a few weeks back before we arrived to Aldervale," Bailon answered taking a swallow from his drink.

Imitating the Lieutenant, Kail swallowed a mouthful of the ale. It wasn't bad, it reminded him of the late fall when the grain farmers cut their fields and the air was thick with dust and grain that made it hard for some to breath and others to get runny noses.

"She looks fine to me," observed Kail, "Why hasn't she gone home yet?"

"No idea? Why don't you go ask her," smirked the Lieutenant as another soldier was hurried away by her glare.

"So Lieutenant I wanted to ask you some things," started Kail.

"I'm off duty, you can call me Will or just Bailon if you want," interrupted the officer with another swallow of ale.

"Um, ok Bailon. I've been thinking a lot about what the army records in Courduff might hold regarding my real parents. My uncle seems to think that my father ran off and joined the army there a long time ago."

"That's a hard question. I couldn't tell you for sure if you would find anything or not. But you don't have to enlist in the army to find out. All that information is public record. You just need to go to Courduff and look. But I do know this, the libraries and records hall has enough information in it to take more than one lifetime to look through if you don't know where to start."

The evening wore on and soon there were several empty glasses on the table between Kail and Bailon. The conversation topics were diverse, Kail particularly enjoyed all the information he could pry from his friend about the city of Courduff. From the airships there to how the train systems worked. Most of the technology had not yet made its way to Aldervale.

"It's hard to even believe some of what you have told me. It's like a completely different world there. I can't imagine what it would be like to fly on one of those airships, let alone command one. And to do battle! That's crazy."

"Yeah, they are something else that's for sure. They are not for everyone though. Most get sick on them." Bailon sat back eyeing the room.

Kail finished the drink in his hand and placed the empty glass with the others. "I think I might go over there and talk her."

"Do you want me to notify your next of kin when she stares you dead?" laughed Bailon.

"It wouldn't be a bad way to die," hiccupped Kail as he looked at the woman at the bar. However, the glare coming from the scarred man surprised him the most. "When did he show up? I swear he creeps me out."

"He came in not too long ago. True he hasn't taken his eyes off you since he got here either," yawned the Lieutenant.

Ignoring the scarred man as much as he could Kail looked around the inn. Things were starting to wind down, the crowd had started to thin and glasses stood more empty than full. The door to the inn opened and in walked four men. They looked like they could be soldiers, but their dress was different than those from Courduff. The noise of the inn hushed for a second as people took in the newcomers. But the hesitation only lasted a few moments and everyone went back to what they were doing. Bailon shrugged that he didn't know anything about the new group. Looking back to the bar Kail was disappointed that the woman was gone. However the man was gone as well. Kail wanted to know if the scarred man had left the inn or gone further inside. He didn't want to run into the guy outside in the dark on his way home.

Chapter 5

The mid-week market was the busiest yet. Soldiers from Courduff along with workers and their families crowded the marketplace. Due to the increased amount of people to Aldervale, they were talking about keeping the market open all week long instead of just a day. Kail had already returned to the farm to restock once after selling out in the morning.

"We're going to need a bigger cart, or do something different at this rate," he commented to his uncle as he made change for a customer with two bags of food and thanked them for their purchase.

"Indeed. But we secured a contract with the garrison that will be at the airstrip for this coming season, so once were done this year, we won't have to man the market anymore." Royce stated, recalling that he had left Kail in charge last week while he had met with the officers that were going to be in charge of the new airstrip and army outpost. A meeting that quickly concluded, and ended with all of them at the tavern to celebrate a new beginning.

"That will be nice. I'm not sure this old cart will make it if we start hauling more than once a week with it," Kail complained. "I don't think it could take the abuse if Mrs. Wilson starts to kick it every day," giving a concerned look to one of the cart legs.

"How has the market been today?" a kind voice asked.

"Oh, hello Ari," Kail replied. "It's been busy; I've already gone home for more once today."

"Yeah, it's getting pretty crazy around here these days," she said hesitantly. Her eyes taking in the busy market place full of strangers. A large clamor from somewhere in the market seemed to startle her. "This must be what it's like all the time in the big cities."

"Probably, you get used to it after a while."

"I don't think I will ever get used to it," Ari said. She turned and got up on tiptoe to stare over the crowd. Her tone indicated something or someone had caught her eye.

Kail moved around the cart to look in the same direction. "What are you looking at?" asked Kail.

"I'm not sure… There, that man, the big one with blond hair who hasn't shaved in a while," she pointed out. "I think he's the one that dropped off that woman a while back. The one that was supposedly hurt on the road."

"I wouldn't doubt it," Kail replied after taking in the big man's appearance. "I saw the woman at your inn last week. He looks like he could be with her." The man looked like a brawler. Few people in the market stood as tall as he did. His clothing was a little odd. A full length duster looked like it had plenty of places to hide a weapon or two. He also drew a cautious eye from some of the soldiers as well. "It does make you wonder though. They don't look like the type someone would want to assault and steal from. More like the opposite to me."

"I hope that's him, it will be nice when she leaves. The complaints about her are getting annoying. Can you get me a small sack of roots and greens for me? I want to get back quickly and let my father know," she said turning back to the cart.

"Sure, I'll get that for you," Kail replied quickly as he gathered the items for her.

"Thanks Kail. Be safe," she replied as he handed her the food and she darted off into the crowd.

"Ah, to be young and in love," ribbed his uncle.

"Shut up."

"You know if you keep giving all the girls free merchandise, what will Mrs. Wilson think?" he whispered to his nephew as they watched her run off.

"You be quiet!" Kail replied with a shove. His uncle continued to mock him with kissy faces and spinning around in a poor imitation of a ball room dance.

Kail made his way to the inn to see if Lieutenant Bailon was around. He had told his aunt and uncle about their talk the week before. With the Kelly farm contracting out the next harvest to the garrison the need for Kail to be around had substantially lessoned. They had all agreed though that before signing up for the army that he should take a bit of time and travel to the city to see firsthand what it was like. Also as the Lieutenant had said, he didn't need their permission or help to inquire about his parents. Both his aunt and uncle had agreed that it would be a good thing for him to do this before he decided anything. It was a lot to think about for Kail. It left him both excited and a little bit scared to head off into the unknown.

The sound of loud fan blades brought Kail from his thoughts and back to his surroundings. The noise grew louder and louder until a massive airship crested the treetops and passed overhead. The massive flying vessel momentarily blocked out the sun as it made its way to where the airstrip was under construction. The noise caused several people to come out of their homes and shops to see what all the commotion was about.

Joining several other people, Kail made his way to the construction site to see the vessel and was curious as to who or what it might have brought to Aldervale. Several soldiers from Courduff had their hands full keeping the crowd back from the construction site for their safety. Several of the officers Kail had seen around town and at the inn were lined up. He could see Lieutenant Bailon standing with them as well. *It might be a while before I could get to talk to him today,* Kail thought. The noise from the airship had lessoned since its landing, but it still managed to kick up a lot of wind and dirt that blew into the faces of the crowd.

Making his way through the crowd of people to get a better look, Kail stopped short. The scarred man was in the crowd as well. The man hadn't spotted Kail. His eyes were focused on the events happening at the airstrip. Behind him towered the blond man that Ari had pointed out at the marketplace. Not wanting to attract any attention to himself, Kail backed into the crowd where he could keep an eye on the two and watch the events on the airstrip.

Several soldiers departed from the landed airship and stood waiting in formation. Their uniforms were different than those of the soldiers already in Aldervale. The engines of the airship had finally quieted down and the air began to clear of dust. Murmurs in the crowd began to creep up as more made the connection that these newcomers were not with the soldiers from Courduff to the west. Kail looked at the airship more closely. On the upper deck he could make out someone standing there looking down on everyone. It looked to be a woman with dark skin and short black hair that moved chaotically with the last bit of wind left from the airship. Closer to the back of the airship, he could see the word "Colossus". *That must be the name of the ship,* he mused.

The noise of the crowd quieted and Kail focused his attention back to the people on the ground. A new figure had descended from the airship and judging by the reaction of the new soldiers as well as the officers from Courduff, this is who they were waiting to meet. He was a tall man and steadfast formal in his appearance. There was no doubt that he was in charge of the airship and most likely a lot more. Formal greetings and handshakes were exchanged. Startled cries from the crowd and shocked onlookers pointed. The girl who had been standing high above on the deck of the airship had jumped over the top rail and was plummeting quickly to the ground a good sixty or more feet below. Kail stood horrified at what was about to happen, but at a mere meter before her body met the earth, the girl's body began glow and a flash of light shot forward from where she had been falling to the side of the man from the Colossus. Just as quickly, the light reformed and the girl from the deck reappeared delighted by the shock her appearance brought to the officers from Courduff and to the crowd.

"Magic!" someone cried from the crowd.

That's all it took for those gathered to panic. Shoved and pushed, Kail tried to focus on not getting knocked down and trampled. He could hear the soldiers trying to calm those that were near them, but several people were already in a full run away from airstrip. Kail found himself staring at the scarred man. The man was staring at Kail and by the wicked smile on his face; he had been for a while. The big man had an angry look on his face but still kept his eyes on the events unfolding at the airstrip. The man motioned with his scarred hand to the brute and they departed into the chaos of the crowd.

Kail found himself running away from the air field like everyone else. He hadn't given thought as to why he was running; only that it was what everyone else around him was doing. Not thinking about the direction he ran it wasn't long before he found himself rounding a corner to a dead ended alley way. Finally stopping to catch his breath he allowed himself to absorb what had gone on moments before. *Magic*, he thought. That's what someone had said when the girl had jumped from the Colossus only to do what? He didn't know, only that one moment she was about to die and the next she turned to light and an instant later stood at the side of that other man. He had heard stories of magic users, the things that they could do and in the past they had control of all the large city states. There were also stories of great wars. *But what was one doing here?* Last he and everyone else had heard that all mages were taken to the council and kept there.

The Mage Council has been disbanded by Therion. The words suddenly came to his mind remembering Lieutenant Bailon's comment the night they were drinking at the inn. He had completely forgotten that part of the night to the ale, but he remembered it now. More confused than ever, Kail tried to make sense of the events that just happened.

"Everything happens for a reason," a thickly accented voice came from the end of the alley.

Startled Kail turned towards the voice. A man stood at the end of the alley that he was sure had not been there before. He had bright blue eyes and unkempt short brown hair. "What? Who are you?"

"Two questions that I have answered already," the man replied as he made his way over to Kail. His clothing was unassuming, if out of place for Aldervale and his speech was hard to understand. "Now I have to go and stop those who would want to rescue you," he concluded after looking at a watch from his pocket.

"What are you talking about?" asked Kail, even more confused than ever as the day became more bizarre.

"Think of it as character building Falconcrest," he said firmly. "You shouldn't have conversations using only questions. It is quite rude. Just remember what Mrs. Wilson taught you." That ended the conversation as he left the alley.

What was going on? Kail thought. *Mrs. Wilson? All she does is kick the cart every week, and what questions were already answered. I need to go home,* he thought.

"Is that him?" a new voice from the entrance of the alley asked.

Kail looked at the entrance of the alley. The man standing there looked vaguely familiar. A second man stopped from a run to stand by the first. "Yeah, that should be him," he stated waiving to others still out of sight. Four men soon blocked the alley and advanced towards Kail.

Once all four of them were together Kail remembered where he had seen them before. That same night from the Inn when he talked to the Lieutenant, four strangers had walked in that everyone had stared at but eventually ignored. What they wanted from him, he couldn't fathom, but he wondered briefly what else from that night he had forgotten. He had not even interacted with them or seen them since until now. He didn't stand a chance when they started to throw punches. Thankfully it was over quickly and the darkness of unconsciousness ended the beating.

Chapter 6

The constant humming noise brought Kail back to the realm of the conscious. He soon wished it hadn't. The metal room he found himself in vibrated to the noise. It was small and cramped with a pair of tiny lamps on either side. Metal tubing ran along the walls and ceiling. One of them fed pressurized gas that kept the struggling flames alive that lit the room. The rest he had no idea of their function. Occasionally loud grating sounds of metal being forced could be heard and the vibrating room would jerk. The walls and floor were cold and slightly damp like the inside of a window on a cold rainy day.

Kail figured he had been there for a while. His face and chest hurt where the men from the alley had beaten him. Judging by how dark some of the bruises on his arms already were tipped him off. His stomach also protested at the amount of time that had passed since he had last eaten. "You've got to be kidding me," he mumbled after assessing the situation. *Why would anyone want to kidnap me? What was going on? Who were those men who had beaten me senseless in the alley? Who was that man right before, and what did all this have to do with Mrs. Wilson?* Question after question raced through his mind.

The small room at the Ebonmore Inn looked ready to burst. The four figures inside all had hostile looks towards each other. "Let him explain himself first Camden Arland," Angela Atagi said standing between the tall muscled blond that glared at the Time Walker across the room.

"Yes, I want to hear what he has to say as well. Weeks in this pathetic excuse for a town and when we're all finally together and find the boy, you show up and stop us from getting him," accused Xavier Ross pointing at him with his scarred hand.

"I say, the time here has been well spent has it not Angela? It's not like when you arrived you were in any condition to be useful. Do try and be more careful in the future. Vacation time is not likely to be had in the future," Mr. Eleazar commented casually in his thick accent.

"That is rich, coming from you Mr. Eleazar. Maybe if you had used someone a little more reliable than a burned rat who spends his time hiding from everything then I would not have been in such a mess," icily retorted Angela advancing on him.

It was Camden's turn to stop Angela. "I get to smash his face in first Red."

"I'm absolutely sure that he will be fine," Mr. Eleazar stated. "At least I'm mostly sure, I was rather busy at the time before I went to that alley," he pondered. "So many things happen in alley ways, I'm sure it was the right one."

Shaking his head in contempt, Xavier lights a cigarette. The light from the flame makes the scars on his hand stand out even more. He took a long drag before speaking. "You're god damned insane, you know that," blowing smoke at him. "And we're even worse for listening to him," including the others in his assessment.

"You try finishing conversations that you haven't heard the beginnings of yet and see how well you do," Mr. Eleazar seemingly agreed with Xavier. "Now, I suggest that we make our way to the train stop, I don't want to be anywhere near his aunt and uncle when they come looking for him." Leaning towards Angela he whispers, "They are going to be a trifle upset, I believe."

"Gladly," spat Xavier who was already out the door, giving The Guardian the finger as he went.

"Cute Mr. Eleazar, real cute," Camden Arland smirked. "Let's go Red." And the pair followed after Xavier.

Mr. Eleazar was the last to leave the room. He was in no hurry to make it to the train station like the others. Being late was not possible for him. The meeting had not gone quite as he planned, but figured it would do. If it didn't, he could always change it later. Reaching the lobby of the inn Mr. Eleazar stopped and pulled a pocket watch from his vest. "And now," he said to himself.

Lieutenant Bailon was just about to stop Camden and Angela as they made for the door. Just as Xavier had exited the inn in front of them; stormed in both Royce and Jessica Kelly. Upon seeing the Lieutenant that their nephew had talked so much about they quickly rushed him demanding answers which allowed Camden and Angela to leave the inn unimpeded. Pleased with himself, Mr. Eleazar casually made his way to the bar and ordered a white tea. "Excuse me young ma'am" he said to the girl passing by.

"Yes?"

"Your name is Ari correct? Ari Ebonmore?"

"Yes. Do I know you?" she questioned.

"Not yet, my name is Mr. Eleazar," he said with a smile.

Kail had no idea of how much time had passed, but it felt like it had been several hours at least since he awoke in the dingy cold room. His best guess had placed him in the car of a train. Where it was headed he could not guess. The passing time had given him chance to go over recent events in his aching head. So far he had the following reasoned out. He doubted that he would be in this room until he starved because the men who beat him up said they were looking for him. That meant he had something they wanted, or he was something that someone else wanted. Either way it confirmed he would not be here forever. Next was the puzzle of Mrs. Wilson. He had remembered the day a while back when he brought her some groceries and she wigged out on him. Something about following the fire, crests and falcons, and something else he couldn't remember. That brought him to the man in the alley. He had called him Falconcrest, and that reminded him of Mrs. Wilson's mumblings, and what did it have to do with her teaching him anything? He couldn't figure it out. He wondered if he had been gone long enough for his aunt and uncle to notice. He hoped they had, given the stir that the airship Colossus had caused. Surely word of magic users and a near town panic had caused them to come looking for him. Though, he doubted what they could do for him.

The screech of the metal door as it opened protested loudly to the last time it had been oiled. The noise caught Kail off guard and startled him. Two soldiers that were dressed like those that had arrived from the airship stood guard. A dark-skinned girl with short black hair in a brown-red dress robe with gold trim entered the room with a tray of food and water.

"Hello," she greeted bubbly and placed the tray in front of Kail. "I'm glad you're awake finally, it's been so boring lately," she said with a roll of her eyes in the direction of the guards. The guards stood unfazed by her comment.

"Um, thank you," he said warily, eyeing the tray in front of him. Drinking the water first, "I saw you at the airstrip. You were on the top deck and jumped off of that airship that landed, weren't you?"

"Yup, that was me," she said. "I'm still in trouble over it too," she pouted sticking out her lower lip.

"So what you did, with the light and not hitting the ground. That was magic right?" Kail questioned in between bites of food from the tray.

"Yes," she giggled and sat down next to Kail. She shifted over close to him and eyed the guards with suspicion.

He paused a bit becoming uncomfortable at how close the girl, that looked to be near his age, sat next to him. Like they were long time friends and not someone he had just met only a moment ago escorted by guards keeping him in this room. "Um, right. I have heard about mages, but never seen one until now."

"I bet. They got very angry when the people in your town started running and screaming after I teleported."

"Is that what you did with the light thing?"

"Yup, it's not too hard to do if you're a Chronomancer," she answered. "My name is Bastiana, my friends call me Tiana. You can call me that if you want," she said moving in even closer.

"Um, ok Tiana. My name is Kail. Kail Kelly from Aldervale"

"I could probably teach you how to do it. Like I said, it's a simple thing to do. Now, turning these guards into piggy's," she threatened with evil eyes. "That's a bit harder to do."

The guards eyed one another and shifted uncomfortably, but held their ground. Kail was pretty sure that she could follow through with the threat if she wanted. "I'm not a mage, I can't do magic."

"Are you sure?" Tiana asked. She moved so close that her face was almost touching the side of his. Kail could hear her take in a breath as she smelled him. "You smell like one to me," she whispered softly in his ear.

Kail jerked away from her spilling the rest of the contents of the tray onto the floor. He was totally unprepared when she licked his cheek and then quickly bit him on the ear. "What the hell?" he said, glancing at the guards for support. The look in Bastiana's eyes was the same as a cat stalking an unsuspecting bird.

"You don't taste like one though," she said with a look of disappointment and confusion on her face. "It's like you have been dipped in bleach and there is no color left."

"What is that supposed to mean?"

"Bored now," Bastiana answered, back to being the bubbly girl when she first arrived. And just like that she closed her eyes and a blue ball of energy glowed from her middle and with a flash she was gone. The guards looked at each other and shook their heads. They closed and locked the door to the metal room and left Kail to figure it out on his own.

"This is the most absurd thing I have ever agreed to do in my life," grumbled Camden Arland. The train that he, Angela, and Xavier had boarded sped through the night in the direction of Courduff. "At least I'm getting paid a small fortune."

"Wait. You're getting paid?" Xavier asked. The look of disbelief and shock spoke volumes on his scarred face.

Camden's loud rolling laugh even brought a smile to Angela's face who sat beside him. "Oh, this is epic," he managed to get out between laughs. Tears were starting to roll from his eyes from laughing so hard. "You're telling me you bought his whole story and are doing this for nothing?"

"Screw you Arland," Xavier cursed as he stormed out of the passenger cabin.

"You should not tease him so," said Angela watching him leave. "I am sure he was promised something as we all were when the Time Walker approached us." She moved to the other side of the cabin now that Xavier had left and stretched her legs out on the seat. One of the Keratin war blades had been removed from its sheath and she looked over the artifact examining the runes etched into its surface.

"Oh, oh, oh, it hurts to breathe," Camden stammered red faced with tears after finding out that Xavier Ross had agreed to follow Mr. Eleazar without asking for something in return. Taking a moment to regain his composure, "Why are you doing it Red? What were you promised?"

"I was not promised anything," her eyes lost in thought staring at the blade in her hand. "Everyone and everything I knew died a thousand years ago," she spoke as her voice took on a somber tone as she recalled the day Mr. Eleazar approached her. "We were gathering a war party after one of our villages had been attacked by men," she said laying the blade across her lap. "We knew of the man who walked through time, so his arrival we took to be a great omen for our victory. He took me aside later when everyone had started to bed for the night. He said he had a choice for me to make. I could either die tomorrow a pointless death that no one would remember, or I could come with him to a distant future. A future that would seem like a living hell for me, but it held a chance to live another day. If I survived long enough I might find something worth living for that was better than getting killed in a war that could not be won only to be forgotten as there would be no left one to sing songs about me."

"Well, that's the worst deal I've ever heard." Camden said when he could tell she was not going to continue anymore. "I would have told him to stick it right up his nose with those choices."

"That is what I told him, if not exactly the same words," she smiled looking at Camden. "However, the next morning, I was one of the first to die. We never saw the ambush the men had set for us. Right before the arrow would have pierced my heart, the Time Walker came again. All around, my people and the enemy stood frozen in place. He let me stare at the arrow as it hung in the air above my breast. Then he asked again if I had given his offer enough thought."

"I guess he made his point- I mean," he stopped, as Angela had that look in her eye that told him to think his next words over carefully. "I'm just going to shut my mouth now".

"Wiser words have not been spoken Camden Arland."

The constant humming that had lulled Kail to sleep had changed pitch. *Maybe they had arrived,* he thought. A few minutes later the door opened repeating its protest of not being oiled. Four guards armed with swords entered the room. "Time to go," said the first one.

"Go where?" asked Kail, but he didn't receive an answer from any of the guards. The hallway outside the room was narrow and cramped with pipes. The floor was grated metal and every few paces he could see more pipes as well as rapidly moving cables as thick as his arm. Rows of doors lined the hallway as well. Each one spaced out evenly, and he could only assume that behind them were similar rooms, no cells, like the one he had just been inside.

"Left, then up," the guard ordered.

A set of narrow stairs led to the floor above. "This is not a train is it?" he commented, not expecting any of the guards to answer him.

"Keep going, all the way to the top."

"At least give me a clue as to what's going on," he pleaded. As expected, he did not receive an answer. The whole placed jerked suddenly and a loud metal clang echoed through the place. "What was that?" Kail demanded as he kept from colliding face first into the wall.

"We're docked. Keep moving. They are waiting for you," the guard said. The group continued to climb flights of stairs passing several floors. The vibrations and humming in the background faded and everything seemed to be magnitudes louder once the constant background noise receded. "Last door at the end of the hallway," the guard pointed.

Kail walked as instructed. The guards stopped a good ten feet before the door and motioned for him to continue. *Well, this is it,* he thought. The door didn't look too complicated to use. A large double handed leaver sat in the center that seemed to work the locking mechanism. Grabbing the leaver with both hands he gave it a sharp jerk. *All metal doors must be alike* he thought. The metal shrieked as he pushed the door open and stepped out of the hall.

The wind gusting into his face was the first thing he noticed. Second was the wind catching the door and that almost flung him off his feet. Struggling to close the heavy door, Kail leaned into it with his weight. Once shut he jerked a handle that returned the securing bolt to its place. Looking around for the first time, he saw that he was outdoors and it seemed to be night time. Where he did not know, but lights were everywhere. *I'm on some platform somewhere,* he thought. Mist whipped up by the wind rushed by him from somewhere. It was cold and damp considering it was still late summer, and the nights were not any cooler than the days.

Movement at the far end of platform caught his attention. Bastiana skipped over to him and grabs Kail by the hand. "Come on," she shouted over the wind, "they are waiting for you."

"Who's waiting? Where am I?"

"You'll see silly," she laughed and led him to the side of the platform that had a ramp leading down to what looked like a flat deck.

Following her down the ramp, it began to dawn on Kail as he looked back. "That's the airship I was on. That's the Colossus," he yelled at her. She didn't answer him but continued to pull him towards the door on the side of the building with the deck. The door opened as they approached and together they hurried inside. "What's going on Tiana?"

The large room had high vaulted ceilings. The walls were made of glass and Kail could see for the first time that they were up very high. Whatever building they were in was clearly the tallest in this city. Other buildings that towered to the clouds stood in all directions. Lights from their windows lit the night sky and blocked out the stars. He could see the massive airship that brought him to this place moored outside as well. It was not the only vessel to be seen. Dozens of airships could be seen flying above and around the cityscape. Small points of light in the far distance showed where the ground was. Street lamps lit every corner and walkway to keep the darkness of night away. Massive parallel lines moving away from the city indicated where rail systems traveled in and out of the city. "Where am I?"

"You are in Courduff," a voice answered. "Though it appears that you are standing in Canyamar," the voice mused.

"What?" Kail questioned. Looking down for the first time he could see that the floor of the room was a large detailed map of the world. As the voice had spoken, he seemed to be standing in the middle of Canyamar. A large area so far to the south of Aldervale that it would take several months if not the better part of a year to travel to by horse. The detail of the map was exquisite. Kail bent down for a closer look. It appeared that if you looked hard enough, every detail was exact. He could see tiny wisps of white that barely seemed to move across mountain chains. The color of the water for the rivers was perfect and they seemed to shimmer as they made their way to the seas. It was like looking down on the world if you were fifty miles tall. "This, this map is real. I mean it's showing me what it looks like in Canyamar right now, isn't it?"

"Yes, it is young master Falconcrest," the voice said. A bald man in formal black robes with red silk trim approached. "A masterwork that has never been repeated."

"Falconcrest? You are the second person to call me that," Kail said still captivated by the map on the floor.

"Indeed," he commented. "Vincent?" looking at the other man in the room.

Vincent responded with a small shake of his head.

"Interesting indeed," the bald man said reaching Kail's side. "Shall we have a discussion then? I'm sure you have many questions."

"Um yeah, I would like that."

"Please come," he indicated to the center of the room. A large table had been set with plates of food and various drinks.

Kail wondered how he had missed it before but gave it little thought as they all sat around the table. Tiana joined Vincent who Kail recognized as the man from the Colossus that had greeted the officers in Aldervale before Tiana had teleported and caused a panic.

"Help yourself. The voyage from Aldervale is a long one. Even by air," the bald man gestured to the food on the table.

"Thank you," replied Kail with a furrowed brow, remembering the cold cramped cell he had been in. The only food or drink was the small amount Tiana had brought him. His treatment on the Colossus was in stark contrast to what was happening now.

Tiana seemed right at home and did not hesitate pouring herself some wine. Kail too after a moment's consideration selected some cheeses and sweet meats from the plate in front of him. Vincent looked like everyone else in the room was invisible to him and ate silently beside Tiana. Only the bald man across from Kail did not seem interested in the feast before them.

"Let us get the formalities out of the way," he spoke. "I trust that you know Vincent and his excitable companion the lovely Bastiana."

"Um, mostly," answered Kail.

"My name is Therion," the bald man offered.

"I've heard of you. You're in charge of Courduff and the Mage Council. Or at least what's left of it from what I've heard," Kail said as he poured himself a glass of some liquid that smelled faintly of flowers.

"It's good to hear that I am known in the far reaches of Courduff's influence. Yes, there is little left of the Mage Council. It was an antiquated system that has lost its usefulness in this age of invention. Its members are either dead or enjoying their retirement how they see fit."

"Does that mean you're a mage as well? I mean if you were its leader, it would make you one of them right?"

"Some would call me that," Therion mused. "I have many titles it seems, depending on whom I'm in the company of. Mage, Governor, Savior and even Tyrant to some, though I am particularly fond of General. That was the rank I held during the War of Antiquities. But a title is nothing more than a way for one man to assert his status on society and those around him."

"Ok, so why am I here?" Kail asked. "Why beat me up, toss me in a cell, take me here and then have dinner like an awkward family reunion?"

"I do apologize for your recent treatment," Therion said as he glanced at Vincent. "But you are very special to us and I needed to be sure that you would arrive."

"You could have just asked."

"Indeed. Now, for the first part of your question. Why are you here?" Therion got up from the table. The lights from the ceiling dimmed slightly and allowed a better view of the city around them. "It's really quite the story. I don't expect you to understand it all, but I will explain best I can."

Tiana left the table as well and walked around the glass walls slowly taking in the view. Vincent remained seated seemingly lost in his own thoughts. Kail refilled his glass with a different type of wine. The last glass that smelled like flowers tasted bitter.

"Are you familiar with the writings and prophecies that tell about the end of the world?" Therion asked.

"Some, everyone has heard of the end of the world stories. But they are just stories right? Meant to scare you when you're growing up so you learn to behave and stuff. I haven't given them much thought though honestly."

"I like the way you think Kail. I agree with your assessments of those teachings. Let me add this to the question. If you believe that your world is going to die in fire, water, or famine depending on your upbringing, and you do? Is it prophecy and foretelling, or are you a victim of your own beliefs?" Therion presented. "In other words, you subconsciously sabotage yourself to where you fall victim to what you have been told."

"Maybe, I haven't ever thought of it like that," Kail said.

"Take the Keratin Nation from history. A race so scared of being conquered by others that they warred with everyone until they were wiped from the planet. Was it fated to be, or did they do it to themselves out of their own fears?"

"I don't know, sir," was all Kail could come up with.

"The Keratins are not alone in this. The Maynooth, Canyamar, and Graal have all vanished to the dusty pages of history. Each of them had their own religion, magic, and beliefs. The constant here is that history repeats itself."

"Alright, I can follow that much" Kail said, "but what does that have to do with me?"

Therion returned to the table for a glass of wine before continuing. Ushering Kail to the glass walls they admired the city around them. The lights in the streets blinked and the massive floating vessels commanded the skies, "Everything you see here is new. In the last fifty years or so the things that men have discovered and built is unparalleled," he motioned to the city. "The mage's are next I fear to fall to pages of history. We were rare to begin with, but recent war and the rise of the alchemy consortiums with their inventers, have pushed us aside. It was all I could do to retain what power and control I had left after disbanding the Mage Council, the ruling body that stood for a thousand years."

Tiana made her way around the room running her fingers along the glass. Ghostly images appeared on the walls. Kail could see robed figures going about their day. "Is that the Council?" he asked.

"Yes, as it was and had been for centuries," Therion answered. "Now, to get back to your questions Kail, I need to tell you of your past."

"My past?"

"What do you remember of your parents Kail? Your birth parents, before you came to live in Aldervale."

"Not much really. All I recall of my father is a black blur of a man, same goes for my mother, but she is a white blur, if that makes sense. I seem to remember that we moved around a lot. I don't have any strong memories of any places," he offered.

"Do you know their names?"

"Uncle Royce said my father ran off when they were kids. But now that you ask, I don't know their names. How is that they have never told me, or that I never asked?"

A smile came to Therion's face. "It's a subtle enchantment really. Very powerful though. It will misdirect you and you will not even know it. You just find yourself deviated and distracted a bit. The focus of your question is then lost."

"Are my aunt and uncle doing it on purpose? Why would they hide this from me?" demanded Kail.

"Oh, I doubt they are intentionally misleading you. I imagine they have been influenced by the same enchantment. It's quite possible that your uncle does not even have a brother. That's why he can only come up with a vague memory of him running off when they were young." Therion concluded.

Therion turned away from the city and made his way back to the table. The food had all been removed and only decanters of wine and drink remained. "Your mother, I do not know. Your father, I know very well," he admitted.

"My father?"

"A great man your father. We fought together in the War of Antiquities. He was the strongest among us," he recalled.

"My father was a mage?"

"Not just any mage Kail. He was easily one of the most powerful mages the Council had seen," Therion said, keeping an eye on how Kail reacted to his words.

"What was his name?" Kail asked, still transfixed on the city around them and the ghosts on the glass that Tiana created.

"His name was Duke Falconcrest," he answered. "I always found it amusing that his first name also served as a title."

"Duke Falconcrest," Kail repeated as he turned away from the view and returned to the table where Therion and Vincent sat. "So my father is, or was, a mage," he continued "What does that have to do with me?"

"Well, as I pointed out earlier, we're a dying breed," Therion gestured to everyone present in the room. "You, young Falconcrest, are also a mage."

"What? I'm not a mage. I'm just someone from a small town that helps around the farm and puts up with mean old ladies," Kail retorted. "I can't do the things that mages can."

"True. You are not a mage yet," Therion said. "One of the great many things your father did before abandoning the Council was to create a binding rune that strips a mage of his powers," he stated while giving Vincent a sidelong glance. "I believe- we believe that this same binding has been passed to you."

"What do you mean," Kail sat confused.

"When your father abandoned the Council, the first mage to be silenced by these binding runes was himself."

"This makes no sense to me, sir. I'm trying to follow everything that you're telling me."

"We believe Kail that because your father bound his powers away, that when you were born, your powers were also suppressed," Therion clarified.

"Are you kidding me? This is getting absurd." Kail protested. "I'm not a mage; I don't have super mage powers locked up inside me like some fairy tale."

Therion's patience was starting to wear thin. "The self fulfilling prophecies are coming about, Falconcrest. I am not about to allow the mages to simply die off like unwanted sheep. The Council has already been broken, your father started that!" he spat. "The ignorant masses are already marching themselves into darkness because they believe in some misunderstood dogma." Therion stood pointing at Kail. "You, Kail Falconcrest, are a mage. You with my help will recreate the Mage Council and bring the rest to heel as it has been for a thousand years."

"Are you mad? I'm a farmer, nothing more," Kail countered.

"The Guardian is back, the council is broken. The masters equip for war," Vincent commented. His words startled Kail who had for the most part forgotten that he was there. "Many religions and races fear what is to come."

Kail stood speechless.

"I know it's a lot to take in for one night," soothed Therion. "Bastiana will see you to accommodations below. We will continue another day, when you have had time to process," he said leaving the table.

Vincent also removed himself from the room and made his way back to the Colossus. Soon only Tiana and himself were left in the map room above the city. "This way," she waved and led him out of the room. Stopping at a door a few floors below where they had been she opened it. "I'm so glad you're here," she whispered to Kail's ear. Planting a soft kiss on his cheek she turned and left him standing outside his room.

Chapter 7

"This is such a waste of time," muttered Xavier as he looked out the window of the café at the impressive skyscraper across the street. Angela had just arrived to relieve him.

"Nothing new is there," she said, sliding into the booth across from him.

"We have been here for days. Mr. Eleazar is never going to show up. They boy is as good as dead at this point," he smirked.

"Camden left this morning," she commented.

"Good for him," Xavier said, as he leaned across the table towards Angela. "This whole thing is falling apart and it's going to get worse as we go forward," he emphasized by banging his fist on the table.

A stern cough came from the waitress on the other side of the café, along with a dirty look when he hit the table. Xavier replied to the waitress with a sneer. "One more day, and were gone, with or without the boy," he finished with a shake of his finger in Angela's face. Xavier left the table. On his way out the door he pocketed some cigarettes from the counter display and tossed a handful of coins on the counter that clattered and some bounced to the floor. The waitress shook her fist and called him a foul name as the door closed behind him.

Angela turned to look back out at the window to the building entrance across the street that they had been watching since they arrived in Courduff. It was extremely dangerous for them to be here. There had been some rough arguments between the three of them when Mr. Eleazar failed to arrive. Angela hated that the Colossus was still here, moored to the top of the building that had served as the last seat of power for the Mage Council. Remembering her last run in with the ship, it had not ended well. All she could do was wait and hope that the mage she fought on board did not try and divine her location. Camden leaving had lowered her spirits as well. That left her with the burned rat Xavier for company, or just flat out abandoning the situation all together.

Therion had not been back to see or talk to Kail since that first night. Kail had a lot of time on his hands the last few days to think about everything. Most of his time was spent up in the map room. Tiana had shown him a bit more about how it worked. Right now he stood over his home town of Aldervale. The map could actually grow or shrink depending on how one focused their mind at it. He had the map dialed in as far as it would go and the entire floor area showed the town including his aunt and uncle's farm on one side of the room, and the airstrip under construction on the other. The map showed tiny people going about their day. There was not enough detail to tell who the individuals were, but he was able to make some good guesses judging how some of the specks moved.

"It's quite the tool is it not," Therion's voice echoed in the empty chamber.

Startled by the unexpected visitor, Kail looked up from the map. When his concentration was broken, the map quickly returned to its original state of displaying the whole world. The sudden change in perspective caught Kail off guard. Vertigo washed over him and he momentarily lost his balance and stumbled part way across the room. "Yeah," he exclaimed. "It's incredible, the amount of information it shows you, the possibilities are endless from city planning, to moving armies, to, to well anything."

"I'm going to be frank with you Kail Falconcrest. You have something I want, and I think it's time for me, to as you put it, to just ask for it," Therion said as he approached Kail steadying himself.

"Alright, sure, what is it?"

"I want to release your power from the bonds your father passed on to you," he said.

"That's it? Why?" Kail asked.

"I have my reasons Kail. But your father was my friend. Let me do this for you," Therion emphasized.

"Can I think about it?" Kail asked. "I mean, I don't know anything about magic or being a mage," he shrugged.

"We can discuss it tonight at dinner," Therion offered and left the room.

Tiana walked into the map room as Therion left and made her way over to Kail. "So are you excited?" she asked.

"What do you mean?"

"Becoming one of us. A mage silly," she smiled. "You know, from what I've learned about your father, I'm guessing you might be as strong as me," she said coyly.

"Why is this so important to you guys? That I'm a mage?"

"Well, lots of reasons really. Mostly because there are not many of us left," she said sadly. "People don't seem to need us anymore. When was the last time you heard about a great healer who walked the land?"

"I haven't thought of it like that," he replied.

"Granted, a lot of people don't like us because of the things we can do. But think about what you might be able to do for them. Like your friends in Aldervale. You would be a natural leader. People would look up to you."

"Do they look up to you Tiana?" Kail asked.

"No... I don't have anything like you do Kail. Vincent found me when I was little. I was abandoned to the streets and he took me in," she said softly. "He's like my father. I would do anything he asked."

"I see," Kail said, not really understanding how that answered his question.

The pair continued to chat in the map room unaware that every word and gesture was being watched. "What are you planning to do Therion?" Vincent asked as he watched the scene play out on the divining wall.

"This game comes to an end tonight Vincent. I will strip his father's binding abomination from him and when his power is unleashed, I will feed it to the focusing stones. And with it I will do what the Mage Council was too weak and foolish not to do," Therion said angrily. "I will grind the world beneath my boot and restore our place of power as the rightful rulers."

"And the prophecy, does this not play right along with what it says?" countered Vincent.

"That's open to interpretation. The power given up shall be returned and the last to rule, shall lord over all. The Guardian will fall and the door will open for revenge yet taken. The childless one will decide the fate of all." Therion recited. "You on the other hand Vincent, better make sure she seduces him. Duke's son could be the end of this whole plan if she doesn't."

"I hope you are correct that if he fathers a child, it will remove him as a threat," stated Vincent.

"Do not let your feelings for your pet get in the way Vincent."

"Of course not," Vincent finished, as he watched the young pair as they moved about the map room.

Angela sighed as the day gradually made its way to the dusk of night. If she had to eat one more dish from this café, she was convinced she would go into a murderous rampage. Xavier had not returned either and she concluded that she was now on her own. Only the demonstrated power of the Time Walker kept her watching from the café. She wondered if he would return her to that moment before death if she left like the others.

"I wouldn't do a thing like that," said Mr. Eleazar from across the table. "I'm a lot of things, but I'm not cruel."

His sudden appearance almost put Angela on tilt. One of the war blades was half way out of its hidden sheath before his first sentence was complete. His physical appearance was different as well. Streaks of white ran through his normally brown hair, and it had been a week or more since his last shave as well. The clear bright blue eyes were the same though.

"Keep doing things like that and you will either kill someone of fright or find a knife in your chest for the same reasons," she chastised.

"Well, tonight's the big night," he said as he reached over and popped a bit of uneaten food from Angela's plate into his mouth.

"Time Walker, we have been here for days. Camden and Xavier have already left. If nothing was going to happen until tonight, why did you send us here?"

"I told you not to be late, I recall. Not arrive four days early," he dismissed. "Don't worry about the others. Camden Arland is spending his money wisely I'm sure and as far as Xavier Ross goes, he will crawl out of the wood work when things get exciting," he said licking the bits of food from his fingers. "Finish your food, we need to get going soon," he finished by looking at his pocket watch.

The dinner was quiet. Vincent once again seemed to zone out everyone and everything around him. Therion sipped some wine but did not touch his food and only took his eyes from Kail when he refilled his cup. Tiana kept glancing at him as well and offered encouraging smiles. Kail wasn't able to get much food down. His appetite just wasn't there given the situation.

"So, are we going to do this?" Kail said cheekily at the atmosphere in the room.

Tiana clapped her hands excitedly, and Therion put his wine down with a smile.

"Vincent, if you please," Therion instructed, and the man left the table. "Come," he gestured to Kail. Once all of them had stood, Therion waved his hand and the table along with its meal vanished.

Vincent returned to the room and brought with him a large rough uncut crystal.

"What's that?" asked Kail.

"This," taking the crystal from Vincent and presenting it in front of Kail, "is a focusing stone" he explained. "They are natural focusing crystals that mages can use for a countless number of things. Tonight we are going to use it to undo what your father did so long ago."

Swiftly, Vincent stepped behind Kail and secured his arms with a vice like grip.

"Hey!" struggled Kail. "What is this?"

Tiana casually stepped up to Kail as he struggled in Vincent's grip. Cupping his face in her soft hands she stared into his confused eyes. "Try not to fight it, this is going to hurt. A lot," she whispered and brought her soft lips to his and kissed him. Breaking the embrace she mouthed the words *I'm sorry.*

In one hand, the focusing stone was glowing brightly, and with the other Therion made a pulling motion towards Kail. Ribbons of silver and orange light seemed to flow from the air around them and gather in his hand.

Kail could smell something beginning to burn. It had that acrid smell of hair being melted off of your arm when it got too close to a fire. The pain started slowly in his wrists and forearms. Looking down he could see strange symbols starting to appear on them. Quickly the pain became intense as the runic bindings began to burn and melt their way out of his skin. It did not stop there. He could feel the same sensations starting around his neck. His tongue soon followed and it felt like it was on fire and ready to explode. The pain from his arms he might have been able to handle, but now with the searing pain other places his mind went into panic mode. *Hot, too hot,* he panicked. Screams filled his ears and if it wasn't for Vincent holding him, he would have been a writhing ball on the floor.

Vincent held his face away from the boy. The runes gave off a blinding light as they removed themselves. He could feel the intense heat they gave off. The smell of burning flesh filled the room and threatened to spill his dinner. Bastiana had unknowingly backed several paces away from the scene. Her eyes were a mix of fascination, horror, and lust at what was going on. She noticed that the map below them was moving, no spinning around wildly. Almost like it was searching in panic for a place to go.

Therion continued to channel the removal spell through the focusing stone. He could see that the pain of removal had most likely shattered the boy's mind as his head was forced back and only the whites of his eyes could be seen. It didn't matter as long as the Duke's power was his. The first rune fell from the boy's flesh to land on the map room floor. Parts of the boy's flesh still clung to the rune and sizzled. The map jerked in response to the runic binding that now rested there. Its power seemed to hold the map down. Soon several more of the runic bindings dripped from the flesh of the Falconcrest boy to the floor.

This is it, this is death. Kail couldn't even scream anymore. He was sure his tongue as well as the rest of his mouth had burned away. He could not breathe past the burning in his throat. He couldn't see, but it felt like his hands had burned away and flames must be traveling up his arms. *Burned alive, one inch at a time. Water, need water* his mind screamed at him.

When the last rune made its way out of Kail's body, Therion stopped the channeling. "Now, let's see what's left."

Vincent released his grip on the boy and let him fall limply to the floor. He felt dead to him, and turned to look at Bastiana.

Falling, I'm falling into death, Kail's mind processed. *No falling into water, yes, cool wet water to quench the fire that is eating me up.*

"Pathetic," muttered Therion, as he looked at the convulsing farm boy on the floor. Placing the focusing stone on Kail's flesh, he then began to prepare for the next part of their plan.

The burning pain from before was nothing compared to what happened next. *Why am I not dead yet*? The sharp pain that pierced his back hurled him back to the realm of the suffering. Whatever it was, he was sure it was pulling his bones out of his body. Screams came again, but were short lived as he felt his will leave him. *It will be over soon,* he thought. *But I want water,* a separate part of his mind focused. *Stop the burning.*

Motes of light began to rise up from Kail's crumpled body on the floor. Therion wove his spell to suck Kail's magical energies into the crystal that began to work its way into his flesh.

"He's going to die isn't he?" questioned Bastiana.

A glare from Vincent was as good as a slap to her face to be quiet and not interrupt the spell.

I can see water, Kail thought. *There in front of me. I can see it. I have to get to the water. I must get to the water! Move, go to the water,* he thought. *Move now or die!*

The lights above the map room exploded suddenly and bolts of multi-colored electricity arched about the room. "What's happening?" yelled Vincent. A blue glow began to surround Kail's body. All the windowed glass walls in the room shattered in unison. Blinding winds rushed into the map room. The glow around Kail intensified until it suffocated all other senses with its intensity.

Move! His mind yelled. The sensation of falling came again. *There, the water, its coming closer. Cool water that will save him from burning to ash.* Kail's body hit the water a lot harder than he expected. *Cool water,* his mind soothed as darkness overtook him.

Slowly, vision began to return to Vincent. Looking about the ruined room he could see his darling Bastiana sitting on the floor hiding her eyes in her clutched legs. Therion appeared to be laid out cold on the floor. The boy, Kail Falconcrest was nowhere to be seen. Neither was the focusing stone. What was on the floor however, was a collection of silvery runes neatly arranged in three circles; one loop for each wrist, and a larger one for a neck.

Mr. Eleazar and Angela stood in the street in front of the skyscraper. Several times lights had flashed from the top of the tower that lit up everything around it. They were not alone in watching. Other people had paused in their activities to wonder at the goings on up there. A distant crash could be heard and the light that preceded it grew so bright that for a moment, the darkness was pushed back and it was brighter than daylight. Even the dark sky flashed blue in the moment.

"Well, that's unexpected," Mr. Eleazar said as he turned and faced the East. "It seems we have miscalculated."

"What are you talking about Time Walker?" demanded Angela.

"For starters, it's about to rain glass. And no matter what anyone says, singing and dancing in that, is nothing we want to experience I can assure you," he scolded. "As for you, Keratin, it's time for you to rescue the young master before he drowns."

"What? How?" was all she managed to get out before Mr. Eleazar grabbed her by the wrist and with unexpected strength tossed her out into the street. Wind was blowing all around her as she fell. The street was no longer there to catch her unyieldingly. A small lake was rushing up at her fast. Instinctively she slowed her fall and stopped about ten feet above the surface of the lake. Hovering over the lake she took in her surroundings and mentally cursed the Time Walker as well. Below her, the lakes water had a ruddy color to it and she caught site of Kail's body slipping into the depths below. Panic hammered her heart and she plunged full speed into the water after him.

Chapter 8

Ari Ebonmore made her way down the foot path to the lake. It was nice to get away from Aldervale for a while. With so many people in town these days, she felt like everything was closing in on and suffocating her. Airships had started to arrive on a daily basis now and the noise some of them made reminded her of the worst night storms that scared her when she was little.

It had taken a bit of begging to get her father to let her go to the lake when it was going to be dark. Pointing out that, that was the only time you could gather some of the herbs and mosses that were fairly valuable and in short supply now a days. What she hadn't told her father was that she was also going to meet a very nice man that had talked to her earlier in the week. She was quite taken with his bright blue eyes and how kind and well mannered he had been to her. Also she found listening to his accent made her heart beat faster and caused her to blush. He said tonight was going to be a special night and that it would be a shame to miss it.

She could see the lake coming into view. The moon was just rising as the sun was setting and cast a mix of silver light to dance with the sunset rays across the expanse. The scene before her was beautiful; this was truly a special night.

A bright flash suddenly lit up the surrounding area followed quickly by a loud splash in the lake. Ari hurried to the lake's edge as large ripples were moving away from where something had disturbed the water's surface. A second flash of light lit the sky and she could see something was falling towards the lake. Before it crashed into the water the object stopped short. It wasn't a something, she could see now it was a person with pale skin, funny clothes and red hair that moved like flames. The woman floating above the lake looked lost as she spun about in confusion. Whatever she was looking for she apparently found quickly, and dove into the water where the first splash had come from.

Ari stood on the edge of the lake trying to comprehend what she had just seen. One thing was for sure, this night was not something she was going to forget anytime soon. At first she thought the woman above the lake was a ghost. *But ghosts wouldn't cause a splash would they?* Also, the woman looked a lot like the one who spent three weeks at her family's inn. And lastly, the woman was flying.

Angela broke through to the surface of the water and filled her lungs with a huge gasp of air. Kail's limp body came to the surface as well. She hurried as much as she could while keeping his head above water. Swimming for the two of them seemed to take ages as each second seemed to take forever when Kail was not breathing.

Once she reached closer to the shore, her feet found purchase on the muddy bottom. It was easier to pull him through the water than it had been to swim. She could start to see some of the extent of the injuries he had. His neck looked like he had been hung until the flesh had come off. Dragging his body out of the water, Angela quickly checked to see if his heart was beating. "Damn," she cursed and placed her mouth on his and breathed. "Damn it," she repeated with each breath that brought no change in his condition. "Damn it!" she yelled as she slammed her fist into his chest. Water gurgled and coughed from his lips.

Kail could feel someone beating on his chest. *Was this torture to never end?* Air suddenly rushed into his lungs. The stinging pain of that first breath as it fought for the right to be in his lungs that the lake water had invaded brought him back to the realm of the living. Coughing out water with each ragged breath was a fight. Slowly, now that he was not in the water, the burning in his neck and arms began to return and replace its pain over the rawness from nearly drowning. The last thing he saw before succumbing back to unconsciousness was the lovely face above him. He remembered that face from the inn. *She must have killed me for kissing her,* he thought.

Ari stood in the darkness watching the woman pull someone from the water and then try to resuscitate them. The sound of the man coughing startled her from her initial shock of the events. "Do you need help?" she called, stepping from the darkness around the lake. The woman spun towards her and brandished two long swords that gave off a silvery sheen in the moonlight.

"Who is there?" demanded Angela when she heard someone call out and approach.

"You are that woman, and… is that Kail?" Ari replied. "Oh my god, what's happened to him?"

"God had nothing to do with this," Angela relaxed seeing that it was nothing more than the innkeeper's daughter and returned her attention to the dying Kail.

With the immediate threat of drowning past them, Angela began to assess the extent of Kail's injuries. The worst of them seemed to be around his neck. His arms and wrists also had similar wounds and a large gash in his back looked like he had been stabbed.

"Those look like burns," Ari commented as she knelt beside him.

"He has lost a lot of blood, and the water has not helped. If we do not stop the rest of the bleeding, he will die for sure."

"Ok," Ari stammered. "I, I, I've been gathering some night moss, If we mix it with some water and apply it to some cloth, it should help stop the bleeding and take some of the pain away." Ari rummaged through the bag she had with her to find the mosses.

Angela once again pulled one of her Keratin war blades from its sheath. Ari stopped what she was doing when the weapon was brandished at her. "Stop jumping like a fawn. Use it to cut your dress for bandages."

"Yes, right, of course," Ari replied, and began to cut part of her dress into strips.

The two of them continued to work quickly in silence. Grinding the moss with rocks and adding it to wet bandages made from Ari's dress. Soon the burns on his arms were wrapped and they moved to the burns on his neck. "The wound on his back will need to be sewn," Angela stated.

Her voice caused a yelp from Ari.

"Calm yourself, where is the nearest place we can take him?"

Still shaking, "Um… Let me think. His place is not too far from here. We could take him there," Ari managed to get out.

Angela stood and moved off into the darkness around the lake. Ari could hear her moving about and hacking at the underbrush in the trees with one of her weapons.

"What has happened to you Kail? What have you gotten yourself involved in?" Ari wondered out loud. This was not what she had expected tonight, not at all.

Angela returned with several long saplings that she had chopped down and began to skin the bark off in long strips. "Wrap them and twist like this," she instructed the girl. "It will hold together for what we need." Soon the pair had a makeshift stretcher. "Lead," Angela commanded, and they made their way from the lake.

The Kelly farm was dark as the two made their way from the forest's edge. Thankfully the light of the full moon lit the area. Ari's arms ached with fatigue from carrying half of the stretcher through the woods from the lake. Her dress had become even more torn and dirtied as it had snagged on everything possible. The strange girl who had introduced herself as Angela Atagi in front of her seemed to be tireless. Several times Ari had stumbled in the dark and nearly lost her hold on the stretcher that carried Kail's body. Each time she had received a harsh word from the woman with swords, but now she only got a harsh glare. Soon the pair crossed the fields and arrived at the back of the house past the barn.

"Set him down," Angela instructed.

Placing the stretcher down, Ari took the moment to sit next to him and rest. Her hands had been worn raw from the wood. Her arms ached so much that she doubted that she could even pick the stretcher back up let alone get him inside the house.

Angela tried the door, but it was locked. That wasn't about to stop her though. Taking a step back she kicked the door hard with all her might and it gave without hesitation.

The smashing of the door just about gave Ari an early death of fright. She did not cry out though because she was so exhausted. "You could have just knocked you know," she scolded.

Jessica Kelly lay awake in her bed with her husband Royce snoring beside her. She had tried to shake him awake earlier when she heard people outside, but all Royce did was roll over and mumble something under his breath. When the door downstairs was nearly kicked off its hinges, her husband had come awake finally and was already across the room to grab a wood cutting axe and making his way downstairs to confront the robbers his wife had heard.

"I'm too tired. My arms won't work anymore," agonized Ari as the other woman seemed ready to make her lift the stretcher by use of her swords. "Watch out!" she yelled as an axe swinging madman came barreling out of the house after the two intruders.

Royce swung the axe at the closest intruder to him. There was no way they were going to get away with this intrusion after his nephew had gone missing earlier in the week. The robber ducked at the last second, tipped off by a warning shout. The axe lodge itself deeply into one of the porch posts. A silvery flash blinked in front of him as he took one confused look at the axe handle in his hands as it had been cut cleanly in two. Before he could take his eyes off the stick he now held, a second flash, but this one a blur of dark and red made contact with the side of his head. Royce didn't feel his body hit the porch as he was already knocked out before he hit the ground.

"Stop it!" Ari shouted. "This is his family," she scolded. "Mrs. Kelly! Mrs. Kelly! Help us, we need help. Mrs. Kelly!" she called into the house.

Jessica Kelly came running out of the house after hearing her name being called for help. The scene before her was one of chaos and confusion. Her husband lay on the porch with someone standing over him holding a pair of swords. Further out she could see her nephew laid out as well and Ari, the inn keeper's daughter, kneeling beside him. "What is going on here?"

Angela grabbed Royce by the feet and began to drag him out of the way and moved back to Kail on the stretcher. "Grab him and take him inside," she commanded to Mrs. Kelly. "She is too weak," indicating at Ari. "Ari, go in and find a place where we can put him."

Ari ran into the house ahead of them and began to turn on the lamps.

"We need a place with a lot of light to sew him up," called Angela.

"Sew him up?" Mrs. Kelly questioned. "What's happened?"

"Talk later, I need to save him first," Angela motioned for Mrs. Kelly to move into the house.

"The kitchen counter will work," Ari called out of sight.

"Have her fetch thread and needle," Angela instructed as they set Kail onto the counter top and she rolled him onto his side to view the wound on his back. "Tend to your man. I will not be as kind if he wakes and tries to swing an axe at me again," she dismissed Kail's aunt.

Ari returned with small kit of needles and thread. Once the bandage on Kail's back was removed, she winced at the site of the wound. The gash on his back was deep and jagged like something had torn into his skin. She helped Angela in silence by bringing clean cloth and water. She watched Angela work the needle with skill and precision. "Call if you need me," she said and left to go sit by Mrs. Kelly.

Jessica Kelly sat on the edge of a divan that she had moved to her husband. "What is going on Ari? He has been gone for days, and now you show up with him in, in, in, this condition. That woman assaults my husband and you break into my house," was all she could get out on the verge of a teary breakdown.

"I don't know Mrs. Kelly, I don't know. I was down by the lake tonight collecting. I heard them, saw them. I mean, I don't know what I saw for sure, but she was there pulling him out of the lake. He was bad, but she saved him. Whoever did this to him, it wasn't her."

Angela finished working on Kail's back. The wound was closed, cleaned, and covered with a fresh treated bandage. She turned her attention to the rest of his wounds by first by removing the bandages that had been hastily put together at the dark muddy edge of the lake. Carefully cleaning each wound brought questions. *What had Therion been doing to him in that tower? If he had wanted to simply kill Kail, why keep him there for days, why torture him like this. The Time Walker has a lot of questions to answer the next time I see him. These wounds would take months to heal in the best of cases*. "We need to get a healer," she spoke softly to herself.

"He is coming around," Angela heard Ari say from the other room.

"Keep him away from here. He will try and kill us if he sees his nephew like this without explanation first," Angela replied still administering to Kail.

Ari and Mrs. Kelly did as instructed. It was not too hard for them to keep Royce in the other room. The lump on the side of his head made sure of that, as well as the knowledge that his wife was not in danger and was unhurt. Ari explained what she could to him. The night eventually gave way to the first rays of the morning sun before Angela came out of the kitchen.

"He will live as long as nothing goes wrong or he gets an infection," Angela reported. "We need to get him to a healer, is there one in Aldervale?"

"No, there hasn't been a healer in Aldervale since the last big war when all the magic users left." Mrs. Kelly answered.

"How is the head," Angela asked Royce with a wave of her hand.

"I'll live," he replied. "That's a mean kick you have there."

"It was quicker, and we did not have time to wait," she smiled.

"Can we see him?" asked Mrs. Kelly.

"Yes, he did not wake or stir at all. I fear whatever has done this to him may have caused him to hide inside his mind. We need to get him help. He is not safe here in Aldervale. Do not tell anyone of this and keep him here at all costs. I will be back as soon as I can," Angela said as she made for the doorway.

"Wait," Ari called after her. "What are we supposed to do?"

The rest of them followed Angela outside. Questions and demands overlapped behind her. However she did not answer any of them. On the horizon something caught her eye. Motioning for them to quiet, Angela continued to stare.

"What are you looking at?" asked Ari. Soon, all of them could see the speck in the sky as it grew bigger.

"Damn," cursed Angela. "Back into the house, now hurry!"

"Why? What is it? What have you gotten us into woman?" demanded Royce.

"It is a ship, and it is not going to Aldervale. It is coming this way," she said. The group returned to the kitchen where Kail remained unconscious.

The faint sound of the incoming airship could be heard as it made its way to the Kelly farm. Angela gave them all brief look and sighed. *A girl, a couple that didn't stand a chance and one potential hero that was more of a burden than anything else.*

"What are we going to do?" asked Mrs. Kelly. Royce stood next to her with a large kitchen knife.

"I doubt that will do you any good," Angela stated. She had both her war blades in each hand. "Is there a place you can hide?"

"No, not really," he replied. "Besides, he's family, if they get past you, they will have to get past us."

"And the girl? Do you speak for her too?"

All eyes swung towards Ari.

"I'm old enough to make my own choices," Ari stated.

Angela shook her head at the sudden bravery of these people. *Fools, all of them*, she thought. *This is where the killing would begin. A random girl, a family, and then what?* She knew well before it got to this point that a lot of people were going to die. But the last month had been so quiet, that she had forgotten to keep her nerves steeled. "Fine, but do not get in my way. Only worry about the ones that get past me."

The noise of the airship was loud as it arrived at the Kelly farm. Clearly stealth was not on their mind. Angela took the front room and debated to whether fight there or outside. She decided to stay inside and let the door way act as a choke point so no more than one or two would get a chance to battle. However she hated giving up the easy exit of being able to fly if things went bad. *No, the doorway was better*, as she looked at the three, no four people she needed to protect.

The anxiety of waiting was building up in them all, as the airship landed in the field just beyond the back yard near the barn. Angela moved to the other side of the room to keep the vessel in view. Two figures descended from the ship and jogged towards the farmhouse. Angela nodded to the group in the kitchen to prepare themselves.

"Angela, Angela!" one of the men called out over the noise of the settled airship. "Are you in there Red?"

"Camden?" Angela said to herself as she made her way to the door. Sure enough, one of the men coming up to the house was the big rough blond, Camden Arland.

Camden and Xavier made their way to the house and greeted Angela. "Did yah miss me Red?" he said with a big toothy grin.

"You are a welcome sight Camden. Even your ugly visage is a relief Xavier," she greeted as she put away the twin blades.

"Do you have the boy? Is he alive?" asked Xavier.

"Yes, he is inside, but he is hurt badly, we need to get a healer," Angela said leading the pair inside. "It is all right," she called to the hiding people.

Ari and the Kelly's came out of the kitchen when called. "It is going be ok, I know these men" Angela explained.

Xavier examined Kail first. "Where did you find him?"

"I pulled him from the lake. It looks like he had something burned out of him and a wound on the back," she said.

"Was that it? Was there anything else?"

"No, just the girl Ari happened to be there and a misunderstanding when we brought him here."

Xavier moved away and sneered at anyone who looked at him from the corner of the room.

"Don't worry about him," Camden told them. "He won't grow on you no matter how much time you give him."

"We need to hurry," Xavier pressed.

"Hurry where?" demanded Royce, "Where are you taking him?"

"Do not worry," Angela said. "We will get him the help he needs and everything will be fine."

Angela and Camden each took a side and lifted Kail off the counter and made their way through the house to the airship. Xavier's glare did a good job at quieting any further questions from the Kelly's and Ari. "I recommend you go back to your little lives and forget all this," Xavier advised them.

Ari, Mr. and Mrs. Kelly stood on the porch and watched them carry off Kail. The events of the last night had left them all a little shell shocked. It wasn't until the airship took off and faded over the horizon did any of them question their decision to just let him be taken away like that.

Chapter 9

Kail slowly came back to the realm of the living. The first thing to return was his hearing. The low humming of the airship in flight was the first noise he made out. *I have been here before,* he remembered, *and I did not like where that had led.* He could make out faint voices as well. He did not recognize any of them, but that did not matter. What did matter was trying to remember how he got here. Images of being beaten in an alley flashed in his mind. *No, that wasn't right, that was before.* All he could remember was a map. *The map room,* that jogged his memory. *Therion, the leader of Courduff and god knows what else. They were talking in the map room. Something about becoming a mage and joining them. Then things went horribly wrong. Therion did something to me and I remember burning. Burning so much that I thought I was going to burn alive. Then water and that woman from the inn was there. It made little sense.*

"I have been at his side for three days. I am not very good at this yet sir," a small voice said.

"Keep at it Suki. If there is any change, notify me immediately," someone answered and left.

The next sense to return was that of smell. Metal and machinery mixed with the tang of antiseptic. Wherever he was, his mind concluded that it was a hospital or something.

Why would I be in a hospital, he wondered? That did not make sense with being trapped on an airship either. The sense of touch slowly returned as well. He could feel the coolness of the bed on which he lay. It was padded but barely. Parts of him felt flat and numb and that made sense with what he heard about being here for three days. His heart skipped a beat when he remembered his arms and neck melting in the map room. He felt for where he had been burned but found no pain. He could feel something wrapped around his arms as well as his neck. *They have me tied down!* His mind began to race. He felt hands at his neck. Fingers reaching around his neck, *NO!* his mind screamed.

Suki Leigh had spent the last three days pouring what little magic she had into the wounds of Kail Falconcrest. Given enough time and treatments she would be able to heal the wounds completely and chances were there would be little to no scarring at all. After Camden left she returned to remove the dressings around Kail's neck. Placing her fingertips on pink wounds, she was totally unprepared for the jolts of electricity that raced through her. Her eyes rolled back into her head and she crumpled to the floor.

Camden Arland, Xavier Ross and Angela Atagi all occupied the bridge of the Snow Break. Another woman occupied the helm, Ellenore Black, who occasionally barked an order into a relay tube or adjusted a break controlling the airship.

"And that's how I came to own the Snow Break," explained Camden.

"That is quite the story Arland. It fits you," complemented Angela. "She has a noble name."

Xavier snorted and lit another cigarette. "Do we even know yet where we're going, or we just going to fly in circles until the boy wakes up or Mr. Eleazar decides to join us?"

"You really should try to stop that nasty habit Mr. Ross," a voice said. Mr. Eleazar coalesced and walked to the forward view of the bridge, wisps of energy floated off of him. "A fine choice Mr. Arland," he added looking around the place. "A fine choice indeed."

They had started to become accustomed to Mr. Eleazar's random appearances however, the crew of the Snow Break had not. Ellenore gave a startled fright and half drew a blade before she realized that no one else seemed to be concerned about the newcomer.

"Now let's have a look at how the young master is doing shall we," Mr. Eleazar invited them.

"I was just down there, I told Suki to notify us when he wakes up," Camden informed him when no one moved to join him.

"Ah, yes, well that would be a good thing to do, if she were not sleeping on the job," Mr. Eleazar countered as he left the bridge to head to the lower deck where the infirmary was located. Angela made her way to follow and Camden joined her. Xavier made no move to be a part of the parade that headed to the infirmary.

Entering the infirmary, Kail still lay on the bed, but Suki lay on the floor. "Not a very good place to take a nap if I say so. And I'm a good judge of places where one would want to nap," stated Mr. Eleazar calmly.

Camden pushed passed him to the crumpled medic and helped her sit up.

"Ouch," she said groggily holding her head in her hands.

"What happened?"

"I don't know. I was healing him and the next thing I remember is you here now," she explained.

"Yes, well I'm sure it was quite a shock. I would want a nap before meeting me too," Mr. Eleazar dismissed. "Now let's see," as he made his way to the side of the bed. "Ten fingers. Ten toes. Scars look like they will fade, all the girls will like that," he eyed Angela and Suki. "Now time to wake up!" Mr. Eleazar said with a hard slap to Kail's face.

Kail's eyes flew open, his face stinging. "Who are you?" he said looking into a pair of very bright blue eyes filled with amusement.

"I think the more appropriate question, is 'who are you?'" he answered.

Kail tried to sit up but didn't do a very good job at it. Angela helped him up. The stitching had been removed from his back, and she could see that only a faint pink line remained where she had sewn him up only a few days earlier.

Kail gave her a strange look when he felt her run her fingers over the fading wound.

"Where am I?" Kail asked Angela as she was the only person in the room that seemed familiar to him, rubbing the side of his face where Mr. Eleazar had slapped him awake.

Angela looked to Camden to answer. "You are in the infirmary of my ship, the Snow Break. You have been unconscious for the last three days or more after Angela pulled you out of the lake."

"Angela?"

"Yea, Miss Red head to your right there," Camden continued. "My name is Camden Arland, happy slap there is Mr. Eleazar, and that is Suki," he pointed. "She has been healing those wounds of yours."

It was a lot to take in as Kail looked at everyone around him. "I'm hungry," was all he could think of to say.

"There are some fresh clothes for you over there," Suki gestured.

"Thanks."

"Galley is up one level. Meet us up there and we can talk about everything. Ladies, shall we?" Camden finished.

They all left Kail to change in private. He had a lot of questions for these people. Where he was going to start, he did not know. He felt different too. Kail examined his neck through a mirror that was hanging on the wall. The pink scars on his neck stood out, but they were not painful when he touched them. The clothes fit well enough, they were nothing special other than they seemed very utilitarian given the circumstances in which he found himself. He wondered how long it had really been since that day in the alley when he was beaten and taken from Aldervale. A small part of him wondered how long it would be before he saw the town again. *First rule of survival,* he thought. *food.* And he exited the infirmary and followed his nose up one level to the galley.

The food wasn't bad. About the same as you would eat if you packed for a long trip to the mountains to go camping. Four others were in the galley with him. The smaller girl, Suki wasn't there. But the pretty girl with red hair from the inn was there, Angela. The large blond Camden Arland, and of all people, the scarred guy he had run into several times back home was there as well. He had been introduced as Xavier Ross. The last person in the room was the one they called Mr. Eleazar. He had been talking nonstop since Kail arrived. The man had been hard to understand at first with his accent, but he was starting to get used to it.

"Wait," Kail interrupted Mr. Eleazar. "You expect me to believe that she," he pointed to Angela, "is a thousand years old?"

"Of course not, that would be ridiculous. It's not polite to discuss a woman's age anyway," Mr. Eleazar chastised. "If you would forget your linear concept of time for a moment and pay attention, I said that was when she was born, not how old she is. There is a difference you know."

"Welcome to the magical land of Eleazar," Camden joked.

"Quiet you," Mr. Eleazar shushed Camden. "Anyway that is who everyone is. Now I am going to guess that your next question is how do you fit into all of this?"

"Actually I think I know the answer to that one," Kail countered. "Therion seemed to think that I was, or am, the son of some great magic user from the war that happened thirtyish years ago. He wanted me to join him in restoring the mages to power."

"The first part is true, and the second part sounds like it follows Therion's motives as well," Mr. Eleazar agreed. "I do regret what happened to you there, but it was necessary."

"Necessary?" asked Angela.

"Oh yes, you see, Kail's father Duke Falconcrest at the end of the war created a runic binding that suppresses a person's ability to use magic. What he did not know, was that this binding is also passed to a person's child if they are born with magic. Thus you inherited your father's choice to abandon magic. He did this so he could leave the Council. Laws back then regarding the use of magic were strictly controlled," Mr. Eleazar explained. "The Duke was careful to leave an out. The bindings can be removed but only by the Council."

"I don't understand," said Kail.

"What he's saying, is Therion is the Council. He is the only one who could remove the bindings," Xavier told him filling the room with smoke from his cigarette. "This has all been about you boy. Think about it. The son of a powerful mage in a world when magic is on the decline. You're a weapon. Every side wants you, and everyone you side against will want to kill you," he finished and flicked his cigarette at them and stormed out of the galley.

Kail sat there and picked at the food in front of him. The unbelievable stories he was being told was starting to churn his stomach. He wished he was home with his aunt and uncle, Royce and Jessica Kelly. *Kelly, that wasn't even my real name, was it?* He didn't care if they were his real family or not, they had always been there for him as long as he could remember. They never tried to make him do anything he didn't want to do. Well maybe they made him work the farm a few times when he would rather have been off playing with his friends.

"I think that's enough for now," Camden said eyeing Kail staring blankly at the food in front of him. "How about I give you a tour of my boat, take your mind of things for a while and I'm sure Suki would like to see you later as well to continue to work on those scars. You don't want to be like Mr. Beautiful who left. Do you?"

"Sure."

"Alright, let's go," Camden slapped Kail on the shoulder and with a big grin like a kid on his birthday the two of them left the galley.

"I won't let you hurt him like that again Time Walker," Angela said icily once they left.

"Angela darling, don't let your feelings get in the way of what you're supposed to do. He has to make his own choices like everyone else. Besides, there will be plenty of time for that later," he smiled.

"You are insufferable. You know that?" she stormed out of the room.

"Here, put these on," Camden said and handed Kail a pair of goggles and a set of ear protection. "It's loud in the engine room."

"Ok," Kail replied and put on the items.

Camden gave Kail a thumbs up and he returned the signal to let him know he was ready. Even with the ear protection it was loud inside the engine room. Steel and copper tubing ran all over the place. Every pipe had valves and regulators on them. There were two other workers there as well. They were alerted to Kail and Camden's entrance by a light that came on when they opened the door that also shut off when it was closed.

Camden lifted the edge of one side of Kail's ear protector and shouted. "That is Harris McAllister," he pointed and waved at one man who responded in kind. "And that is Pyron Redstone," he indicated to the other man. The pair came over and greeted Kail in their own way. They did not try to shout over the noise in the room but used hand signals to communicate.

They made their way to the back of the engine room to a thick metal door with a small viewport in the center of it. "This is the heart of the ship," Camden shouted and motioned for Kail to take a look.

Peering through the view hole Kail was fascinated with what he saw. Inside the room a blue ball of fire seemed to float in a cage of metal bands with runes etched on them. But what caught his eye was the small wispy transparent being that flitted about the room.

The wisp floated around the bound fireball and seemed content with whatever it was doing. When it saw Kail it zipped over to its side of the view port and peered at him with tiny little eyes.

Camden gave Kail and the wisp a big grin and nodded his head. When the wisp saw Camden it put its tiny hands on the glass and pressed its lips like it wanted to kiss him. "Let's go, before she starts to press something else against the glass," he shouted into Kail's ear.

Exiting the engine room, they removed their protective gear and returned it to the holding area. "It all runs off of hydraulics. There's no other ship that I know of like her. Makes it a lot easier to control her, and we can do it all from the bridge instead of having a crew of people below decks taking orders through relay tubes," Camden boasted. "McAllister is a genius when it comes to this stuff."

"That fireball thing was impressive. Is that what powers the ship?" Kail asked.

"Yup, it maintains the chain reaction between the engines and the fuel."

"And that creature that was in there?"

"Oh, her, I don't know really, she showed up in there not too long after we built the chamber. She is pretty playful that's for sure. I told the guys to not encourage her or try to teach her bad habits, but you can see how well they listened," Camden said rolling his eyes. "Let's move to the weapons deck. The boys have been working on a few ideas that could come in really handy."

A few moments later they arrived to the weapons deck. "There is another deck just like this on the other side of the ship," Camden explained. "Are you familiar with cannons at all?" he asked.

Kail nodded his head. "For the most part yeah. You set a charge and when it explodes it pushes a projectile out the open end."

"Yeah, that's pretty much all there is, but we have been working on the shells a bit. The old ones had a timer on them that could be set to explode. See there, that dial, you can turn it and it will count down and then detonate the shell. It's pretty handy, but very hard to get timings down so things blow up where you want them."

It was a simple enough concept for Kail to follow. "Ok."

"These ones here," Camden pointed to shells in a different pile. "We have modified with a proximity fuse."

"What's that mean?"

"They have an eye in them, not a real eye," he corrected at the confused look Kail gave him. "The shell can see. When it gets close to what you shoot it at, it will explode. It gets rid of a lot of guess work and makes it very efficient. Instead of firing all of your ammo at the enemy hoping you get it right, these babies will do it right every time."

"What are these things?" Kail asked pointing at another weapon.

"Ah, this is a prototype. McAllister was working on this for his old boss when I picked him up," Camden explained. "I don't know too much about it, but McAllister says when it's finished it should shoot rounds one after another and not have to reload each time. It should be impressive, or at least that's what he keeps telling me."

They finished the tour on the bridge of the Snow Break which overlooked the outside main deck. "Kail, meet Ellenore Black. She keeps everything running while we're off gallivanting around," Camden introduced.

"Hello."

"Pleasure is all mine sir," she answered Kail with a strong handshake.

"Quite a view isn't it," Camden said as he made his way to the glass viewports.

"Yeah, it's something else that's for sure," Kail agreed as the ship slowly passed high above the ground.

"For me, everything else worth doing pales in comparison to this."

"I can see why."

The pair stood for a while in silence watching the world move by beneath them. "It's getting late and you still have a date with Suki in the infirmary," Camden reminded him. "We had some quarters made up for you. I recommend you swing by the galley again before you bed down. It's going to be a busy day tomorrow dirt farmer."

Chapter 10

The knock on the metal door to his quarters brought Kail from his thoughts. When he didn't get up to answer it, the person on the other side opened the door anyway. Angela stood there.

"May I come in?" she asked.

Kail responded with a shrug.

"Did you get any sleep?"

Kail shook his head no.

"I know it is a lot to process all at once," she stated. "I remember when the Time Walker brought me to this time. Everything that I had known was gone. It took me a while to get used to it too." When she saw that she wasn't going to get anything out of him she advised, "Do what you think is right Kail."

Xavier walked in and eyed the two of them together. "Go to the infirmary, and then meet us on the bridge when you're done," he ordered.

Angela turned and left down the hallway. Xavier watched her leave then turned back to Kail to give him a nasty look and then left to follow Angela.

Suki was in the infirmary waiting when Kail entered. "A few more treatments and you should be all healed up," she assessed.

"I don't think I have thanked you for saving my life."

"Oh, don't thank me for that. You should thank Angela. All I am doing is cosmetic compared to what she did."

"What do you mean?" Kail questioned interrupting Suki's healing.

"You mean you don't know?"

Kail shook his head.

"Well, I wasn't there, but from what I've heard, she and Mr. Eleazar were in Courduff looking or waiting for you. Whatever. And then this happened," she indicated to the fading scars. "Apparently you used Chronomancy or some other form of magic and escaped from Therion. You ended up in a lake."

"I was burning," Kail remembered.

"Well, that probably explains the lake then. Mr. Eleazar then pushed Angela to where you were and she saved you from drowning."

"Pushed?"

"Well, that's what they called it. He teleported her to where you were," Suki explained and moved her healing to another scar. "But it doesn't end there. After she pulled you from the lake, she and someone else carried you to your place. They bandaged and sewed you up," she indicated to the wound that had been on Kail's back. "We came that morning and picked you up."

"She did all that?" Kail asked.

"Yup," she answered. "All done here."

"Thank you anyway," Kail said quietly, his thoughts reassessing the red headed woman as he left the Infirmary.

Kail stepped onto the full bridge. Just about everyone was there. Mr. Eleazar, Angela, Xavier, and Camden were up front having a discussion. Ellenore stood at the helm like she was born to be there. McAllister from the engine room was there as well. One other person Kail had not yet met was there who walked up to him.

"Montoy DeSantos," he offered.

"Kail," he replied shaking the man's hand.

"It's an honor to meet you finally," he replied finishing the shake. "I'm sure we will have more time later," he nodded to Kail. "Ellenore," he nodded to as well and left the bridge.

Kail made his way to the others.

"The man of the hour finally arrives," Xavier mocked as he lit a cigarette off the last embers of the one still in his mouth.

"Good, good," welcomed Mr. Eleazar. "Now that we're all here, let's get started shall we."

"Ellenore, bring her down." Camden ordered.

"Aye sir."

Ellenore called into a relay tube and announced to the rest of the crew to prepare for landing. Her skill at swinging the airship around was impressive. Shadows curved around the bridge as the Snow Break banked and descended. Kail could feel his body press towards the floor. It was a totally different feeling when the ship was being maneuvered like this instead of just cruising in the sky. They all watched as the ground grew closer and in a few moments the airship had settled on the ground.

"Put her in standby," Camden commanded.

"Aye sir," Ellenore answered and began to apply the stopping breaks to the cable system powering some of the drive fans and continued to settle the ship.

Mr. Eleazar's bright eyes shone, it was clear that he had enjoyed the ride. Xavier looked uninterested and Camden clearly looked pleased with himself and the ship. Even Angela had a slight smile on her lips. It took a second for Kail to realize they were all looking at Angela.

"What?" she asked. "Alright, I will admit, it was pretty good." As she walked past Camden, she hit him on the shoulder. "Show off."

The group made their way off the bridge and through the ship to where a ramp was being lowered in the front cargo area.

"Where are we?" Kail asked.

"South of Aldervale a ways." Camden answered. "There is nothing really out here, so we should not be bothered. All of the main sky lanes between the cities are North and to the East."

"Why?"

"It's safer here, is the main reason. And I don't want you to hurt my ship."

"How would I do that," Kail said stopping short as the rest of the group headed out into the open field where the Snow Break had landed.

"This I want to see," sneered Xavier.

"Come, Kail," Angela beckoned.

Mr. Eleazar separated himself from the rest of the group and paced off a distance. Angela positioned Kail opposite of him and told him to listen with an open mind.

"This is magic," Mr. Eleazar said as he lifted his hand in front of him and it erupted in a blue flame. "It is yours to command Kail," Mr. Eleazar continued as the flame changed colors and danced. "I suspect you can feel it already inside you."

"I don't know," Kail replied. "There is something. Like when you wake up in the morning and want to stretch muscles that are stiff."

"There are many schools of magic, some are better at one than another. Some are limited to a few, and rarer still are those that can master it all," Mr. Eleazar stated as he made the flame on his hand disappear. "Try something."

"Like what?" asked Kail.

"Whatever your mind fancies."

Kail took in a breath and his mind could not come up with anything to *try* as Mr. Eleazar put it. Glancing at the others for suggestions, they offered no help but shrugs and anxious looks. *Fire maybe,* he thought? *No*, he dismissed quickly, remembering the burns he had suffered from Therion. His mind wandered back to his home in Aldervale. He wondered how his aunt and uncle were doing. It seemed like it had been forever since he last talked to them. He could picture them sitting around the table worrying about him. He thought of the dark-skinned girl Tiana next. She had been sort of nice to him. He tried to picture where she might be; the map room or maybe with that other man, Vincent, on the Colossus. He could picture her on the outer deck of the airship. Her dark was hair blowing around in the wind. *It was quite a vivid image,* he thought. He could even hear her say, "Hello Kail, I've missed you."

"No!" Mr. Eleazar yelled snapping Kail from his thoughts.

A shimmer in the air flew at Kail and he found himself knocked to the ground. "What was that for?" he complained.

"Who did you see, where did you go?" Mr. Eleazar demanded.

"I didn't go anywhere," Kail said confused.

"I did not think you would try that, but you were already gone before I realized."

"You mean what I was thinking about?" Kail got up and dusted himself off. "I was wondering about my aunt and uncle was all."

"That was all? You didn't go or think about anyone else?"

"No, well maybe. There was that girl Tiana," he remembered.

"Tiana? You mean Bastiana? The girl who follows Vincent around?" Mr. Eleazar demanded.

"Yeah, so what?"

"Camden, we need to leave. Get the ship ready." Mr. Eleazar instructed. Camden and Eleazar hurried back to the ship.

Kail looked at Angela and Xavier. "What?"

Angela gave him a disappointed look and turned to follow the others back to the ship.

"Good job boy. You told them right where we are," Xavier said with a smirk and flicked his cigarette at Kail.

Kail pushed the food on his plate around as he sat by himself in the galley. The steady hum of the airship made it easy for him to slip into thought. He wasn't quite sure why they were so disappointed in him earlier. *Maybe try fire next time,* he thought. But what seemed to bother him most was the look that Angela gave him. It also bothered him that it bothered him. He didn't even know her past sneaking looks at her that night at the inn with Lieutenant Bailon. That all seemed like an eternity ago.

The galley door opened and Camden Arland stepped in. He got himself some food and sat across from Kail. "Don't be too hard on yourself. It's not your fault, and Eleazar didn't do anything to warn you from it. He should have known better."

"I guess," was all Kail could reply.

"Aw, come on, quit beating yourself up," Camden said between mouthfuls. "Everyone makes a mistake."

"I don't know. It makes me feel so guilty for some reason when she looked at me like that."

"What? Oh, ho, ho, so that's what this is about," Camden chuckled.

"Not like that," Kail tried to backpedal. "I mean I know how much she did for me when she saved me from the lake. Suki filled me in on it this morning, and now I apparently have told them where to find us, and we're all in danger."

"Look kid, if I know one thing, it's that I know women. And the one thing I know about that woman, is that I don't get her. My advice is to not let her in your head. You know about Keratins right?"

"No, I had never even heard of them until now," Kail replied.

"They say they have mind powers. Get in your head and make you do things," Camden said giving Kail the crazy eye.

"Great," Kail said buying what Camden was telling him.

"Seriously dirt farmer, you have a long way to go to impress her," Camden pointed out.

Chapter 11

Two days had passed since Kail had used Divination. That's what it was called when he had thought about his home and then found the girl Tiana on the Colossus. He didn't even know that such a thing was possible, but Mr. Eleazar had informed him that Bastiana's specialty was Divination, and it was very rare.

The Snow Break had slowed its speed to a crawl, and the weather outside was very pleasant. A slight breeze could be felt, and the ship hovered high above the ground. Mr. Eleazar had gathered everyone outside on the deck.

"Kail," Mr. Eleazar focused his attention. "What do you know about The Guardian?"

"Not much honestly. Some stories told when I was a kid, but that's about it," he replied. "You're The Guardian aren't you?"

"Yes, I am the Time Walker as our Keratin friend seems to favor. Also known as The Guardian of The Eternal Gateway."

"Not impressed," muttered Xavier.

Mr. Eleazar ignored him. "Throughout this world's history, I act as a guide of sorts. This particular moment of time is pivotal. What happens will shape what is to come. However, don't think about it too much. Time is like a river. In the end you can't change its destination. Remove a stone here, or move a tree there and you might get that river to flow down a different valley, but inevitably it will end at the sea regardless of what you do."

"Then why bother if it all ends the same," Kail questioned.

"Why bother to pull the weeds from your field? The crops will grow just the same, but you do it anyway."

"There are a lot of reasons to clean the fields," Kail began but was silenced by Camden.

"Just let him go, this is his field," Camden said.

"There is a prophecy for this time period: The power given up shall be returned and the last to rule, shall lord over all. The Guardian will fall and the door will open for revenge yet taken. The childless one will decide the fate of all," Mr. Eleazar finished.

"And you think this prophecy has to do with me?" Kail asked.

"I do. I believe the part about the power being returned is you. I have found no other that fits that part. I am pretty sure The Guardian bit is about me, but I don't see how I can fall, and it has that whole child part with it too," Mr. Eleazar pondered.

"Who is the childless one?" Angela asked. "The one who will decide the fate of all?"

"That could be anyone I'm afraid. Do you have any idea how many people there are that do not have children?"

Xavier spoke next "Therion is in there. He was the last to rule the Mage Council. He will end up lording over all."

"Yes, I am afraid that is true. That is one of the reasons I am here to pull weeds, to use that metaphor," Mr. Eleazar confirmed. "The darkness he will create will cause endless suffering. We're going to stop him."

"Why does this even matter to us?" Kail asked. "So what if Therion rules. He ruled the Mage Council, and they ruled pretty much for the last thousand years."

"Because he did not rule the Mage Council, he was simply the last one left when it fell apart. It was a council with checks and balances, not a dictatorship. Once he is free to do as he wishes, he will not stop until everything and everyone is brought to heel," explained Mr. Eleazar. "I am surprised you defend him after what he tried to do to you Kail."

"You have no room to talk! You said it yourself that you let him do that to me, to remove the binding because he was the only one who could do it."

"Yes, he was the only one who could remove the binding, but how he did it was unnecessary. He did not need to pull them out of you leaving gaping wounds. You were tortured. And he did not stop there. That wound on your back. Therion was trying to steal your magical power for himself. Steal the powers given to you by your father. Do you think your father would have made the only way to lift the binding, was to have it ripped and burned out of the person?"

"Why didn't you tell me this before?" Kail asked.

Mr. Eleazar sighed. "Therion and your father were great friends of each other during the War of Antiquities. Therion grew jealous of your father over time. His ability to wield magic with ease infuriated him. For Therion everything was a struggle just to keep up. At the war's end when your father simply gave up his power, Therion felt cheated," Mr. Eleazar continued. "Therion hates you for this as well. If anything know this Kail Falconcrest. Therion wants your power and will stop at nothing to get it and his revenge on your father through you."

"What about the rest of you?" Kail asked looking at Angela, Camden, and Xavier. "Why are you doing this?"

Angela looked away and rubbed a spot above her breast.

"I'm getting paid," Camden simply stated.

"I have my own reasons, and they don't concern you boy," Xavier said and tossed his cigarette over the rail where it faded from view as it fell to the ground far below.

"Fine, let's do this then," Kail said. "If Therion is coming for me, then I won't go back to Aldervale and bring that with me."

Mr. Eleazar nodded in approval. Camden gave him a big smile. Angela still seemed distracted and Xavier walked off the deck and went below.

Kail stood by himself on the outer deck of the Snow Break. His mind wandered on its own as he watched the sun settle over the horizon. He had never seen the sun set from this vantage point. Shadows covered the ground below him, but here, up in the sky the sun was still visible. He hoped that he was doing the right thing by choosing to stay away from Aldervale.

Angela approached. "May I join you?"

Kail glanced over at her and quickly looked back to the setting sun. "Um, yeah, sure." The fading rays of the sun made her striking beauty stand out. Better to ignore her than get caught staring like some besotted fool.

"Sometimes life has a way of taking you places you never knew existed," she said. "It may not seem like it now, but what you choose to do may save countless lives."

"It's starting to feel like I don't have a choice anymore. Why are you here Angela? Of everyone here you seem the most out of place. No one else has been plucked out of some other time."

"You always have a choice," she said, ignoring the rest of the question.

Chapter 12

Camden Arland knocked on the door to the quarters assigned to Kail. "Rise and shine, dirt farmer! You don't want to be late for your first date."

Kail opened the door and took one look at the big grin on Camden's face and tried to shut the door back. Camden stopped it with his foot. "Hey now. You don't want to keep her waiting do you? Woman like that won't wait around forever. Miss your chance and someone else will take it."

"Shut up."

"Aw come on. No pressure, but everyone is up top waiting," Camden said. "I think they are all excited to see what you can do," he finished with a not so subtle whisper. "I know she is."

"What?" Kail said opening the door.

"Oh, you know. Just something she said this morning in the galley," Camden teased and left Kail standing in the doorway.

Kail made his way through the airship to the top outer deck. The only goals that he had for the day was not to embarrass himself, or to do something stupid that would put them in even more danger. The morning sun was bright, and the air had a chill to it from the altitude that the airship floated. Like Camden had told him, everyone seemed to be up and ready. He could see Ellenore inside the bridge with Suki and McAllister. Out on deck were Camden, Xavier, Mr. Eleazar, and Angela who he tried not to stare at too much. Angela's clothes were a bit revealing, and she had both of her swords out of their sheaths, and it looked like she was performing some sort of warm up routine. Kail wasn't the only one who noticed the distraction. Xavier seemed to be stuck in a, cigarette loop, toss, light, hit, toss. Everything to Camden seemed to be just a bit funnier than usual, because the best he could seem to do was at least grin with his mouth closed. Mr. Eleazar looked a bit different, and it took a moment for Kail to accept what the difference was.

"You're older than you were yesterday," Kail stated.

"Only by one day," Mr. Eleazar answered. "But by your yesterday then yes."

"What does that mean?"

"It doesn't mean anything. Today we're going to start your training. I think today would be a good day to just watch though," Mr. Eleazar said with a wink. "Arland, Atagi, if you would be so kind as to give Kail a demonstration of what's expected."

Angela stopped her routine and walked to the center of the deck. Her red hair had been pulled back into a long tight braid. Her angular features and almond shaped eyes stood out much more with her hair that way. Dark red leather bracers with matching thigh high boots were the only bit of color her clothing had. The rest of what she was wearing hugged her skin tight.

"Distracting isn't she," Mr. Eleazar commented. "She is doing it on purpose. Using her visage as a weapon. But it has another function as well. There are no loose bits of clothing that would give an opponent something to grab a hold of."

Camden made his way opposite of her. He didn't seem to have any weapons that Kail could see. He rolled up his sleeves and balled his fists and held them at the ready. "Bring it Red."

Angela charged with both blades. At the last second she ducked backwards and slid under a massive right hook that Kail barely saw. Camden was fast, much faster than Kail had ever seen. Angela was no slouch either. Coming up behind Camden she spun a kick that would have taken his head off if he had been there for it to connect. The pair paced off again. This time, it was Camden that charged.

"He's going to get himself killed," Kail stated. "She's going to cut him to pieces with those swords."

"Watch and learn," was all Mr. Eleazar said.

Angela was being slowly backed up across the deck. Camden's fists were a blur, and Kail could hear and see sparks fly from where Angela blocked some of the blows with the war blades instead of dodging them.

"How?" Kail asked confused.

Camden Arland's arms and fists were a dull black color. The same color as the deck material on which the two of them spared.

"Alteration. One of the ten forms of magic," Mr. Eleazar explained. "His arms are literally made of steel right now."

Angela had managed to turn the momentum back on Camden. The spinning war blades had managed to catch and cut a long slice into the duster that he wore. Camden was unfazed by the near hit and used it to press back the advantage. Twisting the loose clothing around he managed to get it wrapped around the hand and wrist of Angela's left arm. The two of them danced back and forth now that they were tied together. Angela had the advantage with her legwork, but Camden's raw strength kept her from capitalizing on it as he decided where the angles of her attacks could come from. Camden was pushing the fight towards the outer wall of the bridge.

Angela knew that if her back was pressed against the wall, Arland would be free to pummel her into submission if he wanted. She needed to get free of the tangle that snared her arm. Losing the mobility advantage limited her options. As the shadow of the wall crossed over her, she simply walked up the wall backwards and continued up and over the top of Arland. However, instead of landing behind him, she continued up and pulled Arland into the air with her. It was not easy for her to lift the big man off his feet, but she managed to get about fifteen feet above the deck and used her free sword to sever the tangle between them.

Camden had not expected to be pulled into the air by Angela. When he saw her sword flash between them his stomach gave that sudden sinking feeling as he fell towards the deck knowing there was nothing he could do to stop it. Camden hit the deck hard and almost at the same time one of the war blades landed with a metallic tear and stuck vibrating in the deck floor only an inch from his face.

Kail stood open mouthed at the result of the sparing match. Angela still floated about twenty feet off the deck above them with her hand still outstretched from throwing the blade. He continued to stare as she floated back to the deck and helped Camden to his feet after retrieving the war blade.

"You look like a fool with your mouth hanging open like that," Mr. Eleazar said quietly.

"But, what the heck was that?" Kail managed to ask, still processing what he had seen.

"Is this the first time…" Mr. Eleazar pondered. "You didn't know she could fly did you?"

"Fly! Is there anyone on this ship that isn't a magic user?"

"Oh no, it's not magic, not for her anyway. It's as natural to her as breathing."

Camden and Angela walked back over to where the rest of the group was standing. Both wore smiles and slight flushes from the obvious workout they had just given each other.

"Good luck dirt farmer. You're going to need it," Camden said with a smile and slap on Kail's back.

Angela walked up to Kail and offered him one of her war blades. "Is this your first time?"

Kail could only stare at the blade in her hand she was offering him. "Um, yeah."

"Don't worry, I will be gentle," she said with a sly smile.

Camden let out a hearty bawl of laughter at seeing the stunned look on Kail's face from the teasing exchange.

"Any more advice," Kail asked no one in particular.

"Don't let her hit you," Xavier said, as he put another finished cigarette over the side of the airship.

"Hold the blade like this," Angela instructed. "Do not try anything fancy. Just keep it between you and your enemy."

Kail had a hard time focusing on what Angela was showing him. She was all over the place it seemed. Every time she touched his hands to correct his grip, or stand behind him and move his arm in the way she wanted he could feel the heat rise in his cheeks. Several times she had caught him not paying attention and thumped him on the head with her finger. This brought a round of laughter from Camden each time it happened.

The lessons continued until Suki came out on deck to let everyone know that lunch had been prepared in the galley. Kail's whole body seemed to ache from all the places Angela had smacked him with the flat of her sword. He was also sure that there would be several small bruises on his forehead from all the thumps.

The group sat around the metal table bolted to the galley floor. Mr. Eleazar filled his plate and began to eat from it before sitting down.

"Now, there are ten forms of magic. We know that you can use Divination as well as Chronomancy. You saw Arland use Alteration when he spared with Angela. The other forms are Evocation. Evocation magic is offensive magic. If magic had a sword, Evocation would be it. Abjuration is protection or the shield to Evocation's sword. Illusion is the art of making things appear that are not there. Conjuration magic lets you create something from nothing, but it can go both ways. Necromancy is the magic of the flesh, it is what both those who raise the dead and those that heal use, but don't tell a healer that their Necromancy is good. And lastly there is Enchantment. The runes you see on Angela's blades are enchantments."

"That's only nine," Kail said after counting them again in his head.

"The tenth form is not really magic at all. Mokshaism is a form of anti magic. No one can be a Moksha and a mage at the same time," Mr. Eleazar continued. "It's not something that we will have to worry about. There hasn't been a Moksha in several decades. But if you ever do run into one, all forms of magic are useless against them."

"What forms can you use?" Kail asked Mr. Eleazar.

"Oh, I can dabble in anything really. But to answer your question, I use Chronomancy," Mr. Eleazar said between bites of lunch.

"What about you, Camden?"

"Just Alteration," Camden replied. "It's easier for me if I'm near what I want to alter." Camden placed his hand on the shiny table, and it slowly turned into the same metal as the table. When he pulled his metallic hand off the table, it faded back into flesh.

Kail gave a questioning look at Xavier who did not seem to want to eat, just smoke.

"Rely on it too much, and it will be your downfall," Xavier said watching Angela.

Angela had a towel and was drying her exposed skin off and began to undo the braid that held her hair back before joining the table and discussion. "I can fly, that is enough for me."

Kail nodded to himself. *Flying would be a pretty useful thing to be able to do. Divination and Chronomancy,* he thought to himself. *They seemed like they might go together well, if I can divine where I wanted to go and then teleport there. That seemed like it would be a neat trick. Not as useful as throwing fire or lightning,* he recalled, *like some mages being able to do in the stories he had heard.*

"Don't try and think of them as separate independent types of magic. But try and see them each as a piece of a larger puzzle," Mr. Eleazar said. "The less you limit yourself by rules and definitions, the easier it will be to command the magic."

"I'll try and keep that in mind."

When lunch was finished, Kail, Camden, and Mr. Eleazar returned to the outer deck to continue with lessons. Xavier and Angela remained in the galley.

"He likes you," Xavier said in a rare moment when he did not have a cigarette in his mouth.

"A childish infatuation is all. It will pass," Angela said dismissively. "He simply feels indebted to me for saving his life."

Xavier laughed at her comment. "Angela, Angela, Angela. I assure you, to him, it is anything but. I bet you anything that he's up all night thinking about you and that outfit you're wearing. I know I will."

"Your mind is as disgusting as your face and as filthy as your habits," she eyed him across the room.

"Don't hate the truth, I know I don't," Xavier ended the conversation and left Angela in the galley by herself.

Chapter 13

Lately the morning air had a crisper bite to it than normal. The summer was fading fast into fall. The trees and landscape that passed below the Snow Break showed signs of the turning season. It seemed like it had been months since Kail started to train and spar with the odd group of characters he now found himself with, but in reality, it had been only a handful of days. The scars on his arms and neck were gone now thanks to Suki and her healing gifts in the infirmary. Suki also helped when he happened to not pay attention as Angela put it. It would have taken days if not a week to heal some of the bruises and sores he suffered at her instructing hand. Camden had gone easier on him and leaned more towards hand to hand fighting, grappling and all around brawling. Even still he had found himself folded into some painful position more than once at the hands of the big guy.

"Try to conjure a flame," Mr. Eleazar instructed. He demonstrated by holding out his hand and a small ball of flame appeared and danced.

Kail focused his mind on his empty hand and tried to put a flame there. Nothing was happening and he sighed in frustration. "It's no use Mr. Eleazar. Maybe Evocation just isn't in me."

"It should be, your father easily commanded magic. He even used it in ways that no one had even thought of before," Mr. Eleazar said dismissing Kail's doubts. "You used Divination and Chronomancy without even thinking about it remember?"

"That was a little different. I was getting my skin melted off while my magic was being stolen remember? More of a survival reflex than a planned use of magic."

"True as it may be, I have no doubts that the magic is there. You just need to take it in your own way maybe. Give it some time, and I'm sure it will come to you," Mr. Eleazar seemed to end the lesson there.

Kail made his way to Camden who was preparing for a sparring match with him in a bit. Camden had been a bit rough lately so Suki had asked him to wrap and pad his hands to ward off some of the injuries. It was not her job to sit around and mend stupid bruises every night she told him.

"What's going on over there," Kail asked nodding to the other side of the deck where Xavier and Angela stood having a conversation. Xavier caught Kail staring at them and gave him a sneer. He turned to Angela and said something to her that made her laugh out loud.

Camden turned to look at Xavier and Angela when he heard her laughter. "Looks like they are having a fun time about something," he said disinterestedly.

"I can see that," Kail said. "But about what?"

"I don't know kid. Go over there and ask. Or better yet, divine your way over there."

"What does she see in him?"

"Ok seriously dirt farmer, you're bugging the hell out of me right now. Keep it up and I'm taking off the pads and Suki can just scrape what's left of you off the deck if you don't get some focus."

Kail continued to watch Xavier and Angela. It bugged him for some reason that he could not figure out. He never saw Camden sweep his foot and he found himself landing hard on his butt. Kail saw that Angela had seen what had happened, and she seemed to find it funny and turned back to her conversation with Xavier.

"What was that for?" Kail demanded angrily.

"You want to impress the girl that can kick your ass seventeen ways from sideways, then get mad and show her that you were worth saving from that lake. That you're worth the attention The Guardian is giving you. He is practically a god to her people."

Angela wasn't paying any more attention to him or Camden's antics. *Fine,* Kail told himself. *I'll show her*. "Ok. Let's do this," he challenged Camden.

The first exchange was completely one sided. Kail found himself face down on the deck flooring. *Crap, Camden was fast,* was all he could think. Even if he had months to train, he doubted he could stand toe to toe with him for more than a few moments. *A brawl with a brawler wasn't going to work*. The morning passed agonizingly slow for Kail as he found himself on the deck floor again and again. Only a handful of times had he managed to avoid an attack or two but never landed one of his own. He could tell that Camden was enjoying the beat downs but was starting to tire of the ease at which he could beat him. He was simply no match for him, unlike Angela who had managed to beat him in their first sparing match.

"Rest for a moment," Mr. Eleazar called.

Kail was thankful for the old man's intervention, and sat on the Snow Break's deck to catch his breath and work over some of the more sore spots that Camden had so kindly given him. He needed a plan, but his mind failed to come up with anything. He couldn't fly like Angela, and he sure didn't have any real amount of experience that everyone else seemed to have before being brought together. Magic had not really been an option for anything. The only time he had produced anything useful from it was to save his own life, or to endanger it. Simply running away from him did not seem like a valid tactic. Sure if it was a real fight and his life was on the line, he could see nothing wrong with running away from a superior opponent, but it would look foolish running around the deck with Camden giving chase.

"Are you ready Falconcrest?" Mr. Eleazar asked.

"Yeah," he answered. Moving to the center of the deck, Kail watched Camden approach. There seemed to be something different about the way he moved this time. Kail could see him bounce and shift his weight from foot to foot as he circled around him. The movement of his arms started to give tells as to where they were going. *Evade, not run*. That's what Kail decided to do this time around. Every time he had pressed an attack, he now saw, had actually been a feint by Camden to lure him.

"Begin," Mr. Eleazar called.

Kail waited and watched Camden move his feet. He concentrated on the incoming attack to see when and where it would come from. *There, from the left*, he saw it coming and reacted in time as Camden's foot kicked nothing but air and missed the next two punches as well. As Camden missed him, he saw the opening to attack. *Here is my chance,* his mind raced. *No, it's a feint*, he could see that if he had pressed the fake advantage how Camden would have easily wrapped his arms around him and he would be eating the deck floor again. A knowing grin appeared on Camden's face when Kail did not press the attack.

"Getting better I see," he taunted.

The next attack did catch Kail unaware, and he was rewarded with a kick and three punches to his midsection that sent him to the floor. Dusting himself off, Kail chastised himself. *Concentrate more. You need to defend yourself better. Not everything can be avoided, some will need to be blocked, but even blocked blows add up. Make him move more than you. Twice more or three times more. Let him wear himself out and conserve energy, force him to circle around you, four steps for each one of yours*. It started to come together for Kail. Miss, miss, block, dodge. Kail could see how each of Camden's attacks were being followed up with another attack or positioning for a feint. Again and again

Camden attacked. Each time Kail could see where the attack was coming from before it was thrown. Even still, a few of them landed. Camden was starting to take the match more seriously. He was no longer holding back as he had been earlier. Kail still had not had an opportunity of his own to attack back, but he was feeling pretty good with himself so far by not getting pummeled.

Camden increased his assault on Kail. *The kid was getting better,* he had to admit. It was frustrating having the kid evading the majority of his attacks. Even the ones the kid blocked seemed to affect him less and less. The blocks were a lot more firm and didn't knock him around like they had earlier. *Time to step it up a bit*, Camden thought.

Kail saw the change immediately in Camden's movements. *Oh crap,* his mind called out, and he was right in the assessment. Kail's mind showed him several attack patterns and vectors that Camden could take. His only chance was to move and follow the path in front of him that would keep his head attached to the rest of his body. The attacks became relentless in their speed and ferocity, but Kail still managed to see everything Camden was throwing at him. His arms and legs started to feel numb from all the blows they had received and blocked. He no longer could feel them when they landed, just disjointed impact jolts. Suki was going to be angry at them he was sure.

Frustration started to creep into Camden's form. He had not landed a clean blow in what seemed to him to be forever. The dirt farmer still had not thrown a single attack, but Camden had not let him either. *There was something wrong. The amount of blows the kid had blocked should have brought him to his knees, yet still he kept moving and blocking.* That's when Camden noticed it. He had launched a flurry of kicks followed by a backhand that Kail blocked. Except that the backhand had not actually made contact with Kail. It hit a barrier just a hair off the kid's arm. *He was using magic to absorb the blows!* Camden glanced over at Mr. Eleazar and saw him nod in approval.

Camden's attacks were becoming erratic Kail could see. Gone were the feints, and the attacks seemed to funnel from all over to a single point now. A flurry of kicks came fast and hard, but they were easily dodged. The backhand that was sure to follow he would block. *There!* His mind yelled. He saw Camden take his eyes off him and look away. *That's not a feint.* It was the opening that finally came and he pressed the attack for the first time since they had started this match.

Crap, Camden thought when his eyes returned to the kid. He had been attacking for so long that being put on the defense had caught him unaware. The kid came in hot and fast. *Way too fast. Faster than he should have,* Camden thought. Once he had lost the momentum of the fight, it was all Camden could do to not get hit. Some of the attacks he blocked had the same barrier on them. Those attacks started to hurt. Reactively he altered the structure of his arms to match steel. Still the kid did not seem to notice that his blows were hitting forearms of metal.

Kail could see Camden beginning to slow down. Each punch and kick he threw took just a bit longer for Camden to dodge or block. *He is finally getting tired*, Kail thought. He could see it in Camden's face as well. He could see how he was going to knock the big guy down seven moves ahead as clear as day. All he had to do was execute the attack.

Camden could no longer keep up with the kid's blows. Kail seemed to know where he was going to be before he did. He had to do something and something fast. *Just get the kid to back off,* he thought. *A big front kick should do the job. Even if he blocked, it should push him back enough to stop this.*

Five, block, *six*, punch, Kail counted in his head. *Seven* his mind ticked off. The all out front kick he had been counting on came. How Camden had expected to land that monstrously slow attack Kail could not fathom. It was nothing for him to slip inside and under it. Using the big guy's own momentum from the kick, Kail simply helped it up and along.

As soon as Camden executed the kick he knew he was in trouble. The kid blurred past it and pushed his leg up and over the top of him. Momentum did the rest and his back foot came up off the deck.

Everything snapped back into full speed for Kail when Camden went airborne. He expected to knock the guy off his feet by overextending the last kick above him. However, Camden did two full backward somersaults in the air before crashing hard on the metal deck with a clang. That's when he noticed that Camden had made parts of his body metal as when he had fought Angela.

Everyone on the deck looked at Kail in shocked silence.

"Now that was impressive!" Camden yelled as he jumped to his feet.

He wasn't tired? Kail noticed. *How could that be possible,* he wondered? There was no way he could have knocked him down any other way.

Camden walked over and slapped Kail across his back in congratulations. The slap took Kail to his knees. Camden's arms were still made of steel. "Crap kid, I'm sorry."

The last exchange seemed to snap the onlookers out of their stupor. Mr. Eleazar and Angela were at his side to help him up.

"Ouch," was all he managed to get out. The blocked blows and everything else that had happened started to make themselves known.

"That was enjoyable to watch Kail," Angela said. "You were very fast, and paid attention."

Kail could not stop himself from grinning at her praise.

"We can add Abjuration to your list of magic," Mr. Eleazar appraised.

"Yeah, that was something else to block my blows like that dirt farmer, I didn't even notice until the end how long you had been doing it. I had to steel up, because it hurt to hit you like that," Camden said.

"I did what?" Kail questioned. "I thought you were getting tired. You were moving so slowly I could see everything you were going to throw at me."

"No kid. Do I look tired to you? You were fast, freakishly fast. It was all I could do to keep you from running right over the top of me."

"Chronomancy again I would wager, perhaps even Divination again. Seeing where you were going to be ahead of time. Very impressive Falconcrest, very impressive indeed," Mr. Eleazar concluded.

Taking in all the praise he was getting, Kail saw Xavier still standing at the edge of the deck near the rail. The scarred man took one last draw from his cigarette and gave him a nasty look as he tossed it over the edge and left for the lower decks. *Let him be grumpy*, Kail thought to himself. Right now he needed to keep Camden from knocking him down again on accident.

Chapter 14

Kail stood on the outer deck of the Snow Break. The trees had all turned colors and some had even lost their leaves. Skeleton branches showed among those that had turned several shades of yellow and red. He summoned a small ball of flame to his hand and then let the breeze blow it out. Then he summoned another, and another.

"What are you doing?" Angela asked coming up from behind him to take in the view.

"Taking your advice."

"Really, how is that?"

"You said to do something a thousand times. And when I'm done, to do it a thousand more times, and a thousand more until it became as natural as breathing," Kail said.

"It is good that you take lessons serious," Angela complemented. "I see that the scars are almost gone."

"Yeah," he said examining his wrist, the scars were just pale shadows on his skin. "Suki says that they will fade with more time, but she is done with what she can do."

"She is useful to have around," Angela said, returning her view to the landscape that drifted below them.

"Why doesn't Xavier have her do something with his scars?" Kail asked.

"You should ask him that question."

Kail chuckled. "Yeah right, I don't think I would even ask him for one of his cigarettes if the world depended on it."

"Come, I require your assistance in setting up for today," Angela changed the subject.

"Alright..." Kail responded with some confusion. "What is it that we're setting up?"

Kail followed Angela below decks and to the forward hangar area. Several of the cargo crates that they had picked up were arranged in various piles and spaced erratically around the room.

"I don't think Camden would like us moving all the food crates and supplies around like this," Kail said looking at the cargo hold. "You know how he can get sometimes when someone messes with his ship."

"He will not mind, it was his idea and the Time Walker's."

"I don't get it."

"Here help me place these metal poles," she indicated to a pile of spare steel tubing. "Stand them up like this. Here, here, and here," she directed. "Outside when we spar, it is open and flat. It is too basic. Here, it is not so," and she jumped from one crate to another until she stood above his head.

"So you've built an obstacle course?"

Angela shrugged at the assessment. "These pipes and tubes could be trees in a forest. Or you could be fighting in the streets of a city, or inside a building. There will be things that get in your way, block your attack, and prevent you from retreating," she explained as she set more of the piping in place. "Not all danger will come from in front or behind you. Danger can lurk above as well as below."

"Ok, makes sense to practice like this."

"You have improved greatly in a short time Kail, but you focus only on your opponent. Here you will have to focus on what is around you. If you do not, you will find yourself at a disadvantage. A mistake that can be fatal," she instructed. The two of them continued to prepare the hangar for the day's lessons until Suki informed them that it was time for lunch.

Kail put only a small amount of food on his plate and sat on the same side of the metal table as Angela. It wasn't good to fight on a full stomach, but worse on an empty one. Camden soon joined them with an overflowing plate of food. He gave a not so subtle wink at Kail when he saw that they were sitting by each other. It didn't last long. Xavier showed up and without even batting an eye simply forced his way between Angela and Kail at the table. Kail got the hint when Xavier gave him a, *why are you sitting next to me? I will cut your heart out,* look. He quietly moved to the other side of the table to sit across from Angela. Only the food Camden kept pushing into his mouth prevented him from laughing.

Kail, Camden, and Angela returned to the hanger bay together.

"You know you have to put everything back Red," Camden said after looking at the mess the hanger was in.

Angela was busy putting her hair back into a pony tail and didn't bother to answer. She removed one of the war blades from its sheath and handed it to Kail. "Are you ready?"

Kail did not take the blade. "I want you to use both of them this time."

"Alright," she said and removed the second blade and started a quick warm up routine.

"You sure about this?" Camden questioned.

"Yeah, I'm going to use a staff. I think it will work better against her, and I already have some ideas with it," he answered.

Camden and Kail watched as Angela moved about the room warming up. With all the crates and poles set up she moved around like nothing Kail had seen before. Her ability to fly seemed to take on a whole new meaning. It was nothing for her to run up the side of a wall, or flip sideways over a stack of crates. The poles they had set up though worked to her advantage by far. She could grab one and use it to circle around much tighter than she could have done just on her own.

Camden gave a long whistle. "Good luck kid. I'll make sure your family gets what's left of you when she's done."

Camden was right. Angela was in her element here. It was going to take everything he had learned and more if was going to stand a chance. Leave it to her make him feel like he had not been doing a single thing since he got here.

Kail picked up a metal staff and gave it a few test swings. It was pretty stiff, but there was a little flex with it. Its reach was going to be the only advantage he was going to get against her. As long as he could use it to keep himself out of range of her blades, it shouldn't be so bad.

Angela finally settled down and walked to a clear spot in the hanger. Kail left where he was standing next to Camden and squared off with her. The hum from the airships engines vibrated in the floor. She flourished her blades quickly. They were a blur as they flashed around her body, arms, and head before stopping with the points towards Kail. He was definitely in trouble.

They charged each other at the same time. Neither of them wanted to be put on the back foot first. Angela's twin war blades were a blur of fury in front of her. Sparks flew when Keratin blade collided with steel staff. The sound of clashing weapons filled the hangar with their song. Angela was the first to score a hit, sliding the staff under her arm and delivering a hard slap to Kail's ribs. It was easy though for Kail to counter, pulling the staff upwards with it still under her arm, he was able to swing the other end of it underneath and once again push her out of range.

Kail had been right to choose the staff to fight against Angela. There would have been no way for him to try and match her skill with a like weapon. She was forced to use almost every strike to bat away the end of the staff as he swung it at her. When she did manage to get by the staff, it was a lot easier for him to bring the other end around and counter than trying to bring the forward end back into position.

Angela changed tactics from a frontal assault. She started to weave back and forth to exploit angles that Kail left open with his lack of experience. Kail had to concentrate to keep from getting hit. He could feel pressure start to build in the back of his mind. The moving war blades were no longer a blur, but came into sharp focus as the magic helped him fight. She was still faster than him, and her fighting style was not as linear as Camden's was. He could not find a pattern or see the shifts in her muscles that would project where her next attack was coming from.

With his speed augmented by his mage heritage, Kail managed to parry Angela's attacks to a standstill. She maneuvered around him, and it was too late before he realized his error. Swinging the staff around hard, the end of it caught one of the poles they had set up earlier. The collision nearly tore the staff from his grip and left his hands stinging. Angela took advantage of the mistake and quickly disarmed Kail. She had him pinned to the floor with the point of her blades.

"Sloppy. You set the room up. You should know where everything in it is," she chastised kicking the staff back to him. With her back to him she stretched her arms over her head and slid the twin blades against each other. "Again."

Kail glanced at Camden who had been watching the exchange for advice. The shrug he gave Kail only confirmed that she was going to step it up a notch and things were about to get crazy. Kail gripped the metal staff once more and squared off with her.

Angela had yet to face Kail. She could hear him get to his feet and pick up the metal staff. She waited one more breath before launching her attack. She started with a back flip to close the distance between them. On the landing she pivoted into a sideways somersault flip. As expected, Kail brought the staff up and around to block. What she did next, she knew he would not be ready. Instead of landing on the ground, her feet lightly found themselves on the end of the staff. Using her natural ability to fly, she broke gravity's law and advanced down the staff's length to deliver a blow.

Kail's eyes grew in shock. The last thing he expected was for Angela to simply land on the staff he had braced in front of him and then to walk down it. Only at the last second did he manage to duck the attack aimed for his head and toss her back.

Angela wasn't sure what pleased her more. The look on his face when she landed on the staff, or the fact that he had reacted in time and did not let her slap him on the side of his head. It was time to use the room for which it was designed. She jumped to the top of some of the crates that were put out. Having the high ground had many advantages. Using her legs to counter most of the swings and jabs Kail threw at her, let her increase the amount of potential attacks that she would have had otherwise.

This was definitely something different for Kail. Angela was all over the place. He felt like he had climbed into a tree to catch a small bird as it hopped and flittered from branch to branch, and he could only give chase clumsily. He was going to have to come up with something to remove the advantage she held. This became extremely clear when he caught her at the end of the hangar. He was sure that he had the advantage until she simply fought him to a standstill, this would have been normal except instead she had both of her feet on the wall and walked it like it was the ground.

Angela taunted Kail as she fought him on the wall. *This will make his head spin,* she thought. Disengaging the fight, she casually made her way up the wall and out of reach. She didn't stop there until she placed both feet on the roof of the hangar, and stood upside down above him.

"You got her now dirt farmer!" Camden called out.

Angela never saw the staff coming. Pride and Camden's obvious taunt at Kail distracted her. The end of the staff caught her across the shoulder, ricocheted off the ceiling and caught her in the back of the head. It wasn't hard enough to knock her out cold, but she fell like a stone towards the floor.

Kail watched stunned. He hadn't expected that to do anything. He had simply thrown the staff up at her in frustration. His mind flashed some choices. *Catch her, or get the hell out of the way of the staff and two swords that were on the way down as well.*

Was there a choice, his mind asked him? Braving the deadly rain of weapons he managed to get underneath her and catch her before she hit the ground. The clang and clatter of the weapons as they hit and bounced on the hangar floor had Kail tensing with his eyes closed praying that nothing would hit him. When the noise stopped he peeked out. He had caught her and there she was in his arms, she was a lot lighter than he imagined for someone who was not only taller than he was, but could easily beat up anyone he knew.

"I pictured this moment differently," he said before thinking.

She had her legs wrapped around his head in the blink of an eye and using her body for leverage swung around the side and flipped Kail forward to the hangar floor.

Kail found himself pinned to the floor. Angela sat on his chest and had her knees pinning each of his shoulders and arms down. He couldn't stop the heat from rising to his face when the only view he had was one of her legs. Her face came into view above him and he could not decipher the look that he saw. He knew that she must know why this was embarrassing for him. The only thing he could think to do was simply close his eyes and give up.

"Finished?" was all she asked.

"Yes please," he replied and he felt her get off of him. Keeping his eyes closed he was too mortified to move or open his eyes.

"You going to just lie there for the rest of the day?" Camden asked.

"Probably," Kail said.

"Well at least open your eyes, she's gone," he told him. "I will say this, you did a pretty good job against all that." Camden helped Kail get to his feet. "You might want to try wine or chocolate next time before knocking her on her head to get her to fall into your arms."

"Shut up Camden."

"I'm just saying. I don't know how you guys in Aldervale do things, but it's pretty cave man to do it that way."

"Shut up," Kail pleaded.

The ribbing continued as the pair left the hanger.

Chapter 15

Kail opened the door and stepped into the hallway outside his quarters. His heart almost stopped him dead because Mr. Eleazar was standing right in front of him.

"You are going to kill someone doing that you know," Kail complained.

"It hasn't happened yet, besides this way I don't have to waste time knocking, and then you get out of bed and say 'who is it?' and then I reply with some grandiose title, and then you tell me to wait because you have to put on pants, or hide a girl under your bed before you can answer the door." Mr. Eleazar rambled.

"Did you ever actually save time with this, or do you end up wasting it all explaining?" Kail countered.

"Yes indeed it does seem like that sometimes, but until you have had to hide a girl under your bed, or you in her closet… You will understand how precious those seconds can be," Mr. Eleazar said thoughtfully.

"I feel set up with the direction this conversation is going Mr. Eleazar," Kail sighed as he made his way past the man to head to the galley. Grinning Mr. Eleazar followed behind him.

"I see you're progressing well in your sparing matches with Arland and Atagi," he complemented. "It is a clever use of magic, but I think the time has come for you to have some more traditional teachings."

"Alright," Kail agreed. "When did you want to do this?"

"Right now, of course."

"Can we start after lunch instead? I promised McAllister that I would help him with the gun deck, and Camden wants me to spend some time in the engine room too. Something about learning how things work instead of dreaming about farming dirt."

"After lunch will be fine," Mr. Eleazar said.

"Thanks," Kail said and left Mr. Eleazar alone in the galley as he hurried off to meet with McAllister.

Mr. Eleazar found himself in a rare moment with nothing to do. He had planned on having the full day, but decided it wasn't that bad. Half a day should be fine he recalled. Therion would have been no match for him he remembered.

McAllister was elbow deep in grease as he rebuilt the gun. He was still having problems with it jamming as it fed shells out of the hopper. The reaction was just too fast to let the next round fall into place.

Kail walked in licking the last bits of his breakfast from his fingers and greeted the engineer. "Figure it out yet?" he asked.

"No, not yet. It will fire a few times then jam."

"What if you use a spring to load it? That way it's always pushing the next shell into place instead of just letting it fall," Kail suggested.

"That might work," McAllister mused. "I've also been working on this hinge kicker. When the shell moves back it flips like this, you see," he demonstrated. "When it goes forward it pops up."

Kail helped McAllister reassemble the gun, but it would be a while before McAllister could fabricate a spring loader and test out their ideas. They spent the next hour or so going over some of the other weapons on the Snow Break.

Pyron and Montoy spent most of their time in the engine room, and Kail only saw them rarely outside. The first thing they had taught him was the simple hand gestures they used to communicate in the loud room. When they had told him that the main source of fuel was water he did not believe them. It took them quite a while to finally convince him of it. Kail assumed that they were trying to make fun of his lack of knowledge having come from a small town. There was a great deal of things that he had no knowledge of he admitted, but even if it was true, telling people that they burned water sounded crazy. Kail knew that he would never be able to convince anyone from Aldervale that it was possible.

When they showed him the electrolysis chamber housed above the furnace, he started to become convinced. At first he thought the metal rods in the water simply used heat from the chamber the wisp played in to boil the water. That's what it looked like to him with the bubbles coming off of them, and he was familiar with water boilers that used steam to push engines. The mechanics told him otherwise. They said that the water was being torn apart into its base elements that burned when mixed together. Kail told them that it sounded more like magic than anything else when they described it. The downside though he found out was that having water inside the engines after the fuel burned caused problems. It was a constant battle of maintenance and upkeep to keep everything running so it did not all rust.

Kail spent the rest of the morning on the bridge with Ellenore Black. She showed him how the cable breaks worked that steered the airship. She had told him it's better to keep the cables that ran through the ship going at all times, and to use the breaks to hold on to them when they needed to move. The hydraulic systems impressed him the most though. It just did not seem possible to be able to gently push or pull on a lever and have something a hundred times his weight on the far side of the deck swing back and forth. He began to understand how it must have been for the mages in the past. They were the only ones who could do these things. Now some fluid in a pipe with a lever and anyone could move objects on the other side of the room.

Mr. Eleazar stood patiently on the outer deck of the Snow Break. Camden had ordered the ship to just hover and drift with the wind currents so there would be as little disturbance as possible. Everyone on board the ship was either on the outer deck or on the bridge where they could see.

"If you were in a proper mage school, we would spend at least a year reading and memorizing texts, having long discussions about each branch of magic, and debating the morality of how magical powers should be used to better yourself and others. We don't have years." Mr. Eleazar said. "We are going to skip right to what most call the fun stuff. Evocation and Abjuration. These will let you defeat your enemies and keep you alive."

Mr. Eleazar raised a hand out over the horizon as a red ball of energy formed that shot away from him and the ship. A hundred feet or so away, the ball exploded and everyone on deck could feel the thud of the shockwave. "Evocation," Mr. Eleazar explained. "Try it."

Kail walked up to the edge of the deck to the safety railing. He had been practicing every day to create a ball of fire like he had seen Mr. Eleazar do months ago. The ball sized flame appeared in his hand with ease. Imitating what he saw, he raised it in front of him and pushed. The flame shot away from his hand. Instead of shooting away and exploding like The Guardian's had. It made it barely ten feet and evaporated with a funny raspberry sound.

He summoned a second ball of fire and tried again. Like the first, it made it only a little way before puttering out.

He could hear Camden behind him snickering. Ignoring the big man he tried a third time. Same results. The snickering got worse. Each time he tried to generate a fireball it fizzled. Each time Camden's giggles got worse. Finally he turned on the big guy. "What's so funny?" Kail demanded.

Camden's face was dark red. He had tears coming from his eyes and he had been holding his nose shut to keep from laughing out loud. Angela had her hand over her mouth and had to look away else fall victim to the laughter. Even Xavier looked amused at the situation between hits on the cigarette between his fingers.

Kail couldn't help himself. It was pretty funny when you thought about it, and he started to laugh. It didn't take long for all of them to join in the laughing. Camden had to sit down when he called them little farting balls.

After they all had their laugh, Kail and Mr. Eleazar returned to the lesson. The attempt to throw fireballs and have them explode wasn't going very well so Mr. Eleazar tried something else.

"What is better? A huge ball that destroys its target," Mr. Eleazar said and launched a ball that was bigger than the one before; when it exploded it left spots in their eyes. "Or is it better to use several smaller ones to achieve the same thing?" Then he fired off twenty to thirty smaller balls of fire the size that Kail had been trying to form in rapid succession that all exploded at the same distance.

"I don't know. It would depend on the situation I guess," Kail answered.

"True. It comes down to efficiency on one part. Another is that one is a weapon of terror. The other is a weapon of war. Driving fear into an army in front of you can be even more effective than simply killing them."

Kail assumed so. He was not best tactician he knew that, so he had little reason to doubt the man.

"Tell me, after using magic, how do you feel? Do you feel tired or spent?"

Kail thought about it for a moment. "Not really, it still feels like a ghost muscle that needs stretched. Just a feeling, like that it's there waiting unused."

Mr. Eleazar seemed to ponder the answer for a bit. "Let's move to Abjuration. Evocation is fairly easy to practice on your own. Now we have seen you use it naturally when you have sparred with Arland and Atagi. Let's see how you do against Evocation," and without warning Mr. Eleazar hit Kail's arm with a tiny ball of magic. The snap left a tiny burn mark.

"Ouch! That stung," Kail said rubbing his arm.

Mr. Eleazar smiled and snapped another one off his thigh. "Better learn quickly, it's only going to get worse."

Kail scrambled away. Most of the stingers found their mark on his body, but he was able to dodge a few. "This is a weapon of terror!" he shouted at Mr. Eleazar.

Quickly he learned. Soon the attacks were being stopped before they hit him by small barrier off his skin. Still some managed to get through and sting. "Hey, that one really hurt!" he complained after getting stung.

"It should, that one was bigger than the others. You need to do a better job of protecting yourself." Mr. Eleazar shouted and continued his assault.

Kail found it easier if he angled away from the attacks. It didn't seem to take as much to just deflect the attacks away, like you would with a sword compared to just flat out stopping them. Still it seemed better to just to avoid them all together. Everything seemed to begin to slow down for Kail, and he could see the attacks more clearly. It made it easier to dodge the attacks instead of knocking them away. The mistake never occurred to him.

Mr. Eleazar smiled at what he saw Kail Falconcrest try to do. He was trying to use Chronomancy to dodge a man who could walk through time.

Everything froze for Kail. He could see several of the stingers stopped in mid flight in front of him. He could see Camden and Angela standing still like statues. The smoke frozen in front of Xavier's face made him realize the extent of his error. He couldn't move either. But Mr. Eleazar could. There was nothing he could do but watch Mr. Eleazar calmly walk over to him. He didn't say anything. He just stood there assessing for a few moments. Then like it was nothing, he plucked the closest stinger from the air and moved it somewhere behind Kail, and then casually went back to where he stood before. Just before everything jerked back into motion, he swore he saw Mr. Eleazar wink at him.

The repositioned stinger hit him right in the butt. Kail let out a painful cry. That was going to leave a nasty welt, one that he would have to just live with. It would be too embarrassing to ask Suki to heal it.

"There are holes in your defense, but you are adapting well," was all Mr. Eleazar said. "You can do better though. Perhaps we need to use a different motivator." Without warning he shot several of the stingers at Angela.

Without thinking Kail found himself standing between Angela and Mr. Eleazar blocking the assault. "Are you crazy? What are you doing?" he demanded.

Once Angela was blocked Mr. Eleazar doubled his assault and targeted Camden and Xavier. Each time he moved to stop a stinger from hitting one of them, Mr. Eleazar would pepper Angela with stingers. It didn't take too many before everyone was doing what they could to protect themselves.

Angela took to the sky to get away, but Mr. Eleazar simply shot her down. "You are holding back Falconcrest!" Mr. Eleazar shouted.

It became harder for him to block the stingers targeted at his friends. Mr. Eleazar began to arch and weave them around him so simply standing between them no longer became effective. "Stop it!" he yelled at The Guardian.

"You stop it," Mr. Eleazar challenged back.

Kail was the only one left standing at this point. Mr. Eleazar's assault had everyone incapacitated, but he did not stop attacking them or Kail. Seeing Angela lying unconscious on the deck with several blackened burn marks across her body made his heart sink. Even Arland's and Xavier's fallen bodies filled him with anger. The feeling inside of him no longer wanted to be stretched. It wanted to be flexed.

He wasn't sure what or how he did it, but the feeling of raw power flooded into him like an avalanche crashing down the side of a mountain. The stinging projectiles that Mr. Eleazar had been using looked like tiny snowflakes to him now. He easily blew them away from his friends and stopped that assault.

Mr. Eleazar saw the change coming. *Now he is starting to get it*, he thought to himself. Abandoning the attack on the others he focused on the student in front of him. Mr. Eleazar fired off several small projectiles from the end of his hand and charged at Kail.

Kail easily swatted away Mr. Eleazar's attack like shooing away flies. But they were a diversion to let Mr. Eleazar get close. Kail barely raised his defenses in time to stop Mr. Eleazar's attack. A solid blue bar of energy hit him and hit him hard. He was being pushed back across the deck from the force of the attack. He needed more to stop it. Flexing the power and angling the shield like he had earlier against the stingers, Kail deflected the rest of the energy up into the sky and away. Kail countered with an attack of his own. Similar to what Mr. Eleazar had just used against him, he projected a solid stream of energy at the man.

"Good, but you can do better," Mr. Eleazar taunted and simply warped the beam away from him and off to the horizon.

Mr. Eleazar raised his hand above his head and countless red and blue beams of energy shot into the sky that began to curve back towards the deck and rain down on Kail.

Kail sprinted away from the raining energy that exploded around him. He fired off several bolts of energy at Mr. Eleazar in return.

Mr. Eleazar back peddled away from the attack and sent a shockwave of force to push the young mage back.

"Stop this. It is getting out of hand," Angela said.

Kail turned to see Angela standing off to the side. Camden and Xavier were getting up as well. The burns and welts on their clothing were gone. As well as the burn marks on the decking.

"It, it wasn't real?" Kail asked.

"Illusion is very powerful if you believe what you see," Mr. Eleazar explained calmly. "Though I did have to be careful with what you were throwing around. That was quite real."

The energy that had been flowing through Kail left him as suddenly as it had filled him. The loss of the power made the world spin around him, and he crashed to the deck floor in a heap.

Kail slowly came around. He recognized the ceiling of the infirmary. He recalled fighting with Mr. Eleazar, and when they stopped he passed out from the magic. Sitting up slowly he sat on the edge of the bed. He felt tired in a funny way. Like he had spent all day out in the field, but it was more of a ghost feeling instead of physical exhaustion.

"Feeling it now?" Mr. Eleazar asked.

"Yeah, I think so," Kail replied looking around the room. They were alone. "Reminds me of waking up with a hangover."

"That's one way to look at it," Mr. Eleazar considered. "You need a lot of practice Falconcrest. Just like working with a sword, it will get easier the more you use it."

"I'll add that in between beat downs from everyone else."

"Do not overdo it though. It is possible to channel so much that you burn out. Like incinerating from the inside until there is nothing left to contain the magic but a husk."

"Great," Kail said shaking his head. "I think I'll just stick with farting balls then."

Mr. Eleazar laughed. They remembered how Camden had been laughing so hard at his first attempts that he had cried. It seemed an eon ago compared to how the lesson had ended.

Chapter 16

Camden and Kail picked through the tiny market place to replace some of the supplies on the Snow Break. A lot of the food was fresh from fall harvests, but too perishable to consider taking. However, it would be nice for a week or so to have fresh food over the staple diet of dried meats and breads that they had been living on for months.

Kail thought about the marketplace in Aldervale that he and his uncle would sell the food that the farm produced each week. He felt a twang of guilt for not thinking about his home in a while. He had been so busy learning to fight that he had simply forgotten. He took the time now though as he singled out the better pieces of food that would keep the longest. His aunt and uncle would be so busy without him; he imagined that Royce would have to hire extra help. *No*, he remembered, *my uncle had sold the entire harvest to the garrison that was stationed there building the airstrip*. How he had forgotten all of that he didn't know. The airstrip by now was probably completed when he remembered how fast and how many people were working on it. Those thoughts led him back to the young Lieutenant that had become his friend. Lieutenant Bailon. *No his name was Will*, Kail remembered. He imagined what his face would look like when he found out that he had spent all this time aboard an airship. And with the woman that they had spent the evening admiring across the inn that scared off anyone that approached her.

"People might start to wonder if you're right in the head if you walk around grinning at nothing," Camden told him, which returned his thoughts to the present.

"I was just thinking of the marketplace back home in Aldervale," Kail said. "I bet that airstrip is finished by now. What do you think?"

"I think that it's unfortunate that the soldiers are from Courduff," Camden stated. "They eventually all answer to Therion and when everything finally explodes out of control, any place with a military presence is not going to be a pleasant place to be."

"I never thought of it like that. I know some of those soldiers. They are nice people, friends even."

"War can make people do things they never thought of doing," Camden mused.

"Maybe it doesn't have to be like that," Kail said. "What if we just got rid of Therion before it gets to war?"

"I don't think that's going to happen kid. Have you not noticed that Mr. Eleazar is not around much? There are a lot of major players that stand to gain everything and loose even more right now."

"Why doesn't he just, you know, do his thing and take care of it all himself?"

"Honestly," Camden paused. "I don't think that he can. If you look at what he's done since we've spent time with him, and if you believe some of the stories from history, I think it's all beyond his control. Sure he can manipulate, just look at Angela and the rest of us. But take that river bit about time, I don't think one man can change the course of history. All he can do is 'pull a few weeds.'"

The market changed subtlety at first, but eventually Kail and Camden noticed. Commotion from across the way caused heads to turn and a crowd to gather. Kail paid for the food he had picked out, and together with Camden they made their way a few blocks over to see what the fuss was about. A man on a balcony pointed out of town and called something down to the crowd below.

"Do you see what's going on?" Kail asked.

"No, not yet. Let's ask," Camden said. "What's all the noise about?" he asked a stranger.

"Something on the horizon headed this way. An airship they think," the man said.

"Airship?" Camden said looking at Kail with concern. "We need to find out."

The two of them headed inside a nearby building and made their way to the rooftop. Finding the direction that everyone had been looking confirmed what they heard on the street. On the horizon a dark spot was headed this way. "We need to leave," Camden said.

"How long to do you think until they get here?"

"An hour at most, maybe less."

"An hour! It will take us that long to get back to the ship." Kail said.

"We could be in trouble, but the longer we stand here the closer they get," Camden finished as they made their way down to the street and out of town. "If we're lucky someone will spot them before we get there and have everything ready to go. If not, we just got caught with our pants down."

Angela stood on the outer deck of the Snow Break and sighted down the shaft of an arrow aimed at a target she had paced off away from the ship. This was the first time she had gotten to practice in a long while. With the engines off, the ship did not vibrate, nor were there all the bumps and wind gusts that came with being in the air. The arrow flew away from her with a snap of the bowstring. It landed cleanly in its target next to the other half dozen arrows before it.

She floated down to the ground and walked into the wooded area to retrieve the arrows. Each one had either hit the mark she placed out or come very close to hitting the mark. She needed to practice more she told herself. Nine hundred more arrows and she should be back to her old accuracy she calculated. She returned each arrow to her quiver after cleaning the heads off and inspecting each one for damage that might cause it to not fly true. Two of the arrows she singled out for repair and kept them in her hand separated from the others.

On her flight back to the airship she caught the reflection of something off in the distance above the horizon. Pausing she could not see what it was that caught the light. Curious she aborted her return to the Snow Break and instead flew higher into the sky to see farther. She could make out the small town that they had landed near in the distance that Camden and Kail had left for in the morning. Whatever it was she had seen there was no sign of it now. Giving up she started to drop through the air to the landed airship below her. Again something reflected off in the distance. Stopping her decent, she scanned the horizon again. This time however movement on the road coming from the town caught her eye.

"You think she saw us?" Kail asked.

"I hope so," Camden replied. "We saw her flying above the trees and stopping twice before dropping out of sight."

Vincent and Bastiana commanded the bridge of the Colossus as it approached the small town from above. Both wore formal uniforms that bore the insignia of Cahir as well as Courduff.

"The trail ends," Bastiana said stomping her foot. "I still can't find him."

"Locate their ship if you can my dear," Vincent soothed. "Helm, bring us over the town. If we can't find them perhaps a demonstration will," he nodded to a crew member who began to bark orders into relay tubes.

Ellenore Black had wasted no time when Angela reported what she had seen earlier. Even with the warning getting the Snow Break flight ready required time. Adding to the delay was the fact that some of the engine had been opened up for cleaning. She did not want to have Pyron and Montoy make a mistake that would cost them later, but speed was of the essence. McAllister also was in the engine room helping.

Camden and Kail arrived a few minutes later. "Report," Camden ordered.

"One airship is in route. Angela has a visual and says its slowing down as it approaches the town. Engines are still down, but we should be ready for start up in ten minutes," Ellenore reported.

"Who do you think it is?" Kail asked. "This may not have anything to do with us."

"Doesn't matter, we leave as soon as possible," Camden countered.

"What was that?" Kail questioned when the faint sound of an explosion reached them.

Angela came bursting onto the bridge. "It is the Colossus. They are attacking the town."

"What? Why would they do that?" Kail was confused.

171

"They can't find us so they are attacking the town to flush us out," Ellenore said.

"We have to do something! We can't just sit here!" Kail pleaded.

Camden looked at Angela and she nodded. "The only thing we can do is run." Camden said and set about doing what he could from the bridge to ready the ship.

"No," Kail protested.

"Look dirt farmer. The best thing for those people in that town is for us to leave and when they see us, that ship is going to follow. Got it?"

Kail didn't answer but accepted situation as Camden had explained it.

"Keep a sharp eye everyone," Vincent ordered as black smoke began to rise from the town below.

Crew men aboard the Colossus reloaded cannons and awaited the order to shell the town again. Others made their way to the outer deck and strapped themselves to the safety rail and manned the deck guns.

Vincent looked to Bastiana, and she shook her head...

The silence on the bridge lasted for a dozen heartbeats...

"Fire," Vincent ordered with a single word.

The floor of the Colossus shook as each explosive shell was fired from the cannons. Flashes of red soon followed from the detonations. Sound and shockwaves came last and rattled the windows of the bridge.

Camden, Kail and Ellenore all looked at each other when the sound of the explosions reached them.

"Time?" Camden asked as Ellenore moved about the bridge checking valve readings.

A simple nod was all she needed to reply with as the hum and vibrations of the Snow Break's engines stirred to life. Dirt billowed away from the airship as the massive fan blades were brought up to speed.

"Sir, a disturbance has been spotted to the south," a faceless voice announced to the bridge of the Colossus. This time Bastiana answered Vincent's questioning look with an evil smile and gleam in her eye.

"Helm, bring us about and intercept," he ordered.

Angela met the rising Snow Break half way and made her way to the bridge. "They have seen us and are coming," she stated.

"Give us all she's got." Camden ordered and Ellenore pressed a button near the helm.

A green light lit up in the engine room followed by a yellow one.

"That's my cue," McAllister motioned and left Pyron and Montoy to head to the weapons level and prepare.

The two mechanics went back to the engine and powered it to full capacity. Even the little wisp seemed eager to help.

The yellow light also lit inside the infirmary and Suki strapped herself down and waited as she felt the ship lift into the sky.

Xavier sat in the galley with a pile of spent cigarettes. He hadn't moved since they landed here the night before and he could care less about the situation going on outside.

Vincent and Bastiana watched as the Snow Break left the ground and cleared the tree tops around it. The Colossus made its way through the sky towards the smaller ship. Black smoke rose high into the sky from the burning town they'd left behind.

"Can we out run them?" Kail asked.

"I don't know," Camden answered. "Even if we can, where are we going to go that they can't just follow?"

"We fight them," Angela said.

"Maybe, but not here," Camden said. "We need to find a place where we can maneuver, but everything around here is just flat lands and trees."

"Fire a warning shot," Vincent ordered.

"We are still out of range and closing sir," a crew member answered back. Moments later the shell being fired was felt throughout the Colossus.

Vincent and Bastiana watched in silence as the shell exploded in the distance near the smaller airship.

The sound of the explosion was shockingly loud around the Snow Break and Kail covered his ears.

"That was a warning shot," Ellenore called out from the helm.

"Damn," Camden cursed. "Go higher, if we get lucky head for the clouds if you can find any."

"They cannot out run us," Vincent said. "But they can out maneuver us," he finished as he watched the Snow Break take for the sky. "Bring us up helm."

"Kail, go help McAllister, we're going to need all the hands we can if we hope to make it out of here alive," Camden ordered.

Kail sprinted best he could through the decks of the ship and found McAllister loading each of the cannons with the modified proximity shells.

"When the light turns red," McAllister pointed above them. "Point and fire," he shouted over the noise.

Kail nodded and manned the cannon. He could feel his ears pop and the air cool as they went higher and higher into the sky. The shadows around them began to swing and elongate as Ellenore brought the ship around. Several more times his ears rang from the explosive shells the Colossus fired at them, but none of them reached the Snow Break.

Kail felt his stomach rise and a few of the loose unsecured items around them lifted off the floor. They were coming about and dropping down at the same time. The massive airship that had been trying to knock them out of the sky finally came into view below him. Kail saw several tiny flashes blink along the top of the Colossus's deck. The light turned red.

Kail pulled back on the firing trigger and the cannon slammed into him hard. His ears rang painfully and he missed whether or not his shot had hit the Colossus. He felt more than heard McAllister's shot follow his. Following McAllister's lead, he reloaded the cannon for a second shot. Return fire exploded around them and the hail of shrapnel could be heard bouncing off the hull but making no direct hits.

The screaming sound of a shell buzzed the bridge of the Colossus as it missed wide. "Seems she has some teeth," Vincent stated. A second shell exploded in the path of the Colossus and the massive ship shook from the blast. Two of the crewmen outside on the deck were dead from shrapnel, and more debris clattered against the front windows. "Bastiana," Vincent nodded and the short dark-skinned pixy haired girl teleported through the glass and emerged on the deck of the Colossus.

"Stay above them," Camden ordered. "It's the only advantage we have."

"Aye sir," Ellenore responded as she twisted and turned the more agile Snow Break through the air above the Colossus.

Angela had made her way outside and stood holding on to the frame of the door that lead to the outer deck. The Snow Break was moving extremely fast, but not so fast that if she timed it right she would be able to get back when Ellenore brought it around again. Of course if she timed it wrong, she imagined that the ship would hit her so hard that she would be killed.

Kail and McAllister held ready to fire against the Colossus when it came into view. Again the light above them turned red as Ellenore provided them a firing angle. This time when Kail lined up the shot, he did not flinch when the cannon kicked him. The shot exploded well before arriving at the Colossus and a blue ripple expanded out like it had hit a pool of water. McAllister's shot had the same result.

"Did you see that?" McAllister yelled.

Kail could only nod his head that he did. *Tiana,* he thought. *It has to be her.*

Bastiana's laugh was lost to the blowing wind around her as she detonated the Snow Break's fire harmlessly out of range. "Hello Kail," she called out. A beam of hot energy shot skyward from her hand towards the Snow Break.

The Snow Break lurched from the impact of the magical attack. Protesting metal screamed as the energy cut along the side of the ship.

Suki felt the harness jerk and she kept her head down as medical supplies were torn free from shelves where they were secured.

"Damn it," Camden called out as parts of the hull were torn free.

Ellenore fought with the helm to break off the approach she had planned. Dodging cannon fire was one thing, but there was no way they could survive the mage as well.

Angela used the momentum of the banking airship to launch herself harder than she could have managed on her own into the air.

Kail unhooked himself from the cannon and made his way to the bridge as best he could as the airship jerked and bucked underneath his feet despite McAllister yelling at him to return to the cannon. He knew that the only way for them to make it was for him to get to the bridge and try to fight off Tiana's attacks.

Vincent smiled as white hot metal poured off the smaller ship above them. It delighted him to see his Bastiana in her element. "Keep up the chase," he ordered the crew.

Bastiana watched with delight as the Snow Break tried to turn away from her attack. Her only warning of danger was the shattering of an arrow that hit the metal deck of the Colossus to her right. The second cut across her right arm. The shock of the attack caused Bastiana to lose focus. No longer secured to the deck of the Colossus, she was knocked off her feet and was blown and tossed to the safety rail where one of the deck crew helped stabilize her. It had saved her life as well. Several more arrows rained down where she had stood just moments earlier.

Vincent's eyes squinted in anger at what he saw happening to Bastiana.

Once again under control, Bastiana walked back to the center of the deck. With elated eyes she focused on the turning airship they pursued. Her mind raced excitedly, *She was up there. The woman who could fly. That beautiful deadly angel,* which she desired. With a high pitched scream Bastiana let loose another blast of magical energy.

Kail arrived on the bridge in time to see Tiana's attack race towards their ship. Time seemed to slow down as the magical attack came at the Snow Break to tear more of her apart. He felt the power coming to him as he pushed his own magic at the incoming attack.

The magical energies collided off each other below the Snow Break. The collision was blinding to behold as the Snow Break continued through its turn unharmed. The airship's floor shook as McAllister fired off another shell at the larger Colossus below them.

Angela flew as fast as she could towards the airship that had been her home for the last few months as it pulled through its evasive turn.

"What was she thinking?" Camden called out over the chaos of the battle as he spotted Angela flying towards them.

Ellenore had the maneuvering breaks pressed as tight as possible as unsecure items rolled and bounced to one side of the bridge.

Kail watched as Angela angled to meet the ship ahead of them. It didn't take much to see that she wasn't going to make it as the Snow Break was moving just too fast for her to catch them.

Angela could see Camden and Kail on the bridge of the airship stare at her as they flew by ahead of her.

"No," Kail called out. "We have to go back for her!"

"We can't!" Ellenore shouted as one of the maneuvering breaks gave out and the airship lurched as the turn was cut short.

Kail watched as Angela drew farther and farther behind them. "No." The power inside him surged and the words that Tiana had spoken to him so long ago whispered inside his head. *It's not hard if you're a Chronomancer.* Instantly Kail found himself being beaten by the wind around him. He had Angela wrapped in his arms from behind.

The shock of Kail teleporting on top of Angela caused them both to fall uncontrollably from the sky.

Again the power surged and both Kail and Angela appeared on the bridge of the Snow Break. The differences in momentum however caused the pair to crash hard into the back wall after taking out the command chair that Camden had barely managed to escape from.

"There!" Ellenore called out and pointed in front of her.

Mr. Eleazar stood on the outer deck of the Snow Break.

The last shell that McAllister had fired managed to score a hit on the Colossus. It did little to deter the airship.

Bastiana was delighted that Kail had blocked her last attack and prepared to launch a third as smoke blew around her from the shell that she hadn't bothered to stop. This time her attack would bring the ship from the sky. She closed her eyes to fire off a third blast of energy.

Mr. Eleazar watched as Kail teleported himself from the bridge to the open sky to catch the distant Keratin and then return the both of them to the bridge. He watched as the incoming attack from Bastiana made its way towards them. A moment before impact, Mr. Eleazar snapped his fingers and said a single word. "Stop."

The entire battle froze in place. Both sides of the fight hung in the air. The magical energy from Bastiana hung frozen in the sky a heartbeat away from cutting into the airship. Suki in the infirmary held her hands over her face as loose objects hung in the air that had been bouncing around. Camden and Ellenore were looking right at him. Mr. Eleazar took a deep breath and calmly walked to the bridge.

Bastiana watched stunned as her attack simply cut through empty air that the Snow Break had occupied.

Vincent tilted his head at the sudden change of events. Their prey was almost in hand, and they simply vanished. "The Guardian," he said to no one in particular.

Chapter 17

Kail sat in a chair in the infirmary of the Snow Break. There had not been enough beds for everyone. Suki had checked him over when Camden and Ellenore brought him and Angela off the bridge. He was the least injured. He looked over at the beds. Angela lay in one, he felt bad that she had been hurt when he went after her. Crashing through the bridge of the ship with her like that was not what he wanted. He just didn't want to leave her behind. It just proved a point that he had so much more to learn about magic and how dangerous it was to use.

In the other bed lay Mr. Eleazar. Camden and Ellenore said that they thought they had seen him outside on the outer deck during the fight, but then he was gone. Suki said that when the fighting stopped, he was just there lying like that on the bed. She also said that there did not seem to be anything wrong with him, but he had not woken up for two days.

"Can you keep an eye out for a little while? I need to take a few moments for myself," Suki asked him.

"What?" Kail said as his thoughts were wandering. "Oh, yeah. I can do that, sure."

Suki looked at him and raised her eyebrow questioningly. "Alright, but if anything changes, you come find me, ok?"

Kail nodded that he would as she left the infirmary. He stood up and moved next to the bed with Mr. Eleazar on it. "What did you do old man?" The strangest event so far was that the Snow Break was fighting the Colossus and then just like that, they found themselves someplace completely different. The Colossus was nowhere to be seen. Camden eventually concluded that they were several hundred miles east of where they had been. Most likely south of Cahir now instead of south of Aldervale like they had been before. He wasn't positive until they could find a town or city he could look up on a map, but the terrain seemed to fit. Kail and the others agreed that Mr. Eleazar must have teleported the entire airship away. That much magic must have been more than he could handle and that's why he was like this.

"I hope you have not been looking at me like that when I am asleep," Angela said.

"Yes. What? I mean no," Kail said caught off guard. "Yes, Suki left and asked me to watch, but not like that. I'm just going to shut my mouth now."

"You are a funny man Kail Falconcrest," she said looking at him flounder.

"How do you feel?" he asked quietly.

"I feel like Camden Arland should get a softer chair," she said jokingly, bringing up that the chair had been destroyed.

"I'm sorry about that," he apologized. "You saved my life once when you didn't even know me. When I saw you miss the ship, and they said we couldn't go back... I didn't think. I just reacted."

"You should start thinking more. Who knows what could have happened using magic like that. It is like giving a child a sword then expecting them not to cut themselves."

"You're right. I do need to think things through more."

"I am not ungrateful though. I have been chased by that ship once before, and it is not something I wish to repeat," she said.

"When Suki lets you out of here, we could practice," he offered.

Angela looked at him questioningly.

"You know, you could fly and I could grab you again. Seems like if we did it nine hundred and ninety nine more times. We should get the hang of it," Kail said nonchalantly.

Angela laughed at the offer. "No, no, I think once was plenty."

Kail felt better once she smiled.

The door to the infirmary opened and in stepped Camden. Interrupting the pair, "Ok, isn't this creepy. The two of you having your obvious bonding moment next to the guy passed out," he said.

Kail closed his eyes and then turned away from Angela to face Camden. "Do you need something?"

"Yeah, we need to go help with the repairs," Camden said.

"Suki told me to stay here and watch over them."

"She can watch over the place. See she's awake, and besides Mr. Eleazar will probably just disappear on us anyway," Camden argued. "Come on dirt farmer, she will be here when you get back. Right Red?"

Kail looked back at Angela.

"Go, I will be fine. If the Time Walker wakes, I will find Suki," she assured him.

Camden and Kail left Angela and Mr. Eleazar and headed out of the infirmary. "Head on outside, McAllister and Ellenore are out there. I am going to swing by the galley and grab some food to bring them," Camden pointed. "I'll meet you there."

"Ok," Kail replied as he made his way through the ship. Rounding a corner he found himself face to face with Xavier coming from the opposite direction. Kail tried to just nod and to make his way past the scarred man, but Xavier intentionally blocked his path.

Kail sighed. "Can I get by Xavier?"

"So pathetic," Xavier said looking Kail up and down. "It's just one accident after another with you."

"At least I tried. I didn't see you anywhere." Kail retorted trying to muscle past him.

"Watch yourself. You wouldn't want anything bad to happen to her."

"What's that supposed to mean?" Kail demanded.

"You won't be a natural leader. No one will look up to you," Xavier answered cryptically, and he pushed past Kail.

"What a psycho," Kail muttered under his breath as he continued through the ship.

The Snow Break rested on the ground protected by surrounding tall trees. The engines were on standby. Neither Camden nor Ellenore wanted the mechanics to take them offline for maintenance after what had happened. Kail walked down the loading ramp from the cargo hold and joined the others in repairing the ship.

McAllister was welding some plates over the damage Bastiana had caused. "This whole section will need to be replaced," he told Ellenore who was marking down the information.

"Do the best you can. I don't know the next time we will be able to birth up at a place with a metal works," she told him. Ellenore spotted Kail and greeted him. "How are the wounded doing?"

"Angela seems fine. Mr. Eleazar is still the same though. Camden will be here soon too. He's getting some food for you guys," Kail summarized. "There anything I can do to help?"

"Sure, the main damage is easy to spot and McAllister is working on it. You can help me go over the rest of the hull. Look for anything, even if it's just a small hole, crack, or scratch. Mark it with this," she handed him a stick of chalk. "I'll note down what we find."

"Ok," Kail said as he took the chalk and started to search for damage caused from the battle. "I don't think I would have ever thought to look for small stuff compared to that," he indicated to where McAllister was working.

"Small problems can become big problems if you don't take care of them," she replied.

The two of them had only scanned a small portion of the hull and already Kail had circled more than a dozen places where the hull had taken damage. "You think the whole ship is like this?" Kail asked.

"Not likely. You can see the pattern already if you look at it. One of the shells they fired at us exploded I'm guessing fifty feet or so off in that direction," Ellenore pointed away and towards the front of the ship. "That is all shrapnel that hit us, or that we flew through."

"Is this going to be a danger to us?" he asked.

"Not right now, if we don't eventually do something they can start to rust out and maybe fall off or something. Worse case would be we ignore it and the next time it gets hit or the time after that it might cause the plating to fail," she told him.

Kail and Ellenore continued to mark up the hull of the ship with chalk when Camden arrived with some food from the galley. Everyone took a short break to eat.

"How did you learn all this stuff Ellenore?" Kail asked.

"My father and brothers. They ran a metal shop that did commission work," she said.

"Your family worked or built airships?"

"No," she smiled. "More like decorative work. Things that went inside buildings like fancy doors and such. They did some metal sculpting as well for some of the larger towers in Courduff."

"They are still in Courduff?" Kail questioned.

"No, not anymore. A few years back they were taken away. Their shop was confiscated and converted when they started to mass produce airships," she said sadly. "It's a lot easier for them to just make the people disappear and take what they want."

"Taken away? You mean you don't know what happened to them?" he pressed.

"No, I have not seen them since," she said effectively ending the conversation. She picked up her notebook and went back to work.

Kail felt badly for her. He had not known anything about the woman that flew Camden's ship for them. He wondered if maybe someday she would find out what happened to her father and brothers. He mulled over what she had said and thought about the airstrip in Aldervale. Old man MacDonnell had sold his land and left for the city so they said. He wondered now if that had been true or not. He remembered his friend Wilhelm Bailon and tried to picture him doing such a thing. No that couldn't have happened he concluded.

Chapter 18

Suki sat by herself in the infirmary, well, mostly by herself. Mr. Eleazar was not exactly what she would consider company. She had tried to keep Angela there as long as she could, but the headstrong red head had finally had enough and left. The place was lonely when there was no one to take care of or just to talk to as it had been with Angela. *Not that I wished more people got hurt,* she quickly thought. *Maybe I should talk to Camden about doing more.*

"Thank you," Mr. Eleazar said unexpectedly.

Suki nearly jumped out of her skin. Mr. Eleazar sat on the edge of the bed and was straightening his clothing.

"You are the most valuable person on this ship. No one else can do what you can. Don't forget that," Mr. Eleazar told her.

"Are you alright? You have been in here for three days. What happened to you?" she asked and tried to get him to lie back down.

"Three days?" he repeated and he looked at a small watch from his pocket. "Suki, I assure you that I am fine, but if you like, you may accompany me outside. It's time we all had a little talk."

Ellenore was going over the repair information and damage reports with Camden. McAllister was still working above them with the welder on the heaviest damage. Xavier had managed to create quite a pile of spent cigarettes and had begun to arrange them in little patterns. Supervising is what he told everyone he was doing.

"What's going on?" she asked to no one in particular when she saw Suki and the mechanics Pyron and Montoy make their way to the rest of the group. Her answer came right behind them as Mr. Eleazar walked into view as he exited the Snow Break.

"Can you go find Angela and magic boy," Camden asked Ellenore. "This looks important."

She nodded and took off in the direction Angela and Kail had gone earlier.

After a few minutes the entire group was together as Ellenore returned with Angela and Kail.

"I know you all must have a lot of questions for me," Mr. Eleazar started. "I will try and explain, but first there is something new that we need to discuss."

"I can think of a few questions," Xavier mumbled.

"It is time to go to The Eternal Gateway," Mr. Eleazar said. "Things are accelerating, and it will have the answers."

"The Eternal Gateway," Angela said.

"What's The Eternal Gateway?" Kail asked. "Have you been there before?"

Angela nodded. "It is where and how the Time Walker brought me here."

"Whoa, whoa, whoa there. Hold on," Camden stopped them. "A Gateway, that you used, to pull her through time? I don't think so. No way in hell we're going there. Over my dead body are you taking us to another time."

"I don't intend to do that. The Gateway will show us what we need to know," Mr. Eleazar told them. "Something has changed and I, we need to know what."

"Where is the Gateway?" Kail asked.

"In the heart of Canyamar if the legends are true," Xavier said looking at The Guardian.

"Yes, that is where the Gateway resides. It is hidden though," Mr. Eleazar said. "But as its guardian, I can show you where to go."

"Why not just zip zap and do your thing to take us there?" Camden questioned with a flourish of his hands.

"Like I did to bring you here?" Mr. Eleazar countered. "I do enjoy doing the unexpected, it tends to take people by surprise, and you saw the results of how that went."

Camden looked at everyone there. One of the things that had never sat well with him was as a leader making choices for others. No one from his crew had questioned or spoken their own opinion regarding what was being discussed. "Fine," he decided. "I hear there are some interesting animals to hunt in Canyamar."

With that declaration Ellenore quickly took charge of the crew and had them all hustling to get the Snow Break ready to fly.

"What are you not telling us?" Xavier asked when the crew had left.

"I don't know until I get to the gateway," Mr. Eleazar answered. "A simple time stop should not have incapacitated me for three days," was all he offered and took his leave from the group.

Angela glanced with concern at Camden, Kail and Xavier. Xavier just nodded his head and lit another cigarette.

A few short hours later the engines began to turn the massive blades that lifted the Snow Break into the sky. Mr. Eleazar had confirmed what Camden had suspected about their location. He instructed them on the general area where The Eternal Gateway lay.

They had several days of travel time ahead of them and Kail found himself spending most of it with McAllister. "You think the new feed is going to work for the gun?" He asked.

"It's looking promising," McAllister grinned as they loaded the gun. "Hit that yellow button so they know we're going to do some test firing," he said pointing to the back wall.

Ellenore called out when the amber light turned on in the bridge. "Test fire soon."

Camden sat in what was left of the salvaged command chair. "Give them a green light," he ordered.

The light on the weapons deck turned green. "All right, let's see how she does," McAllister said as he loaded the first round into the firing chamber and pulled back on the engaging hammer. "Fire in the hole!"

Kail held his hands over his ears as McAllister held down the firing trigger. A steady round of fire leapt from the gun. Kail could feel each round thump in his chest almost as fast as his heart beat. It did not take long, and the new feed to the gun was empty. McAllister turned to give Kail a big grin and a thumbs up.

"That sounded impressive," Camden said when the firing stopped. "Looks like they've got it working."

"That gun would have been handy a week ago," Ellenore agreed with Camden's assessment.

Angela stood on the outer deck of the Snow Break with Mr. Eleazar when the test was performed. The ground below them had changed to dense jungle and the air was thick with heat and moisture. "New weapons to kill each other with," she said.

"From bows to catapults that are replaced by cannons and missiles," Mr. Eleazar said. "It is the way with all things I'm afraid."

"Why go back to The Gateway? When we were there last, you said that to use it again could undo everything that we had worked for."

"I don't have a choice in this it seems," Mr. Eleazar answered. "I did not see that attack happening in the plan. If I had not stopped Bastiana, she would have destroyed the ship. Something has changed, and what I know is no longer correct."

"And what of our deal?"

"I don't know my dear. I have no intentions of going back on anything, but I will do what's necessary to save this world from the darkness of Therion."

"Maybe it doesn't need saved from Therion, but saved from you," Xavier said coming up on their private conversation.

"The Guardian will fall and the door will open for revenge yet taken," Mr. Eleazar quoted from the prophecy. "Perhaps you are right. Maybe this is fate telling me that I've gone too far."

"The childless one will decide the fate of all," Xavier quoted. "Sure, you don't have a child, but I don't think you are the one it's talking about," he said tossing a spent cigarette to the wind.

"The door will open," Angela repeated. "Do you think that someone else can use The Eternal Gateway?"

"I don't think so, but anything is possible," Mr. Eleazar said thinking over the question. "If it came under control of the wrong person, it could erase all of time."

"Now there is something to look forward to," Xavier said.

"There lies The Eternal Gateway," Mr. Eleazar pointed from the bridge of the Snow Break.

"I don't see anything," Kail stated the obvious.

"If you could just fly over it and find it, then it would not be much of a secret now would it?" Mr. Eleazar said.

"The jungle is pretty thick around here. I don't see a place to set down sir," Ellenore reported.

"There is a clear area about ten miles to the north of The Gateway where you can set down. We will have to make the rest of the way by foot." Mr. Eleazar said.

"Wonderful, a ten mile hike through the jungle. Just what I was looking forward to." Camden said, letting everyone know how he felt.

A few minutes later the ship settled into a small clearing and the group began to gather for the journey.

"It's going to take at least three hours to go ten miles in this jungle," Camden told Ellenore. "Then we have to do whatever and hike back," he said checking some of the gear they were taking with them one last time. "The ship is yours."

"Aye sir, we will be here and ready when you return," Ellenore assured him. "Good luck."

The group of Camden, Kail, Angela, and Xavier disappeared into the jungle with Mr. Eleazar leading the way. The rest of the crew settled in for a long wait. None expected them to return today.

The jungle was as thick as Camden had feared. But they seemed to make good time. Mr. Eleazar seemed to be able to lead them through as if following a path that no one else could see.

"So, you said you had been here before Angela?" Kail asked.

"Once, a thousand years ago, when the Time Walker came. This is where he took me to bring me to your time," she answered.

"What was it like? The gateway and coming here I mean."

"The jungle is the same."

"And?" he pressed.

"You will see soon enough," she said with a smile but not answering his question.

"What do you think Xavier?" Kail asked when Angela dodged his questioning.

"I think you should watch where you're going," Xavier told him.

Kail tripped and hit the ground hard losing a few items from his pack in the process.

Xavier added insult to injury by flicking his cigarette butt at him, and not stopping to help as he walked past.

Kail dusted himself off and retrieved what he had dropped. "Thanks!" he called after the scarred man.

Xavier simply waved above his head without turning around.

Camden was the next to ask. "Are there still Imaeras in these jungles?"

"Yes, but they are rare," Mr. Eleazar answered him as they continued through the jungle.

"What's an Imaera?" Kail asked.

Xavier shook his head at the annoyance.

"An Imaera is a large jungle cat," Angela started to explain. "Most of them are dark black, and they are larger than the horses you use."

"Are we in any kind of danger from them?" Kail wanted to know.

"With the amount of noise you're making. They are all a hundred miles from us, or about to jump out and kill us to stop the sound of your voice!" Xavier said.

"He's probably right Kail. But Imaera are also known for their hides. The leather from an Imaera will not wear out. If you cut it, it will mend itself in time. Also from what I've been told, it does a decent job of nullifying magic," Camden explained.

"If it can do all that, how would you ever kill one to skin it?" Kail asked.

"That's the trick now isn't it," Camden said with a mischievous grin.

"We're here," Mr. Eleazar said stopping in front of the group.

Everyone made their way to where Mr. Eleazar stood. The jungle thinned in front of them and sunlight found its way to the small clearing.

"That's it?" Camden asked. "A pile of rocks that have fallen on each other?"

The Eternal Gateway stood in the clearing. Two large pillars of rocks jutted from the ground. One of the pillars had been taller, but it had broken off sometime in the distant past and now rested against the other forming a broken arch.

"You see what you want The Gateway to be," Mr. Eleazar countered.

"What's that supposed to mean?" Camden continued.

"I see a wooden door standing in the middle of the jungle," Kail spoke up.

"A carved stone archway," Angela added as she moved to stand next to Mr. Eleazar.

"Hey, how come your Gateways are better than mine?" Camden wanted explained. "What does that mean?"

"It doesn't mean anything," Xavier finished. He ground a cigarette into the ground and moved closer.

"What do you see Xavier?" Camden pressed hoping someone saw The Gateway like he did or worse.

"I see a door with a sign on it that says, 'Arland's an ass.'"

"Seriously? It has a sign on it?" Camden said. "What?" Camden asked of the various looks everyone was giving him.

"The Eternal Gateway has and will always be here," Mr. Eleazar started. "I have seen it when the world was new, and it is still here when the world is old and its children have moved on. Everything changes, but The Gateway remains."

"So how does it work?" Xavier asked.

"I don't know honestly," Mr. Eleazar admitted. "It is its own being as far as I can tell. It does not use magic, nor is it alchemy or technology. It shows me the past, as well as the future. When I step through, I exit in that time. I can also bring people through with me," he finished nodding at Angela.

"And if someone else walked through it?" Xavier continued with another question.

"Oh, nothing. It only works for me. If you look into the door, or archway, all you will see is the jungle on the other side. But as the Guardian, I see the life of the world in front of me."

"I don't see jungle," Kail said.

Kail's words seemed to alarm Mr. Eleazar. "What do you see?" he asked very seriously.

"Well, I see the door, a wooden door like I said earlier. But it's closed, I don't see what's on the other side," Kail explained.

"Interesting," Mr. Eleazar mumbled.

"What does that mean?" Xavier asked.

"What? Oh sorry, I don't know for sure. It's not like I make it a habit of bringing everyone I meet to The Eternal Gateway. But everyone that has been here described it similar to what you all have. An arch or some other similar open doorway in the middle of the jungle," Mr. Eleazar told them. "No one has seen The Gateway closed."

"So… what do we do then?" Camden asked.

"I guess the obvious thing would be to go open the door Mr. Falconcrest," Mr. Eleazar answered bluntly through his accent.

"Is that a good idea? You said it yourself you're not exactly sure how it works." Xavier protested.

"Alright, I recommend you open the door Kail, but don't walk through it if you see something other than the jungle on the other side," Mr. Eleazar corrected.

Xavier tossed his hands into the air with frustration when it was clear that Mr. Eleazar did not seem to have any problems with what was going on here.

Kail turned and gave a questioning look at Angela. "Was it like this at all for you?"

"No, I see the same archway as before. When the Guardian walked through with me there was still just jungle around us. When we traveled away from here, that is when I could see that the world had changed," she answered.

Kail hesitated for a moment and then stood in front of the closed wooden door. He stopped and turned to look at Mr. Eleazar. "Should I knock first?"

Mr. Eleazar smiled. "It is your Gateway Kail Falconcrest."

Returning to the door, Kail resolved himself. He placed one hand on the handle, and with the other he knocked and opened the door.

"I don't know. It reminded me of the past. Therion was there though, but he looked different. He had hair for one thing and when I saw him in the tower in Courduff, he was bald. He was fighting with someone, but I don't know who," Kail said with a sigh. It had been over an hour since he opened The Gateway and looked through it. "Maybe it was him when he was younger and fought in the war."

"But you saw him several times. Go over each again," Xavier pressed him.

"It is important Kail," Mr. Eleazar said. "What you have seen, The Gateway has not shown me."

"It was all just Therion. I couldn't tell where he was. Every time I did see him, it was dark though. Like night time," Kail added. "Could that mean something?"

"It might be significant," Mr. Eleazar mulled.

"And then that girl, whoever she was, I swear slammed the door shut," Kail finished.

"She probably caught you looking in her room," Camden teased him.

"I don't know. She reminded me of Angela. Same look when she's mad. She had two swords like Angela too. Like I said, when I saw her, she looked at me. Flew down and shut the door."

"A Keratin at the Gateway," Mr. Eleazar puzzled.

"Her hair was all funny too. Like it didn't know what color it wanted to be. Parts of it were black, and others red," Kail added.

"I know the history of the Keratin Nation, but not of whom you speak," Angela said.

"Nor have I encountered a Keratin like you described," Mr. Eleazar agreed.

"Was she fighting Therion?" Camden asked.

"No, I don't think so. Each time I saw him everything shifted sort of. The same happened when she shut the door."

"I wonder why The Eternal Gateway chose to show you the past." Mr. Eleazar said to himself. "Well one thing is clear," He told the group. "We're on our own going forward."

"What does that supposed to mean?" Camden wanted to know.

"I think it's clear. What I know, what we know is wrong. The only logical thing to do is continue forward with the objectives we had before," Mr. Eleazar said. "For now, I suggest we stay here the night. It is a long walk back to the ship, and I for one do not want to walk there in the dark." Mr. Eleazar excused himself from the group and went back to stare at The Gateway. No one wanted to ask what it was showing him, if anything.

Xavier seemed the most agitated about what Kail had seen. He had been smoking non-stop since Kail began to describe what he saw.

"What do you think?" Kail posed the question to Angela and Camden.

"I don't think it means anything," Camden said. "I think it's one of those things that you could spend the rest of your life wondering about."

Angela had no advice to offer him either, and she set about making camp for the night.

"Xavier?" Kail asked the scarred man.

"I think it's clear. It's not us," He said.

"What do you mean?" Kail wanted to know more.

"All you saw was darkness and Therion. Then someone shut the door in your face. Don't you get it? You didn't see any of us," Xavier finished as he walked away from the group.

Chapter 19

The night in the jungle was not a restful one. The Eternal Gateway had not given any of the answers they had hoped to find. It only left them with more questions. The fact that the night had more sounds than the day did not help either. Mr. Eleazar had spent the whole night in front of the door looking through it. When questioned, he only replied to say that it had not shown him anything new.

"So what's the plan then?" Camden asked after everyone broke camp.

"We go back to the ship. Get the repairs finished for starters," Mr. Eleazar said.

"And then what?" Camden said. "Fly around for a few more months?"

"One step at a time Mr. Arland. One step at a time," Mr. Eleazar finished and headed back into the jungle.

The group departed after Mr. Eleazar. Xavier followed behind Mr. Eleazar still trying to get the Guardian to give up more information. Camden was next and Kail and Angela brought up the rear.

"You haven't said much this whole trip," Kail told her.

"What is there to say?" Angela replied.

"I don't know. Aside from him, you are the only one who has any experience with all this."

"My experience in walking a few steps pales compared to what you have experienced Kail."

"I guess you're right," Kail said. "But it just seems like this is completely messed up. I mean look at us. From Aldervale, to Courduff, to Mr. Eleazar saving us and now here. In the jungle thousands of miles from anywhere. Only to have some door show me the man who tried to kill me and then some girl who slams it in my face."

"Once I came to grips that I was a thousand years removed from my home. I have accepted that my fate is tied to the Time Walker," she said.

"Why is that? Everyone seems to have some sort of deal or reason why they are doing this. What is your story Angela?" Kail pressed.

"It is simple. I was a soldier, I was given a choice and I chose wrong. I died and the Time Walker offered a different path," Angela told him.

"What? You died?" Kail repeated confused.

Before Angela could reply the faint sounds of explosions in the distance could be heard. The normal sounds of the jungle also faded away as more explosions followed. Camden came running back to the two of them.

"Did you hear that? We're in trouble!" Camden said. "Angela go and see."

Angela nodded and dropped her pack as she took to the trees above them and out of the jungle canopy. The rest of the group waited for her to return.

"That was cannon fire," Camden said while they waited.

"What's going on?" Kail asked.

"I think the ship is under attack. But how or by whom I don't know."

Angela dropped to the ground next to them. "It is the Colossus. The Snow Break is firing on them and is in flight."

"How in the hell did they find us here?" Camden demanded looking at Mr. Eleazar.

"I don't know. This is all wrong. Just like they found us before," Mr. Eleazar said. "Angela, you are the fastest by far. Go, your skills will help."

Angela nodded and retrieved her bow and a set of arrows from her dropped pack giving everyone one last look she disappeared into the jungle above them.

"The rest of us, we need to hurry," Mr. Eleazar stressed and started to run in the direction of the fight. Everyone dropped their packs and headed after Mr. Eleazar. As before the jungle seemed to part for them as they made their way through it much faster than they should have been able to do. A rapid succession of faint explosions could be heard.

"That's McAllister's gun," Camden shouted through the jungle.

Kail remembered the gun that he had helped McAllister get working before they landed in the jungle. He hoped that it was doing a good job of defending the Snow Break. Without himself or Mr. Eleazar there to counter Tiana, their ship did not stand a chance if she decided to throw her magic at it.

"Stop!" Kail yelled. When he had thought of the dark-skinned girl, an image of her in the jungle flashed into his mind. That small warning saved their lives as a blast of intense energy cut across the path that Mr. Eleazar had been leading them.

A peal of laughter filled the jungle silence. "Oh, you don't fail to disappoint, do you Kail?" Bastiana called out from somewhere.

Everyone had scrambled for cover following the magical attack. Kail found himself near Camden and they could see Xavier several yards away pressed up against a tree. Mr. Eleazar was not in sight.

"Come out and play with me Kail. You can bring that pretty friend of yours who can fly too," Bastiana's voice sung out followed shortly by a second magical attack that cut through the jungle around them.

Xavier motioned for their attention and pointed ahead of them. Looking in that direction Kail and Camden saw a pair of soldiers from the Colossus making their way through the underbrush in their direction. They both nodded that they had seen the two men.

Xavier pulled out a metal ball from under his coat and twisted the timer and then threw it at the men as he ran into the jungle. The two soldiers reacted to the device Xavier had thrown as well as spotted him as he ran away. The explosion of the clockwork bomb destroyed the jungle where the men had been. Bits of dirt, jungle and soldier landed all around them.

Kail's ears rang from Xavier's bomb, but he heard Camden when he told him to run while there was confusion. The two of them cut through the trees keeping their heads down. Another errant blast of energy sliced through the air next to them. The magical energy burned through the trunk of a tree that had spent its entire life reaching for the sky. The cracking sounds of shattering wood from above stopped the pair in their tracks as the ancient tree collapsed through the jungle sending all manner of debris to crash and fall around them.

Mr. Eleazar came charging out of the jungle next to them. "Run you fools!" he said as ran past them. Another explosion detonated in the jungle nearby. *Xavier*, Kail thought and took Mr. Eleazar's advice to start running again.

Kail did not know when he became separated from Camden, but he noticed the big guy's absence when he rounded a tree in the jungle and found himself face to face with another pair of soldiers from the Colossus. Each of them was armed with a long sword and immediately charged at him. Weaponless Kail panicked as they ran at him. Even though he had trained with Camden and Angela aboard the Snow Break it had not prepared him for the real thing.

The collision took them all by surprise as Camden barreled out of the jungle and tackled the two soldiers. Camden had one of the soldiers on the ground and was grappling with him. The other soldier got to his feet and abandoned his partner to continue after Kail.

Kail held his ground as the soldier advanced on him. The soldier had the advantage with the reach of the sword, but Kail doubted the man had any experience fighting someone who could use magic. As it had been when he spared with Camden, the soldiers' formal training made it easier for him to see the patterns in the man's attacks and it was not that long before he had his opening to turn the weapon on its owner.

Camden stood up from the undergrowth after dispatching the soldier. Kail saw that his hands and arms were all twisted snarled knots. "Tree roots," he shrugged and took note of the dead soldier at Kail's feet. Another explosion sounded through the air demanding their attention.

Mr. Eleazar had made his way through the jungle keeping Bastiana after him. He checked the small pocket watch and noted the time before putting it back. He turned around and waited.

Bastiana skidded to a stop when she found Mr. Eleazar waiting for her. "Hello," she said with a tilt of her head. "You're dressed funny."

"And you should not be running around the jungle by yourself," Mr. Eleazar replied.

"You're not like the others," Bastiana said eyeing Mr. Eleazar.

"No, I'm not."

Mr. Eleazar and Bastiana circled each other. Her hands began to crackle with red and white electricity and her lips twisted into a mischievous grin. Quickly raising her hands above her head, the ground in front of her tore itself apart as the force of her attack raced towards him.

Mr. Eleazar stood his ground until the last moment and then sidestepped the ground rushing at him. His answer to her attack was one of his own. The magic was subtle but the results were not. Undergrowth that had just been upturned animated and turned against Bastiana. Roots and vines made their way towards her and began to ensnare her legs.

Bastiana watched as the plant growth made its way up her legs. "You're pathetic," she informed him. She focused her magic and teleported herself skyward as a blue ball of energy. She reformed and let the momentum carry her up. At the same time she focused several blasts of magic back to the ground where Mr. Eleazar stood. Before gravity began to pull her back to the earth, she teleported once more and shot through the trees to emerge on a thick branch that overlooked where her attack had landed.

Mr. Eleazar watched as the talented young mage shot through the sky and attacked him. It really is too bad about her he thought. Her magic crashed down around him in several concentrated explosions. His magical barrier held though and when the dust cleared, he still stood looking up at her. "You're going to have to do better than that," he taunted her and vanished.

Kail and Camden made their way through the jungle. They had come across another pair of soldiers from the Colossus and had taken them out. They could hear Bastiana and Mr. Eleazar fighting it out somewhere in the jungle near them.

"How many more do you think there are?" Kail asked.

"No idea, but that ship is big. They could have as many as fifty troops or more on it," Camden said. "We need to keep heading to the Snow Break."

Kail nodded and the pair headed in the direction of the airships.

Xavier stepped out of the jungle and into the clearing of The Eternal Gateway. He had managed to kill another soldier from the Colossus along the way and had a nice set of knives to show for it. Eyeing The Gateway he lit up a cigarette and made his way to stand before it. He had not told the others what he saw, but it was not jungle on the other side.

Bastiana eyed the jungle floor where Mr. Eleazar had been. She wrapped her magic around her in a protective barrier just in case. *This old man apparently has a few tricks up his sleeves.* Once again she teleported through the air, this time emerging next to three soldiers from the Colossus. "Keep your eyes open," she told them as they began to move through the jungle towards The Eternal Gateway.

Mr. Eleazar stepped into the clearing of The Eternal Gateway. Xavier was there smoking. Mr. Eleazar let the shroud of invisibility fall from him. "Xavier," he acknowledged.

"Come to guard the door Guardian?" Xavier asked.

"It can take care of itself," Mr. Eleazar replied moving closer. "I expected you to be half way to the Snow Break by now."

"I had a run in with a few friends," Xavier said showing the pair of daggers he now had. "Besides, I want to know what you really saw."

"You first," Mr. Eleazar said.

"Well, if it isn't the old and the ugly," Bastiana's voice floated like liquid silk from the edge of the clearing.

Chapter 20

Angela left her companions as she took to the sky again. As she cleared the tree tops, she could see the massive airship, Colossus, bare down on the smaller Snow Break. She could see the flashes of cannon fire long before the sound reached her. It would be several minutes before she would be able to do anything for the crew that had remained behind as the rest of them had traveled to The Eternal Gateway. She had to give Ellenore credit. If the Colossus had caught their ship while it was still on the ground, they would not have had a chance.

Vincent stood on the bridge of the Colossus as they made their attack on the Snow Break. She would not escape them this time. He was a tiny bit disappointed that they had to give up the element of total surprise, but it was necessary to let Bastiana and the troops have time to depart to the jungle. The markers they had been following had continued on ahead when they came across the ship parked in the clearing. This had allowed the smaller ship time to get airborne. *No matter,* he thought. *This time there would be no escaping them.*

Ellenore cursed, without Camden and the others, the Snow Break was severely undermanned. She was alone on the bridge and it was up to her and the rest of the crew to do what they could to survive. They had been lucky that the Colossus hadn't just charged in and obliterated them. Instead they were given half a chance when it had stopped and soldiers dropped into the jungle. She didn't have time to wonder if the ground party would be ok. If she didn't save the ship, then it wouldn't matter either way.

Suki's heart was pounding in her chest. She had followed McAllister to the weapons deck as ordered and he gave her a crash course on how to load the main cannons. Her job was simple. When he fired, she reloaded while he fired again from the next cannon. Repeat until they had escaped, or they were dead.

The bridge of the Snow Break vibrated each time the cannons were fired. "Come on," Ellenore called to the ship as she tried to will it faster and to get ahead of the Colossus before it opened up on them.

Vincent gave the order to fire at will to the cannon and gun crews. The air around both ships was filled with explosions from opposing fire. Crewmen lined the outer deck of the Colossus and manned smaller deck guns while crew a few decks down took aim with larger cannons.

Angela flew hard to the air battle unfolding in front of her. The deck crew was her first priority followed by going after the larger guns. She wasn't sure how she was going to shut them down just yet, but one step at a time. The gun crew of the Colossus never saw her coming until it was too late for some of them. She landed on the deck of the Colossus and slid down its length. She fired off six arrows that each landed in the backs of crew manning deck guns pointed at the Snow Break. Angela ditched the bow and shot back into the sky.

Vincent watched silently as the red head killed six of his crew in a matter of heartbeats and managed to silence half of the guns that were firing on the other airship. The clatter of her discarded bow as it hit the front window of the bridge was just insult to injury in his eyes. "Re-man the deck guns," he ordered. "Send an armed escort as well to deal with her if she tries to return."

Ellenore let out a loud whoop when she saw Angela join the fight. The Snow Break had yet to deal any significant damage to the Colossus, but at the same time, she had managed to keep the larger ship from blasting them out of the sky. With the smaller guns silenced she felt the first stirrings of hope in her chest that they were going to survive this mess.

Angela's successful attack had not gone unnoticed by McAllister and Suki. They both cheered as well. "That's going to make them think twice," McAllister yelled.

Suki had to admit, it was the most impressive display she had ever seen. It was like a fiery avenging angel that swooped down, saved them and then took to the heavens again.

McAllister brought his new gun to bear on the Colossus and held down the firing trigger. He was rewarded with the satisfaction of seeing the gun leave a line of holes in the side of the Colossus as they passed.

Kail and Camden ran through the jungle as fast as they could without falling over themselves. Without Mr. Eleazar it was much more difficult to maneuver. The sound of explosions in the distance as the Snow Break squared off with the Colossus spurred them on as the jungle did its best to keep them away.

Ellenore swung the ship around to expose the undamaged side to the Colossus. She hit the signal light to the weapons deck to let them know that they needed to man the cannons on the other side of the ship.

Suki and McAllister unhooked their securing harnesses and scrambled to the other side. "Load that one," McAllister pointed. "I'll get this one."

The Colossus slowly came into the firing arc of the Snow Break. The angle was bad for both ships, but the Snow Break was better off. As they cut across the front of the Colossus, the larger ship did not have a firing solution other than the deck guns that had been silenced by Angela. McAllister fired the first shell and watched as it missed wide. He traded places with Suki so she could load the cannon again while he tried to damage the Colossus.

Angela assessed the situation from the air above the ships. She watched as the Snow Break cut in front of the Colossus. The problem for her was that once they finished that maneuver, they would be exposed to a full set of guns. She was going to have to go back and kill the gunners on the other side. Angela pulled her twin war blades from her back. She watched as more soldiers came out onto the deck to replace the ones she had killed. Even more followed to protect them. She chose to fly down and come in from the back of the Colossus. The crew on the deck would not see her until she was on top of them.

Angela dropped from the sky. The wind whipped her red hair behind her. One of the shells from the Snow Break missed and it exploded deep in the jungle below. Using gravity to assist she pulled out of the drop and buzzed past the side of the command bridge and onto the deck. Two of the soldiers on the deck never saw what killed them. She let her momentum carry her to the front of the outer deck. The shadow of the Snow Break crossed over her as it continued to swing around. She charged the closest crewman who was bringing his deck gun to bear on the Snow Break. Only at the last moment did he see the danger.

Xavier and Mr. Eleazar turned to watch as Bastiana and three of the Colossus's soldiers entered the clearing.

"It seems like I get to try this again," she purred. "Alive if you can," she instructed the soldiers to go after Xavier. "As for you old man, I will let you live if you tell me where Kail is."

"That's simple. He is in the jungle. You may leave now," Mr. Eleazar said looking at his pocket watch.

"Old and funny, I think the world will be a better place with one less mouth to feed," she retorted.

"Bastiana, you are better than this."

She squinted her eyes at him when she heard her name spoken. "How do you know my name?" she demanded.

"You don't understand dear. I am The Guardian of The Eternal Gateway. There is nothing I don't know," Mr. Eleazar said.

Bastiana rolled her eyes at Mr. Eleazar's bravado. "When I die, I will let everyone know that you were nothing more than a delusional old man." She held out her hand and with a crack of light she held her staff covered in runes.

"Where did you get that?" Mr. Eleazar asked cautiously.

"You're the master of time. You should know everything," she mocked him.

Xavier made his way away from Mr. Eleazar and The Gateway. The last place he wanted to be was next to a pair of mages squaring off with each other. Of course the three armed soldiers that were paralleling him wasn't exactly his idea of a good alternative. He had already used the last of the clockwork bombs in the jungle. *One more of those*, he thought, *and this would be easy*. He took a couple of deep breaths. Now was not the time to get excited and get himself killed. Everything he had been through was for this moment here and now, he would not let it slip away.

Angela had her hands full. These soldiers were well trained and did a good job holding their ground against her. They worked well as a team, and it was clear that they practiced that way. None of them had fallen to her blades, and she could not get any of them to come at her by themselves so she could cut them down. The deck crew was disciplined as well. Even with her there, they continued to do their job and began to fire on the Snow Break.

Ellenore did what she could at the helm and barked into the relay tubes to the engine room. This pass was going to be rough. Several times already the Snow Break had shook from incoming fire. At this rate, they would be blown from the sky in a few minutes. She could see Angela on the deck of the Colossus fighting it out with crew. She did not know what Angela could do being that outnumbered but was thankful for anything at this point.

McAllister hesitated on firing at the Colossus again when he saw Angela fighting. The last thing he wanted was to blow her to smithereens. When the Colossus opened fire again he prayed that she would not be a simple casualty of friendly fire, but he had no choice. Aiming the best he could, he fired at the deck of the Colossus hoping it would land high near the bridge.

Angela could see that they were preparing to charge her. She had an easy out to the sky of course, but that would not do her, or the Snow Break much good, and she was not about to abandon them. She had to somehow hold them off and buy time for the others to arrive and help. The proximity shell from the Snow Break exploded onto the deck of the Colossus. Several of the gunners and a few of their guards were killed instantly. Angela got lucky that only her ears felt seriously hurt. A pair of soldiers with shrapnel wounds lay screaming on the deck where the shell had landed.

This was her chance to attack, and she did not let it pass. She ran one of the war blades through the chest of the nearest soldier still disoriented from the blast. The soldier could do nothing but stare at the blade in his chest while his brain refused to admit that his body was dead. The other war blade she used to parry the attack of his buddy. She yanked her blade free from the first man and let his body fall to the deck. The rest of the soldiers had recovered enough from the earlier blast to attack.

Angela dodged attack after attack. The war blades caused the soldiers weapons to chip and spark when they collided with the indestructible blades. She ducked under the sword of a soldier who tried to take off her head. She brought her foot up high and hard and was rewarded with a crunch as she felt his teeth break on each other inside his mouth. A second soldier had thrust at her and she caught his arm underneath hers. She followed up by simply bringing her other blade around and severed the limb and literally disarmed the man. Now the deck of the Colossus was in total chaos. Several of the deck crew had abandoned their guns to flee from the carnage unfolding around them. From the blood and dead caused by the Snow Break to the wrath of the red headed woman slicing up soldiers, there was panic.

"Stop for a moment," Camden called out to Kail.

"What?"

"I don't hear anything," Camden said while motioning for Kail to not make any noise.

"What do you suppose is going on?" Kail asked.

"I don't know. I don't think either ship has gone down. We would have heard that I'm sure."

"Angela?" Kail said. When he thought of her he caught a glimpse of her covered in blood surrounded by carnage. The quick vision caused him to miss a step and he fell.

"Watch it," Camden chastised him. "What was that all about?"

"I saw her. Angela. I don't know, but we need to hurry, she was covered in blood."

Bastiana moved closer to Mr. Eleazar and The Gateway. Mr. Eleazar held his ground in front of the gate and did nothing but watch as she squared off.

Xavier tightened his grip on the pair of daggers he had in each hand. His eyes bounced back and forth between the soldiers as they came closer and began to surround him. Xavier made the first move. He threw one of the daggers end over end as hard as he could and was rewarded with it sticking out of a soldier. *Things are looking better. Only two more to go, but only one more dagger.*

Mr. Eleazar wrapped himself with invisibility and moved away from The Gateway. He did not get very far when Bastiana slammed the end of her rune staff to the ground and a pulse of sound reverberated from it. The counter spell washed over him and the invisibility magic dissipated.

"Not so fast old man. That tricky trick won't work again," she sung out.

Mr. Eleazar responded by firing off a dozen small fiery orbs in her direction. Bastiana's eyes lit up as she started to run through the clearing. The orbs exploded behind her where her feet had been. She brought up her hand and a bar of energy leapt from it towards The Guardian.

Mr. Eleazar blocked the attack with a barrier of his own. However the sheer force of energy behind her magic lifted him off the ground and sent him through the air backwards into the clearing.

Bastiana's laughter filled the clearing as she sent Mr. Eleazar flying backwards. "Everyone can fly!"

Mr. Eleazar landed in the underbrush and tumbled backwards a few extra yards before getting back on his feet. *I'm getting too old for this*, he thought. Dusting himself off and picking a few pieces of jungle off of his coat he focused again on the girl in front of him. He lifted one arm and fired his own magical attack back at her.

Bastiana reveled when the magical energy came in contact with the rune staff in her hands. It absorbed the energy and didn't even stir the air around her. *This so called guardian didn't stand a chance,* she thought. Mocking his attack, she started to walk towards Mr. Eleazar ignoring his assault. She felt like defeating him the old fashioned way.

Xavier had his hands full keeping the soldiers at bay. He had managed to stick a second one with his knife, but the soldier was not out of the fight yet. He charged the soldier that was still a hundred percent and the two of them danced to a deadly song. Xavier went low with his blade and the soldier went high. Both of them caught each other's attack with their free hand and it was a contest of muscle at this point. Xavier saw the wounded man come at him from the side to try and finish him. As the man thrust his sword at him, Xavier reversed his push and pulled the soldier closer to him and watched as the wounded man's sword stabbed through his comrade. Xavier continued through the pull and spun around and caught the wounded man through the back of the neck with his dagger. He watched as the blood spilled out of the two soldiers. He turned and watched as Bastiana used her staff to block Mr. Eleazar's attack and advance on him. *Such a wicked girl,* he thought.

Mr. Eleazar aborted the attack and changed tactics. He ran towards The Eternal Gateway and fired off another set of magical blasts into the air behind them. They were not intended to hit the girl, but the ground around her and explode. The staff might absorb his magic, but it would not absorb the debris.

Bastiana saw him make a run for it and chased after. "All you do is run away!" she called after him. The rain of explosions around her brought her up short. She had to close her eyes and shield herself from the debris being thrown around. She blindly fired off several volleys of her own not caring where they went.

Mr. Eleazar batted away several of the random attacks. They flew away from the clearing to explode in the jungle around them. Chunks of trees were shattered into splinters that rained down. He continued to attack the area surrounding her.

Xavier made a mad dash for The Gateway. They were tearing the jungle apart around him. He saw Mr. Eleazar making his way to the gate as well with Bastiana also closing the distance. He was only going to get one chance. Even then he would be lucky to get that. Reaching The Gateway first he set up and waited for the moment to attack.

227

Mr. Eleazar was getting tired. The time stop from earlier had left him weak. A long hike in the jungle followed by a fight and lots of running did not help either. How the young mage had found that blasted staff he wanted to know as well. This whole fight would have been a lot easier if it wasn't here. Mr. Eleazar saw Xavier at The Gateway waiting to throw a knife. *It might work,* he thought and fired several more balls of magic at the ground in front of the advancing Bastiana. He saw Xavier reach back to throw the knife. An errant blast of magic buzzed past Mr. Eleazar's head as it made its way directly towards Xavier. Mr. Eleazar reacted; he brought his hand up and snapped his finger at the scarred man just as the knife left his hand an instant before he would have been melted in two by her attack. The magic passed through thin air as Mr. Eleazar teleported him away. Xavier's dagger sank deep into his shoulder. He looked at the handle of the blade sticking out of him. *Of course, it all made sense now. The scars from being burned. The cigarette butts that had left a trail for them to follow.* He should have known better, no he did know better.

Bastiana swung the staff and delighted in hearing the satisfying crack as she hit the old man in the side of the head. It was funny to her the way his body rolled away. *All this over a pile rocks surrounded by jungle,* she thought.

Angela had them on the run now. She was leaving a wake of dead bodies and blood behind her as she cut down soldier after soldier. Her clothes and hair stuck to her body from all the blood.

Vincent stood calmly on the bridge of the Colossus and watched her deal death to his soldiers. One after another they fell to the blur of her blades. It was almost comical. "Would someone please remove her from the ship?" he ordered.

Angela stood alone on the deck of the Colossus. She could see Vincent looking at her through the glass. She lifted one of the war blades and pointed it at him.

Bastiana walked over to the fallen man's body and pushed him onto his back with her foot.

The world for Mr. Eleazar spun and he could not focus his eyes on anything. He felt himself get kicked onto his back and tried to keep from passing out. The pain in his shoulder was intense, but the blow to the head was worse. He could make out the shape of someone standing over him.

"Last words old man?" Bastiana asked. "The Gateway is ours now."

"Not on my watch."

Bastiana saw Mr. Eleazar smile and tried to figure out what was so funny. Then she saw it. The old man had a small pocket watch in his hand, and she watched as he closed his fist and crushed it.

The blast leveled the jungle around The Eternal Gateway for several miles. Angela took her eyes off of Vincent and watched as the blast wave pushed the trees to the ground like they were nothing. Camden and Kail heard the jungle scream around them. They ducked for cover and Kail managed to shield them from most of the blast as it passed over them. Ellenore was speechless as she saw the explosion in the distance.

Mr. Eleazar was gone. The Eternal Gateway lay shattered.

Chapter 21

Camden and Kail crawled out from under the jungle that had fallen around them. The glare of the sun was shockingly bright now that there was nothing to block its light from reaching the ground.

"What the hell was that?" Camden said surveying the destruction around them. The trees lay shattered, and they all lined up like they had been pushed over by a giant hand.

"I, I don't know," Kail said. "It came from the direction of the door," he pointed.

Camden turned to look in the direction that they had been running. Bits of the jungle still floated in the air and cast a haze in the direction of The Eternal Gateway.

"What do we do?" Kail asked.

Camden didn't answer. He turned from where the explosion had come, and he spotted his airship circling at a higher altitude above the Colossus. "I'm getting to my ship."

"What about Mr. Eleazar? And The Gateway, and Xavier is out here as well," Kail said.

"Right now I don't care. What I do care about is my ship and the people on her."

"We can't just leave them," Kail protested.

"If you want to go look for them, go ahead."

Kail stood torn in what to do. Go with Camden and see what they could do for the Snow Break and the Colossus, or head back through the debris of the jungle and find Xavier and Mr. Eleazar. "I'm going to look for them," he decided.

Camden gave him a hard look. "Find them, and then we get the hell out of here dirt farmer."

Kail nodded and left the big man to head back towards The Gateway.

Xavier found himself standing in the infirmary of the Snow Break. The disorientation quickly faded when he realized what Mr. Eleazar had done. His face twisted with rage. "Nooooo!" he screamed and began to tear the room apart. "No! Oh, no, I will not be cheated again."

Camden watched Kail leave, then turned and jogged towards the edge of the blast zone towards the circling airships.

Xavier left the infirmary and calmly walked into the galley. The years of pent up rage had centered him to a resolved calm. He would have the revenge that was promised him one way or another. He looked at the long kitchen knife as it hung on the wall. He could see himself in its reflection as he reached to grab it. Scars disfigured him to the point where even the people who did this to him did not recognize him.

Kail scrambled through the ruined jungle calling out for Xavier and Mr. Eleazar. He could see the small rise of the clearing near The Eternal Gateway.

Xavier walked onto the weapons deck of the Snow Break. He could see Suki and McAllister manning the ship's cannons. *So easy,* he thought to himself.

Suki did not understand. She watched the Colossus swing around outside in front of the guns. She could see Angela down there. She looked so small, but so bright and full of life, life that fought for all of them. The pain through her back was sharp, but did not hurt too much. She had felt more pain from lesser wounds as a child. She looked down and pulled her fingers away from her chest. She could feel the tip of the blade sticking out of her. Her fingers were stained red. *Is this blood? My blood.* She did not understand as her legs gave out underneath her.

McAllister caught movement out of the side of his eye. "Xavier? You guys are back," he said spotting the scarred man standing behind Suki. He watched confused at what he saw. A red stain was growing from the center of the medic's chest. Everything seemed to move in slow motion as he watched her fall to the floor. Xavier stood there with a blood covered knife in his hand. "No!" he screamed and charged her killer.

So easy, he thought as McAllister charged him. *What was the man going to do? Stop him.* Xavier brought the knife around.

Suki could feel the cold of the floor. She couldn't move, but she could feel her blood pool around her. She could see shapes moving above her and shadows dance. *Was that McAllister yelling?* A body landed next to hers. Then she saw it being dragged off and watched silently as someone rolled it off of the ship. *Are those Xavier's boots,* she wondered as the darkness took her?

Kail had not had any luck in finding Mr. Eleazar or Xavier. He stood where The Eternal Gateway had been. He could see parts of it scattered around him. Things were spiraling out of control fast. That much he was sure of. He had not let himself think about it before, but now he could not help it. *What if they were gone? Gone as in dead?* He tried not to panic about what it would mean if Mr. Eleazar was dead. *Xavier is gone as well,* he thought. *What about Tiana?* The flash to his mind made him drop to his knees. Tiana was still alive. He knew it when he saw her, but she wasn't unhurt.

Bastiana was angry. She was angrier than she ever cared to remember. She didn't mean to kill the soldier that had found her smoking body lying in the corridor of the Colossus. But when he had stood over her and touched her, she lashed out. *Someone else can clean him off of the walls,* she thought. What few others that crossed her path quickly removed themselves from it. She did not spare the time to find a mirror, but if the looks on their faces were any indication, she was frightening.

What was left of her uniform barely hung onto her body. Most of what she had been wearing was pretty much gone on the entire left side. She had spared a few glances on her way to the bridge and saw that her left arm along with her exposed stomach and left leg were covered in runic symbols. She knew that she would most likely kill someone when she did look at her face. She didn't have to guess where the burnt smell of hair was coming from.

Xavier felt better, but not much as he casually stood in front of the door leading to the engine room. He mulled over the goggles and ear muffs hanging on the wall. "Don't want to damage that sensitive hearing now," he spoke to himself and fitted a pair of hearing protection to his ears. He pulled on the heavy door and stepped into the engine room and shut it behind him. It only took a few moments inside to kill the mechanics. Like the others they never knew what killed them. Only a pair of tiny eyes looking through the thick glass in the heart of the ship saw their killer walk away.

Camden made his way through the jungle under the airships in the sky. Everything felt wrong to him. There had not been any cannon fire in quite some time. What could have happened that had both ships in a stalemate? He grinned when he the thought that Angela maybe had taken out everyone on the Colossus. *That would be nice,* he thought. *It might actually make up for this lousy day.*

Something crashed through the canopy above him and landed just out of sight. Camden looked up but could not see much, only hear the sounds of the massive engines and fans that kept the airships in the sky. He made his way to where he heard the object fall. *Is that a body?* he asked himself. Camden ran over, and his heart froze in his chest. He looked upon the broken body of McAllister, his friend that he had talked into coming with him after he bought the Snow Break. *What the hell was going on up there?* The silence of the guns became even more ominous.

Kail got to his feet and shook his head. He was even more confused than before. Tiana looked like hell from what he saw. He called out again and again for Mr. Eleazar and Xavier. No one answered his call.

Xavier jogged up the flight of stairs to the bridge of the Snow Break. *One more to go. One more to go.* He stopped and pressed his ear to listen through the door. He could not hear anything, not really. It was about amusing himself now more than anything. He could feel Ellenore on

236

the other side of the door bring the ship about and start to dive behind the Colossus. He opened the door and slowly entered. He could hear her curse that no one was firing the cannons at the larger airship. *Such foul language,* he thought.

Ellenore cursed out loud as they passed by the Colossus and McAllister and Suki did not fire on the ship. The angle had been perfect and with Angela silencing the deck guns, they were not going to get a better shot than now to make something happen. She knew that the next move would be reckless even by her standards, but she didn't see a better way to go. She grabbed the breaking throttle and swung the ship around. She shed altitude and dropped the airship down behind the Colossus. The jungle came into view as the ship began to make its dive.

She felt the ice of the blade slide across her throat. That was minor compared to the sudden inability to breathe. She tried to call out, scream, or do anything, but her lungs were being filled with her own blood. She got weaker each time her heart beat. The last thing she saw was the jungle rushing up at the ship. Death was quick.

Bastiana stormed onto the bridge of the Colossus. "Look at what he did to me!" she demanded and tossed the rune staff at the nearest person.

The bridge crew was caught off guard and so was Vincent at the sudden outburst. They had been staring at the bloody woman on the deck of the ship that threatened to kill them all and the sudden destruction of the jungle below.

Vincent was speechless at the site of his darling Bastiana. Half of her hair was nothing more than melted stubble. The runes of protection from the staff crisscrossed her delicate skin. He would worry about that later. He knew that look that radiated from her eyes and if he didn't channel it away there was a good chance she would destroy everything in a fit of rage. "She's waiting," was all he said and pointed to the Keratin standing on the outer deck of the Colossus.

Angela stood scanning the ruined jungle from the Colossus. Her mind raced through a thousand possible outcomes of what had happened and none of them were good. She heard the crack and sizzle as Bastiana teleported near her. By reflex alone she leapt into the sky to flee the ship. She did not get far when the air around her exploded with electricity. Her nervous system was completely scrambled, and she landed back on the deck of the Colossus.

Bastiana watched with uncontrolled pleasure at the sight of the pretty flying girl as she dropped from the sky and landed before her. She fired off another blast of electricity just to relive the moment and walked slowly to where Angela lay twitching on the deck. She looked down smiling at her as Angela stared back but unable to move. Even the drying blood seemed fitting. Bastiana straddled Angela and brought her face down next to hers. She rubbed her cheek along Angela's and took in a deep breath through her nose and closed her eyes. "You even smell pretty," she complemented. "And now you're mine."

Soldiers from the Colossus surrounded the two women on the deck.

Chapter 22

Camden moved away from the body of McAllister and now stood in the clearing where they had left the Snow Break before following Mr. Eleazar into the jungle. He could see his ship in the sky above him. *What was she doing?* as he looked on in horror as the ship began to dive behind the Colossus. "Come on Ellenore, you know better," he said out loud. The airship should have pulled out of the dive by now. He couldn't look away as the ship fell from the sky and plunged towards the ground.

Xavier saw the jungle rushing up at him through the windows of the bridge. "Whoa, whoa, whoa," he said as he stepped over the body of the first mate. He grabbed the helm and released the breaking leaver and pulled hard. He let out a mad laugh as he brought the ship out of its suicidal dive. The ship bucked and protested as some of the giant fans shredded the tops of the trees, but he had stopped it from crashing into the ground and killing him. He kicked the maneuvering breaks and brought the ship to a halt just above the trees. Xavier left the bridge and made his way outside to the outer deck of the Snow Break; he shook his fists and yelled at the Colossus above him.

Vincent kept one eye on the events in front of him with Bastiana and the other on the Snow Break. He saw it loose control and almost crash into the jungle, but it pulled out of the dive at the last moment and now just hovered at the tops of the trees. His men had picked up the Keratin and were dragging her by each arm to a holding cell. He saw Xavier walk out onto the deck of the other ship and signal him. "Fascinating," he said to no one in particular. The scarred man who from the beginning had led them to Angela on the roof tops. Who had found the boy that Therion wanted so badly and again left behind a trail of markers in the form of spent cigarettes. The man who had delivered everything he said he could even the location of The Eternal Gateway and the death of its guardian. Therion would be pleased with the results. They had no use for the man now. "Helm, take us North. We are finished here."

Xavier watched the Colossus turn away and begin to leave. At first he cursed that they were leaving him behind, but it didn't matter. Xavier knew more about Vincent and Bastiana than they could possibly know. Xavier started to laugh so hard that he began to cry. Finally after everything he had been through, he had won. He dropped to the deck and lay facing the sky. The euphoria that filled him was rewarding as he watched the clouds float in the sky. He had more work to do and claim his prize, but for now he settled for the moment of long fought victory.

Kail stood at the center of the destroyed jungle and tried to fathom what was happening. He saw the smaller airship almost crash out of the sky and then the Colossus just seemed to not care anymore and left. "Why are they leaving?" he said out loud. "I am the one they have been after. Why leave now?"

Camden kept his eyes to the tops of the trees as he made his way to where the Snow Break hovered. The ship's engines blew the trees around. He waved his hands at the ship above him and yelled. Someone was up there that much he knew when he saw the ship pull out of the dive. Now he just needed to get their attention so he could get on board to help.

Suki's hands trembled so much from shivering that they were near useless. She had woken up in a massive pool of her own blood. She had used as much of her healing magic as she dared to stop what little blood she had left from flowing out of her. She was so tired, but she knew that if she went to sleep she would not wake up again. She was sure of one thing though, she needed to get help. She had used her legs to push herself along the floor of the weapons deck. It wasn't the easiest thing to do and she left a wide smear of blood behind her. When the ship had dived she had rolled down a corridor and now rested against a maintenance hatch. The hatch gave access to the underneath of the ship so the crew could use it to load weaponry for the ship's cannons directly and bypass the loading hanger all together. It also had a view port where she could see Camden Arland on the ground below waving at her.

Camden continued to try to get the ship's attention but was not having any luck. "Come on!" he yelled as loud as he could. He saw the access hatch for the weapons deck slide open above him and the hauling cable came down. He ran over and caught the end of the cable and stood confused as it continued to spool out and pile up at his feet. Finally the winch halted as the last of the cable was deployed. *Whoever lowered the cable apparently, wasn't going to raise it back up*, he thought. He grabbed the cable and used his magic to bond his hands to it and began to climb to his airship that hovered above him.

Camden hauled himself through the access port and onto the weapons deck of the Snow Break. He slapped the button and the winch began to haul the cable back. The other button, the one that lowered the cable was smeared in blood. *Something is very wrong*, Camden thought slowly looking around where he stood. There was blood smeared all over, like someone had decided to mop the deck floor in it. Then he saw a boot sticking out from a section of piping. Cautiously he stepped around wide to see who it was. "Oh my god."

Camden rushed to where Suki lay against the corridor wall. Her head slumped forward and her clothes were saturated in blood. The sight of her brought him up short. He didn't know where it was safe to touch her, or if she was even alive. "Suki, Suki, can you hear me?" he spoke softly. Camden gently lifted her head to see if she was alive. Her eyes fluttered open and looked at him. The overwhelming relief was short lived when the urgency that she was near death hit him.

Suki tried to open her eyes, but they refused to listen to her. She felt someone tilt her head back and finally managed to get them open. She was so light headed, cold, and never felt so tired in her life. A tiny smile tried to lift her lips when she saw Camden in front of her. She could see his mouth moving, but she was not able to hear any words. She watched in silence as emotions rolled across his face. *Camden was here,* she thought. *I'm going to be safe, I can sleep now.* A tiny part of her called out a name. *Oh, that's right. I should tell him before going to sleep.* "Xavier."

"Xavier? Xavier did this? Come on, come on, stay with me!" Camden spoke to her. He watched as her eyes closed and her body relaxed. "No, no, no. Don't do this." He gathered her small body into his arms and made his way as fast as he could through the weapons deck. He had to get her to the infirmary his mind raced. "Come on girl, you're going to be ok. You're going to be ok," he kept saying out loud. The infirmary seemed to be miles away as he carried her through the ship.

Finally, he thought. He kicked the door open so hard that the heavy metal door almost tore free of its hinges. He set her down on one of the beds. *So much blood,* he thought. *How could there be so much blood inside such a small person.* He quickly scanned her but could not see any obvious wounds. The wettest blood was on her chest so he started there. He tore the shirt she wore open like it was tissue paper. There, a wound on her chest was still leaking a small amount of blood. *Ok, ok,* his mind raced, *she is still alive*. He looked at her face and her blue lips spurred him along. "Stop the bleeding, I need to stop the bleeding," he spoke to himself.

He grabbed the first aid kit from the wall and tore it open, its contents spilling all over the floor of the room. "Calm down dumb ass. You can save her," he chided himself. Franticly he cleaned away the blood around the wound. It was such a tiny wound he thought. *How could that have done all this?* his mind wondered as he packed and taped the wound. *It couldn't have.* His hands froze above her as it came to him. "Oh god," he whispered. Gingerly he removed her arm from her torn shirt and rolled her onto her side to look at her back. Despair began to creep into him as he saw the much larger wound. "The son of a bitch stabbed her in the back." This was more than he could fix. "No, I will not let that bastard win," he scolded. He set to work cleaning all the blood away. Camden scrambled through the room until he found thread and needle. He was no surgeon or a tailor, but it couldn't be that hard.

It was all he could do to not scream and tear apart the room. Threading a needle was an impossible task it seemed, but he finally had it and set to sewing her back shut. He prayed that she would live as he finished. It wasn't pretty that much was sure, but it did not bleed anymore. Like her chest, he covered the wound with packs of cloth and taped over them the best he could. She looked dead to him. But he could see her chest rise and fall a tiny bit. It was out of his hands now.

One thing wasn't though. Xavier was out there somewhere. If he did this to Suki, then it was most likely him that killed McAllister too. He needed to be sure though. There were three other people on the ship too. Camden left the infirmary and glanced back at the frail woman laying there. The rage was just beginning to simmer as he made his way to the engine room.

Camden exited the engine room and suppressed the urge to empty his stomach. Xavier had been brutal to the two mechanics. War was one thing, but this was different. It was personal on some level he did not understand. You kill and move on in war. You don't take the time to make sure they suffer. He made his way through the ship. It was different now. The normal vibration of the engines seemed changed without the crew. It was as if it knew that its keepers were gone.

He stood in front of the door to the bridge. He mentally prepared himself for the worst before stepping inside. Ellenore was not at the helm. As he stepped further into the room her body came into view. There was no mistaking that death had claimed her. Camden knelt down and closed her vacant eyes; eyes that would never shine again piloting the Snow Break through the sky. He focused on a long galley knife that lay next to her. His mind flashed at the cuts and wounds he had seen on his crew. *This was the knife Xavier had used to kill my crew*. Camden picked up the knife and looked it over. He was going to use it to kill the man. It seemed appropriate. He stood up and looked out the bridge windows, and his heart started to race and skip a beat. *There is Xavier, on the deck of my ship. Sunning himself without a care. If it is the last thing I do in this world,* Camden vowed, *it will be to kill that man.*

Xavier's moment was coming to an end. There was still so much to do. He planned to start by claiming The Eternal Gateway; it was the centerpiece of his plan. It always had been. Even before that wretched child and that infernal guardian stood in his way. He hauled himself to his feet and made for the bridge. He came up short when Camden Arland stepped out on to the deck. He had a lot of blood stained to his clothes and then Xavier noticed the knife in his hand. Xavier smiled, *fate seemed to be granting all of my wishes today.*

Camden watched his crews' killer get to his feet. He tightened his grip on the knife in his hand. The thundering of his heart rushed through his ears. He felt the growl fueled by rage rise in him as he charged the man.

Xavier laughed at the big man. It was easy to sidestep at the last moment and watch him run passed. "Camden Arland has finally arrived," he taunted. "To think, that this is where it all begins."

"You're a dead man," Camden spat back and lunged.

Xavier danced away from the blade in Arland's hand. He wasn't foolish enough to fight the bigger guy straight up as he wanted. Arland was on tilt though, that gave him the advantage as he punched him hard in the ribs as he passed. "A dead man. I assure you, I am anything but," Xavier said as

247

he dodged another wild swing of the knife and landed a kick that brought Arland to one knee. He followed it with a hard kick to Arland's chin that rewarded him with a line of blood as Arland was thrown to the deck floor.

"I will make sure you suffer," Camden said spitting blood from his mouth and getting to his feet. The two of them circled each other.

"I learned long ago that it was better to let the thugs do the fighting," Xavier mocked. "It keeps me from getting filthy and besides they like it."

Camden advanced, and again Xavier dodged the knife. He did manage to slice open the scarred mans shirt. "A death of a thousand screams awaits you."

That last one was close, Xavier thought. He needed to enrage the man even further. "We've known each other for so long Arland. I am going to let you in on a secret. She dies and there is nothing you can do to save her. I wished you could have been there, the knife slid in so easy and she was too stupid to even know what was happening." The taunt had the desired effect.

Arland went berserk swinging the knife and screaming as he tried to kill Xavier.

Xavier took advantage of the situation he had created and landed blow after blow with his fists. Each time Arland over extended himself he made sure the dumb blond felt it. Punches and kicks are not going to be enough though. The knife Arland had was not going to do him any good. The idiot had fused it to his hand and would not be letting it go.

Camden couldn't believe what was going on. *How could this murderer who did nothing but sit around and smoke be beating me?* The sound of Xavier laughing at him caused his thoughts to fill with static, and he charged again. He swung the knife at the man's face, but at the last moment Xavier ducked. He felt the kick to his stomach, and his own momentum sent him airborne to land hard on the outer deck.

"Just lie there and bleed for a while," Xavier said.

Camden slowly got to his feet. He expected Xavier to be there, but the man was walking away. "Don't you turn your back on me," he screamed.

Xavier turned to look back. He enjoyed what he saw. *The breaking of Camden Arland*. But he wasn't finished yet. "I still have someone else to kill," he told him casually and left the deck of the airship.

Camden charged to the door where Xavier had disappeared. He slammed into it, but it was jammed by something behind it. Again he rammed it with his shoulder and it budged an inch. Again and again he slammed into door. He welcomed the pain in his shoulder, it helped clear his head, as the door finally opened enough for him to squeeze through. He pushed past the door. He almost tripped over whatever it was Xavier had used to block the door. His vision turned red as he saw the body of Ellenore. Xavier had used her body to block the door, and he had just beaten and smashed it to get past.

Xavier stopped for a moment and listened to the tortured screams of the ship's captain and smiled as the agony echoed throughout the ship. He tried to picture the man as he discovered the present he left for him. The thought gave him a better idea as he changed direction and headed for the engine room.

Camden's mind cycled through the various ways he was going to crush the life out of Xavier. He figured the killer was going to make his way to the infirmary where he had left Suki. At the last moment before leaving the bridge to save her, a small light lit up on the helm. Someone had opened the engine room door.

Xavier stood in the center of the engine room. The blood and bodies of the crew would make it easy for him to finally kill Arland. He had found a large heavy wrench that he now held in his hands. *A fitting weapon,* he thought. *It would do a smashing job.*

Camden could see Xavier standing in the engine room with the door open waiting for him. *There was no escape for the man now.*

Xavier watched and smiled as Arland approached the engine room. He could see the sanity on the man's face shatter as he stepped into the room of carnage.

Camden felt the wrench smash into his hand as Xavier brought it up to block the knife. He ignored the pain and shoved the scarred man away from him. He watched as Xavier swung the wrench down and club one of the mechanics bodies on the ground. The wet crunch sounded through him as if it were his own body that had been smashed.

"Come on Arland! Show me what you got!" Xavier taunted.

Camden charged with a scream. Xavier stepped to the side and brought the wrench around across his back. The blow sent Camden to the ground. As he tried to rise Xavier brought the wrench around and caught him under the ribs. The pain was nothing like he had felt before as fire stabbed through him.

Xavier swung the wrench again and delighted when it slammed into the side of Arland's head. It sent the larger man sprawling through the blood on the floor. *Revenge is so sweet*, his whole body shivered with it.

Camden's head rang and his vision spun all around. He found himself lying on his back in the engine room. Too stunned to do anything, he looked around blankly trying to shake away the disorientation. All he could see was red. The floor, walls, the faces of his crew staring at him from the void, all covered in red. Even he was covered in red. *No, it can't end this way*. He rolled over and tried to push himself up. *So much red*.

"I've waited so long for this moment," Xavier said and approached Arland from behind, bringing the wrench up to finish the man off.

Camden could hear Xavier behind him ranting about something. A flicker of blue light caught his eye. *At least it won't be red that I see last*, he thought. Now he focused on the blue light that fascinated him. Tiny little blue eyes looked at him from behind a thick plate of glass.

"The Guardian has fallen, the door will open for revenge." Xavier quoted. "My revenge!"

Camden reached up and pulled open the door to the heart of the Snow Break. The blue light from the power core saturated the room and made all the red turn to black. He heard Xavier scream like he had never heard anyone else scream. Camden propped himself up against the back wall. What he saw would haunt him for the rest of his life. The tiny playful wisp surrounded Xavier. He could see the man's flesh boil and tear as he was ripped apart one tiny piece at a time and incinerated. When it had finished, the wisp returned to the engine core and the door slammed shut.

Camden sat there for a few moments in silence. Only the hum of the airship and the vibrations comforted him. He wanted to die right there and then, or just pass out. *That hurt too much*, he thought. He staggered to his feet and left the engine room. He refused to look back to see if those tiny eyes were watching him.

Chapter 23

"Come on Camden, let me help," Kail pleaded.

"No! I am going to do this myself," Camden cut him off. He jabbed the shovel into the jungle ground. The layers of rot and fallen leaves and sticks were hard enough to get through, but the ground with the eons of roots twisting through each other made it almost impossible. That was fine with Camden. He could think of nothing better to do than dig. Dig the graves of his crew. Four cloth covered bodies lay in the shade just out of sight. Harris McAllister, his friend who had jumped at the chance to come with him. Ellenore Black, the first mate and pilot that asked if she could show him what she could do when he interviewed her instead of telling him. Montoy DeSantos and Pyron Redstone, the pair of mechanics who could have complete conversations with each other without ever saying a word. And then there was Suki Leigh. The medic who had the rare talent of healing, she now lay in the infirmary in a coma, and he had the privilege of watching her starve to death, and there was nothing he could do to help her.

Kail watched his friend take his grief and frustration out on the ground for a few moments more. "I'm going to go check on Suki… If you need anything, you know where to find me." Camden didn't bother to reply. He would check back on the big guy in a few minutes. The bandage that wrapped around his head already had blood seeping through it again. Kail made his way to where the Snow Break rested in the clearing.

Suki was another story. Kail still had a hard time believing that Xavier had done all this. True the scarred man had never been friendly, but to just suddenly snap as Camden had described him and kill everyone did not make any kind of sense to him. They had lived with each other on this ship for months now. Fought battles and survived. But to have it end like this. It didn't make sense. Camden wouldn't talk about what happened to Xavier either. All he knew was that it ended in the engine room.

Kail gently checked the bandages on Suki's back and chest. He wished he had spent more time with her instead of the others. It never even occurred to him that she might be able to teach him how to heal. He had been so caught up in learning to fight instead. The desire to try pulled at him each time he saw her, but he didn't dare to try to experiment on her. The last thing any of them needed was another dead friend to bury. Also he feared that Camden would instantly kill him right now if he even looked at her wrong.

Camden pounded the last of the grave markers into soil. His hands were blistered from all the work. The pain did little to mask the losses. He shooed Kail away when the kid tried to get him to change the bandage on his head. He sat on the ground in front of the graves and did his best to purge the images from his mind. He never noticed the sun set or the dark of night settle around him.

Vincent watched as the city lights in the distance caused the clouds to glow. They still had a few hours before arriving at Courduff. Therion would be pleased at the death of The Guardian and that they now knew where the location of The Eternal Gateway stood. "Keep us on course. You have the helm," he ordered and departed from the bridge of his ship. The corridors were empty at this hour as he made his way below decks to the officer's quarters. He wanted to check a few things before they arrived.

His darling Bastiana's welfare concerned him the most, not that he would let anyone know. Her encounter with The Guardian in the jungle of Canyamar did not return her unharmed. Volatile did not quite describe her personality, and now it might even be beyond his control.

He checked Bastiana's quarters first and did not find her there. He continued to the next logical place she would be, the holding cells. The soldiers on duty saluted him when he approached, and they opened the main security door for him. Only one of the cells was currently occupied, and an extra set of guards stood at attention at the locked cell. He did not have to ask if Bastiana was in there with their prisoner. He could tell by the looks on their face that she was. He stood in front of the cell and nodded his head. The guard opened the metal door for him.

Bastiana stood with her back to him. She had taken the time to clean up and replace her destroyed uniform. He was not pleased at her choice to shave her head bald. True half of her hair had been burned away, but he hated that she resembled Therion in any fashion. The runic tattoos that covered her body were a concern as well. He could make out some of them on the back of her neck and her left hand was covered in them.

"Bastiana, we are almost at Courduff. If you are done playing with her, she needs to be cleaned up and presentable," he said. Angela, the red headed Keratin that had caught the attention of his Bastiana in ways he could not understand, sat chained to the wall by her legs, arms, and neck. The woman had refused to talk since they had captured her. He did not care, but Therion was sure to want to know why The Guardian had brought her to this time. Therion also had ways of making her talk. Most of those ways were unpleasant.

Bastiana turned and looked at Vincent. "She is beautiful isn't she?" as she glanced back at the chained prisoner. "She won't fly for me though," she pouted.

"Motivation my dear. Motivation," Vincent replied. Bastiana exited the cell in front of him. The guards outside all stiffened. They had heard about the soldier she had killed earlier. *True it was an accident,* he mused. *But a healthy dose of fear could do them some good after their miserable performance against one woman from a race that died out an eon ago.* A performance issue he intended to remedy soon.

Vincent ordered the prisoner to be made presentable. He did not care how, but found it amusing that the crew given the dubious honor of cleaning her up, approached the task with the same fear as they would have if ordered to feed each other to a wild animal. *Discipline is severely lacking,* he decided.

Bastiana strolled down the ramp of the Colossus to the landing platform outside of Therion's map room. She was upset and missed that her hair was gone, but the chill damp air caressed her bare scalp and sent tingly chills down her spine. That she liked. The runes that crisscrossed her body infuriated her though when she looked at them. Two more crew members were already dead when she caught them talking about her. She made sure to clean up any bodies or evidence this time. Vincent had been upset when she had left a mess in the corridor. She did not like how she felt when he was angry at her.

She was the first to open the door and walk into the map room. The world spun beneath her feet as she gave it a mental spin and then stopped it over the location of The Eternal Gateway. The jungle around it was cleared from her battle with The Guardian. She smiled that she had caused all that. Vincent followed her in shortly as did several soldiers with Angela in tow. Therion was not there yet. She didn't care really, he did not like her, and she felt the same towards him, besides she could play with the map until he arrived.

She walked around the stoic pale beauty and ran her finger across the red head's shoulders and was rewarded with defiant shrug. "Is this what the world looks like to you?" she asked. "Flying through the sky looking down." She did not expect to get an answer, and she was not disappointed. "You can move the map on the floor with your mind. See," Bastiana demonstrated by spinning the map again. "Can you make it spin?" Vincent cleared his throat in a quiet warning. Therion had arrived it seemed. She continued to stare at Angela until they began to talk.

"I see you have brought back a trophy it seems. I'm sure there is a fascinating story behind it," Therion said.

"There is a lot to report, but I shall skip to the more important developments first," Vincent spoke. "This," he indicated towards Angela. "Is the Keratin that The Guardian pulled from a thousand years ago to our time."

"Fascinating,"

"The Guardian as well, is no more," he said and then turned to face her. "Bastiana had the pleasure of watching him die," he complemented. She felt a warm glow inside from the small praise he gave her in front of Therion. She looked to the bald mage at the center of the room and anger began to creep into her. Therion looked unconvinced at what Vincent had told him.

"I see that you have found the location of the legendary Eternal Gateway," Therion indicated by zooming the map in so the entire destroyed jungle in Canyamar filled the room. She did not like that he could take control of the map from her so easily. "And did your best to make sure everyone else could find it as well," he finished harshly.

Bastiana knew enough to keep her mouth shut, but shot him an angry glare none the less. She had killed The Guardian. Something he had not been able to do. She did feel some satisfaction that The Gateway had been shattered. Wait until he heard about that.

"The spy was true to his word. He delivered on what he promised," Vincent continued.

"And I trust now that his usefulness is over, you have taken care of the loose end?"

"Yes," Vincent answered.

"And the boy? I noticed he is not standing here," Therion's patience seemed to be thinning.

Kail. They did not know his whereabouts. She was sure he was in the jungle with them when she killed the old man, but there was no sign of him when they left. She was not able to use her Divination arts to try to search either. Whatever The Guardian did when he died, it played havoc with the area. It was like it was still shrouded in Enchantment.

"We are unaware of his location. The Keratin might be able to help with that." Vincent offered to appease him over the fact that they had failed to find the Falconcrest boy.

Bastiana watched as Therion inspected her prisoner. She felt pins and needles slide over her as he looked at her. The pretty Angela was hers. She captured her from the sky. She was not his to interrogate or decide anything about her.

"Filthy work breaking someone. Let your pet fetch the information out of her. I'm sure she would like that," Therion said and gave Bastiana a disgusted look as he returned to the center of the room. She threw daggers from her eyes at his back.

"Thank you," Bastiana said with a false smile. "I will start right away sir." *Anything to get out of this room,* she thought. Besides, it was a lot more enjoyable to play with Angela. She motioned for the guards to take her prisoner back to the ship.

"I think a room here would be better suited," Therion stopped her.

"Of course," she bowed and led the way out of the map room to the lower chambers. *Filthy pig,* she thought. As she left the room, she could hear Therion and Vincent continue to go over the recent events. She could care less about that. She had one desire on her mind, the woman who could fly, Angela.

Chapter 24

Kail left the stale infirmary and made his way to the galley. Suki's condition continued to remain unchanged as far as he could tell. Yawning from exhaustion he checked on her several times during the night.

Stepping into the galley he was brought up short by the sight of Camden sitting at the metal table. He had not expected the big guy to be there after the way he had been yesterday. He only hesitated a moment before fixing himself something simple, and sat down across from Camden. After several bites in silence, he decided that now was as good as ever. "We need to think about leaving soon. We can't stay here forever, and we need help for Suki."

Camden responded by filling his mouth with food instead of answering.

"Camden, I understand about the others, but this has to stop. We do nothing and Suki will die. We do something, she has a chance to live," Kail pleaded. "And what about Angela? We don't know if she is alive or dead."

Camden pushed his food away from him in disgust and just stared at him.

"What are we supposed to do? You, Angela, and Xavier spent more time with Mr. Eleazar than anyone."

"Don't ever mention that name again."

"Fine, but what was the plan, before all this," he waved to include the whole room. "What do we do?"

"We do whatever the hell we want I guess," Camden said. "This little adventure is over. I should have known from the beginning it was nothing more than a waste of time."

"So that's it? Just give up, go on with our old lives like nothing happened?"

Camden just shrugged. "Mr. Eleazar never let in on any grand plan. He only told us enough to get us to go along with his little game."

"What did he tell you?"

"Nothing really, just provided me with the means to do whatever I wanted in exchange for a few services. I always wanted to captain an airship so it wasn't that hard to say yes when a man offers you everything you want," Camden said.

He didn't know what to think. "What about the prophecy? And what about Therion? All that talk about darkness falling on the world and about us. You remember, about not letting it happen."

"I say we cut our losses and go our own way dirt farmer."

Bastiana watched as the soldiers secured Angela's wrists and ankles to the wall with chains. She wanted to do it herself but settled for watching. Once they were finished, she dismissed them. *Alone finally.* "Such pretty eyes, and hair," she said bringing her hand to feel her bare scalp. *Hair.* Rage filled her and she screamed.

Dark red hair filled her hands before her rage subsided. The Keratin held a defiant stare but one filled with tears. "I'm so sorry," cooed Bastiana. She did not want to see her new toy like this. She wanted her to be beautiful. "They want me to torture you, break your mind and get you to tell me all of your secrets," she started. "I just want to know about Kail."

Angela simply blinked.

"You see, the last time he was here," Bastiana said as she began to pace about the room. "He left without saying good bye. Why would he do that? Do you know?"

Angela knew the answer to that question, but feared what the dark mage would do if she put voice to it. She was not sure what happened to any of the others in the jungle. Only that something happened at The Gateway after she left, and then she had been captured.

"I know you can talk, so stop pretending that you can't," the mage said.

She ignored the woman.

"I said talk!"

Angela's body shook as the mage filled her with the same electricity that she used to capture her. She gasped for breath when the mage stopped the assault.

"Don't make me hurt you any more than I need to, I won't like it." the mage said. Angela noticed that the tone of the mage seemed different.

"Now, I am going to ask again," she said, this time she had come closer so she could whisper it to her. "Where is Kail?"

"I do not know"

"See, now that is much better," Bastiana said backing away enough to look into her eyes. "But not what I want to know."

Angela's scream echoed down the hallway.

Camden had left the galley and Kail was not sure where the big man had gone nor did he care. He made his way down to the infirmary to watch over Suki. She was better company than Camden right now. He brushed aside her hair as she lay there with her eyes closed. *Fine,* he decided. If Camden wasn't going to do anything to help her, then he was. He hesitated before trying to use magic on her. "Camden first," he said.

Kail turned to leave the infirmary. He would convince Camden to let him experiment healing on him before Suki. Given the man's current state of mind, he was sure he could convince him. If Angela were here, she would help hold him down.

The thought of her made his mind flash.

Angela.

He could see her; she was chained to a wall. There was someone else there as well. A hand pinched her face. A dark-skinned hand. Angela's scream filled his mind and his body with pain.

He found himself on the floor of the infirmary. He tried to shake off the dizzy feeling in his head. His whole body hurt like each inch of it had a knife point on it.

"What the hell," he said climbing to his feet. *That was Angela,* he thought, *what was all that pain, and what was going on?* Before he had fully figured it out, he was already running through the ship.

"Camden! Camden Arland!" he yelled as loud as he could for his friend. He knew one thing. *Angela was alive.*

Bastiana attached the new chain in place. It trailed from the floor to a new steel collar she had placed around Angela's neck during one of the moments she waited for the Keratin to regain consciousness. The rest of the restraints were removed. *This would be much more fun*, she smiled.

She slapped her toy across the face to wake her up. "That's better. Since you were born to fly. I decided that from now on, that is what you will do."

She watched as Angela took in her new situation.

"Fly for me my little bird." When she did not obey Bastiana lashed out, and a red welt appeared on her pale skin.

"I said fly!" she demanded. Another welt appeared. "Fine. You can sit there then."

She placed her hand on the floor of the room and concentrated. She looked at the defiant woman and started to smile. She watched as Angela began to squirm on the floor. Heat shimmers began to rise from the floor as she poured her magic into it. The challenging look the Keratin gave her sent chills down her spine. She would have her way, or cook the woman right here.

Angela could hold out no longer. The searing pain was more than she could bear. With a scream of protest she lifted herself off of the floor to escape the pain.

Kail continued to call out for Camden as he ran through the Snow Break. The engine room was empty as he took all the stairs in one leap. He slapped all of the controls that started up the engines that Pyron and Montoy had shown him. He was rewarded with the familiar loud hum and the first vibrations began to make their way through the ship.

Camden could hear Kail yelling his name as he sat on the bridge but choose to ignore the kid. He finally sat up when the light for the engine room door lit up on the console beside him. When the engines started he had had enough.

Kail ran to the bridge. He had stopped yelling for Camden after starting the engines. Rounding a corner he slammed head on with Camden coming the other way. Kail lost the battle with physics and bounced off the bigger man. "Camden, we have to go," he said and tried to pass Camden to get to the bridge.

"Go where?" Camden stopped Kail from running by him.

"She is alive Camden."

"What are you going on about?"

"Angela, Angela is alive. We have to help her," Kail told Camden.

"Alive? So what? The two of us are going to just fly in there and rescue her?" Camden spat.

"What? We have to help. She is being tortured," he pleaded.

"Give it up kid. It's over."

Kail had finally had enough. "No, you listen to me Camden Arland," he started. "You are going to help me fly this ship. You are going to find help for Suki. You are going to help me save Angela."

Camden looked down at the dirt farmer. The kid had fire in his eyes, literally. Also the kid had managed to back him up all the way to the door to the bridge in his speech. "Alright dirt farmer. Let's go save the girl," he said with a half smile. *If I am lucky, I might get killed in the attempt. That was better than sitting here,* he decided. *And if lady luck saw fit, I might just get to see that fire unleashed.*

Kail smiled back. There was something funny about the way Camden had finally come around, but he didn't care. The two of them set upon the bridge and got the ship ready to fly.

The jungle shook in protest as the giant fans lifted the Snow Break into the sky. Four graves stood vigilant watch as the dust settled around them. One of their own, the woman born a thousand years ago, needed help.

Chapter 25

Flying the airship with just the two of them was a lot harder than they expected. They had a long way to go to catch up to the Colossus. Camden had made Kail go to the engine room to see what he could do to get every last bit of speed out of her. Of course he could have done it, but it still bothered him to be in there, and he really didn't want to right now. Not by himself at least.

Kail returned to the bridge. "I think that's the best were going to get," he told Camden.

"We're doing good. Can you hear and feel that?" he asked. "It's almost like the ship knows."

"Yeah, I can feel it."

"Anymore flashes on Angela?"

"No, and I've tried. I'm positive it was Bastiana I saw there as well," Kail continued. "We need to get to Aldervale as fast as we can. We can take Suki there to my aunt and uncle's place."

"Sounds good to me," Camden agreed. It was easier now to forget the pain that ate at his soul for leaving his crew behind. Kail was easy to follow. He did not want the responsibility. "What is your plan after that?"

"I've been thinking about that. We can't just fly to Courduff, they will see us coming, and we wouldn't stand a chance," Kail said. "Suki first. There is time for me to come up with a plan."

Camden just nodded.

Kail excused himself from the bridge and headed down to the weapons deck. He would have preferred to practice outside on the outer deck. But the speed at which they were moving, it made that choice prohibitive. It was also starting to get cooler the further north they moved.

He started simply enough. Creating a ball of fire and pushing it out of the ship. It went out almost instantly. He tried it again, this time he managed to get the ball of fire to stay lit for a nice little pace from the ship before it went out. "This isn't going to cut it," he scolded himself.

Camden manned the helm of the Snow Break. The flashes of light coming from the side of the ship caught his attention. *Dirt farmer was going to have to do better,* he thought. He had seen Kail do some scary things in their time together with magic. But he seemed to only let loose when things were bad. Things were bad right now, and a few fireballs being blown out by the wind we're not going to be enough to save Angela.

Kail became frustrated with himself after failing to make any progress. He remembered what Angela had told him about practicing something a thousand times, and then practicing a thousand times again until it became second nature. He sighed; he didn't have time to practice a thousand times, and then a thousand more. His thoughts wandered to Suki, lying in the infirmary, then to Angela. He recalled the pain he felt when he saw her in his vision. He remembered when he sparred with Mr. Eleazar, and he had thought that they were being hurt.

Camden was suddenly taken aback by the bright stream of magic that burst from the side of the ship. The bar of energy streamed off to the horizon and continued out of sight. "What the hell..." A second bolt of energy followed shortly after the first. Again Camden watched stunned. "That's not a little farting ball." The display continued for over an hour. Sometimes they were bars of bright energy, other times they were balls of fire that exploded at different ranges from the ship. What really sent shivers down his back was when several dozen smaller beams of energy leapt from the ship at various angles and shot into the night only to explode once they had flown out of sight. "Well, we just might give them their money's worth with this hair brained idea."

The magic that Kail was throwing out of the side of the Snow Break quit almost an hour ago. Camden had not seen or heard from Kail. He suspected that the kid was passed out down on the weapons deck. "Now what is he doing?" Camden said to himself as he spotted Kail walking onto the outer deck of the ship. "Kid is going to get himself killed."

Kail braced himself against the wind as he made his way onto the outer deck of the ship. The night air combined with the wind was a lot colder than he had expected. He was tired from practicing earlier, but he had an idea and if it worked it would save them a lot of time.

Concentrating he pictured a barrier at the front of the airship. *Off of the ship,* he decided, *out in front.* A light green shimmer began to appear in front of the Snow Break. *Now add more*, he thought. He felt the magic bend to his will.

Camden watched in silence from the bridge as the air in front of them started to glow. It reminded him of the auroras that he had seen once. He wasn't sure what the dirt farmer was trying to do. Suddenly, a bright blue flash caused him to look away for a moment. When he looked back, large defined circular glyphs rotated in front of the ship. A smaller one glowed at Kail's feet on the floor of the deck. The entire airship started to buck as the glyphs spun faster and faster. Camden could only watch and hope that Kail did not destroy them or worse get them killed.

The rotating glyphs grew bright and then suddenly stopped. It was like they had locked into place and they glowed a soft white color. The turbulence that the Snow

Break had been experiencing suddenly stopped. Even the normal vibrations the ship experienced from the engines had lessened. "This is new," he said to himself. What did catch his attention was the airspeed indicator. His eyes grew wider as he watched the needle move around its housing until it stopped. The needle was pegged out at the maximum that was listed.

Kail wasn't sure if he had done it correctly, but it felt right to him. The wind around him had settled to a slight breeze, and he could see the magic anchored to the glyph at his feet. Gently he lessoned the magic he was pouring into the spell. The spell held once he had stopped channeling into it. He could see that it would hold for quite a while on its own or if he decided to dispel it.

He returned to the bridge to find Camden there giving him a scary eye look. "What?" he asked.

"What are you trying to do?"

"I had an idea. I think it will help get us to Aldervale faster," he explained.

Camden pointed at the indicator. "We will be there in a couple of hours, maybe sooner seeing how it doesn't go any higher."

Kail looked to where Camden pointed. "It worked! We will get the help she needs," he said with a smile.

They had to land the Snow Break quite a ways from the Kelly farm as to not alert anyone to their presence. Kail had to dispel the enchantment early as well when other airships came into view on the horizon. They flew as low as they could to avoid silhouetting the ship and getting spotted.

The two of them carried Suki through the dark as the farm came into view. "Set her down here," Kail instructed. "We need to make sure everything is going to be ok. I heard what happened last time with Ari and Angela."

Camden nodded and stayed with her.

Kail ran low the last distance to the farm house. The lights inside were off, and he could not tell if his aunt and uncle were home. The back door was locked, but he knew where a spare key was and retrieved it from the bottom of a potted flower. He slipped inside and made it about ten feet to the stairs when he ducked and something smashed into the wall just above his head. "Whoa! Stop, stop," he called out. "It's me Kail!"

"Kail?" his uncle's voice said out of the dark.

Light at the top of the stairs came on as Jessica, his aunt, turned on a lamp. "Kail! It is you," she cried.

Kail was suddenly crushed by his uncle's arms as he hugged him. "Where have you been?" he demanded. He did not get a chance to answer when a second pair of arms from his aunt joined.

"We have been so worried. When they took you months ago you were dying," she cried.

"I know, I know, I'm sorry, I will explain everything, but I'm not alone and we need help," Kail said breaking free from the reunion. He returned to where Camden and Suki were to relay the news and help bring in Suki. "Where can we put her?"

His aunt scrambled and cleared off a place for them to set her.

"What is going on?" his uncle demanded. "The last time you were here, it was you lying there. What have you gotten yourself mixed up in?"

Kail explained the best he could, and Camden did what he could to fill in the holes.

"Think Royce, what do you remember about your brother? My father," Kail said. "You can't because the truth is; you did not have a brother."

"That's absurd. Of course I had a brother. His name is…" Royce's voice trailed off as the enchantment started to distract him.

"Royce, stick with me here. Remember what I told you." Kail said as he shook his uncle.

"But that means, that means we're not your real family," his aunt said.

"No, that's not true, you are my family," he countered. He was not prepared to have this argument with them. "We need you to take care of Suki."

"You're leaving again aren't you," his aunt said.

Kail looked at his aunt and uncle before answering. "You remember Angela? The red headed woman that saved me from the lake with Ari's help," he said. "They captured her when this happened," he indicated to Suki. "I have to go save her."

"There will be questions. What do you want us to say?" his uncle asked.

"Just tell them the truth. Someone dropped her off in the night," he replied. "Tell them who ever did it, stole some horses too. We will leave them tied at the old tavern so you can get them in the morning."

"And then what? Live the rest of your life on the run? They will come after you," his uncle argued.

Kail looked at Camden. "We know. But she saved my life, all of our lives and we can't just let her be tortured and killed."

"You have changed so much, Kail," his aunt told him.

"You don't know the half of it. I will tell you everything, but we have to leave now," Kail insisted and hugged his aunt and uncle as they headed out the door.

"We need to be careful," Camden said as the first rays of the morning began to rise in Aldervale. "This place has changed since we were last here."

Kail nodded in agreement. He could hardly recognize the place after being away for a few months. "This should be a good place to leave the horses," he said.

The streets of Aldervale were empty at this early hour. Only a few early risers would be awake. The town had grown considerably with the garrison and completion of the airstrip. They quickly ducked into the darkness when a door slammed open ahead of them and several drunken soldiers from Courduff stumbled out into the street. Kail and Camden just eyed each other.

"Why are we sneaking around? They can't possibly know about us," Kail whispered.

"Haven't you figured it out yet?   Aldervale is occupied, and they don't even know it. There could be some sort of curfew enforced. They could hold us, and when your aunt and uncle show up with Suki, we will be the prime suspects," Camden whispered back.

"Ok, we need to get to the train station, and find one that is going to Courduff," Kail said.

They waited until the soldiers had left to make their way to the old train station. The cover of darkness was quickly fading when they arrived. Again there were soldiers, this time they were on duty and not returning from a long night of drinking.

"We need a distraction, or just take out those two over there and sneak on board," Camden suggested.

"No, look. People are starting to arrive. This time we're just going to buy a pair of tickets and board like anyone else," Kail whispered as he held Camden back from doing something rash. "Come on this is going to work. Besides do you want to fight soldiers the whole way? We sneak on as stowaways, and they find us, that will be just more we will have to fight."

"If you're wrong, this whole rescue ends right here."

Kail nodded, stepped out of the shadows, and walked down to where a line began to form in front of the ticket counter. Camden followed closely behind him. "Settle down Camden, you're acting weird," he chided him.

It was his turn to approach the next open ticket counter. "Two for the next train to Courduff please," he said with a smile. The ticket master behind the counter smiled back and prepared to hand over the tickets, but hesitated when she saw Camden. Kail glanced at the big man behind him, and he looked like someone who was guilty of punching babies. He quickly explained, "First time on a train, you wouldn't happen to have any extra scented bags for, umm, accidents would you?"

The ticket master handed over the tickets along with a small stack of bags. "Boarding begins in thirty minutes, it's open seating so feel free to find a spot away from others if you need to," she said eyeing Camden's condition.

Chapter 26

Angela slowly woke up on the cold floor of the cell. Eyeing the room, she was alone, alone at least for now. She got up and was still chained to the floor by her neck. She took the free moment to get rid of the stiffness and find all of the bruises and sore spots from earlier. She did not know how she was going to get out of this mess. But she knew that if even the slightest opportunity arises, she would take it, even if it meant certain death. She was not going to spend the rest of her days as that mage's plaything. She froze at the sound of the door opening and heard several people enter.

"Awake so early. Me too, I spent all night dreaming about you," Bastiana cooed.

Angela turned to see that the dark-skinned mage along with four other soldiers had entered the cell with her. The soldiers left a bowl of water and food at the edge of her reach. She had no desire to eat or drink anything that they brought her, but she also knew it was important to keep up her strength. She highly doubted it was poisoned because the mage could simply kill her on purpose or accidently during one of her outbursts. She reached out to take the food when the mage lashed out at her hands.

"No, you can't use your hands darling. Eat only using your mouth," Bastiana teased by inching the bowls closer with her foot.

Angela would have nothing of it. She would not eat off the floor out of a bowl like a dog. "You eat it," she said defiantly, kicking the bowls at Bastiana. She knew it would get her punished, but she did not care at this point.

Bastiana's mouth hung open as her clothes were covered in food. Her laughter was the last thing Angela expected as she watched the mage pick bits of food from her face. "Now there is nothing for you to eat," Bastiana said.

Angela only had a moments warning when she saw the change in her eyes. Laces of electricity arched across her entire body. Bastiana did not have to demand her to fly. The force of the punishment alone lifted her into the air. Her muscles convulsed and contracted out of her control. She held back as long as she could, but finally she screamed.

Kail and Camden had found an unoccupied private cabin on the train to Courduff. Camden was explaining to him where the tower was that Mr. Eleazar had them watch. Camden figured that was the best chance where they were holding Angela. "Unless you can divine her location better."

"She is in Courduff, of that much I am positive. Where though I don't know," Kail said. "None of my visions have been intentional. More like my mind just wanders in a day dream, or I get slammed when I think about someone."

"Something to work on I guess," Camden said between mouthfuls of food that his aunt had given them before they left.

"Yeah, I guess," he agreed. "You hear that? Sounds like someone is screaming."

Kail found himself in a room. He could see Tiana in front of him. She was wild looking with no hair and strange markings on parts of her skin. She did not seem to be able to see him standing there. The screaming he heard was much louder now. He turned to see Angela chained and floating in the air as miniature lightning raced over her body. "No," he called out at the sight of Angela's torture. Spinning to face Tiana, "Stop this!" he yelled.

Bastiana stopped channeling her power across Angela and took a step back as if someone had slapped her. The screams from Angela turned to moans as she fell to the floor.

"Everything all right ma'am?" one of the soldiers in the room asked.

"Everyone out," she ordered looking around the room. "I said out. Now!" she yelled when they were too slow to react.

"I know you are there Kail Falconcrest," Bastiana said as she continued to search the room.

Angela watched from the floor as the mage circled around. Her eyes looked up when Bastiana spoke Kail's name. *Kail is here,* she thought. She suppressed the sudden rise of hope that grew in her. *If he was coming, then so would the others. Foolish of them,* she thought, but it made her smile as it was exactly the type of thing they would attempt to do.

Bastiana searched the room. She knew Kail was there, she could feel him, like before, but this time it was harder. Like catching him in the corner of her eye but when she looked, he was not there. She focused her mind inward and began to divine the room. "There you are," she whispered as he came into view. "You're stronger now," she complemented him. "You're coming to rescue her aren't you," she said tilting her head curiously.

She watched as he looked at her pet lying on the ground. Mixed emotions swirled inside of her: jealousy, anger, and anticipation. "You feel for her!" then it dawned on her. "This is not the first time you have seen here is it!" she demanded.

Kail nodded his head. "I saw you before."

"She is mine! Come, Therion and Vincent will be delighted to know that you are on your way here," she taunted. "I will make sure she gets to watch as Therion tears your powers from your soul."

Kail found himself back in the private cabin with the steady noise of the train. "They know we are coming," he told Camden.

"I figured as much when you spaced out there."

Chapter 27

Kail and Camden departed the train after it arrived in Courduff. Now that the enemy knew they were coming, they needed a plan. The waitress of the café brought two coffees to their table as they looked out the window at the entrance to Therion's tower.

"Ironic, to think that we sat here, in this same spot waiting on you," Camden said. "You were right about not taking the Snow Break here. We would never have gotten within ten miles of this city," he finished referencing the sky that was filled with airships.

"She is up there Camden. They all are," Kail stated.

"What do you want to do dirt farmer?"

"We go in the front door," he nodded across the street. "Do the unexpected, it will take them by surprise."

"Mr. Eleazar would be proud," Camden said with a big smile. "I like it."

Camden walked to Kail's left as they approached the front entrance of the tower. Two guards eyed them as they approached and shifted to block the door. He glanced at

Camden and nodded. Camden smashed one guard with a fist made of stone and his limp body rolled down the steps. The guard in front of him flew backwards when he lifted his hand and pushed. The guard's eyes rolled up into his skull when it made contact with the building and like his partner, Kail sent him rolling down the steps. A few people started to run away from the scene, not wanting to get involved. Camden held the door open.

The lobby of the tower was grand to say the least. It was constructed long before they were born when it served as the central hub of power for the Mage Council. Bureaucrats, politicians and military leaders with their aids moved about the lobby not paying any attention to them. Camden shrugged at him as they made their way over to an elevator and waited. A small group of people walked over and joined them at the door. A commander and a group of officers were busy going over reports when one of them pointed out that Camden's hands were made of stone.

"What is going on here," the commander demanded. "Who are you people?"

Kail looked around as they were drawing a lot of attention. "So much for surprise," and he hit the commander in the nose as hard as he could. Camden dropped two more of the officers before the shouting and chaos began.

"No going back now," Camden stated as several guards started to rush towards them.

"We need to make this quick before they have a chance to organize."

Camden tore back into the lobby area; the incoming guards didn't stand a chance as he took them down. It did not matter if they came at him separately or in groups. Kail had his own problems as several guards started to gather near him and prepare to take him down. "I offer you this one chance to leave. I am here to get my friend," he told the guards.

The guards looked at each other and they attacked. Power flowed through Kail and the attacking guards seemed to slow down. It was not hard to sidestep the first wild swing, step under the second guard's attack and disarm the third. Using the sword he had taken from the third, he parried and attacked the others. One of the guards swung his sword and he watched as it passed by less than an inch from his face without flinching. He let a ring of power explode from him that washed over all three of the guards and sent them slamming against the walls and floor.

Kail ran to join Camden in the wider lobby away from the elevators. One of the guards who had just seen him blast the last three away with magic did not seem scared. The guard drew his sword. He pulled a second shorter knife which he held in a reverse grip as he squared off with him. Kail took a couple of swings at the guard and studied how he reacted. The guard was experienced and easily blocked his probing attacks before coming at him. One sword against an opponent with two was not the smartest choice he had ever made, but his time sparring against Angela had taught him a few things. Kail swatted away the guard's sword and spun his own around to catch the shorter knife before the man had a chance to stab him with it. The guard caught off position had no defense for what he did next. Placing his free hand on the man's chest he released a blast of magic. The bright flash and small explosion sent the guard through the air with a burning hole in his chest. The man's body crashed through a table. A pair of interns who had been hiding under it fled screaming towards the exit.

Camden stepped quickly between two guards. Before they had a chance to react Camden leapt and kicked one guard in the side of the head. It wasn't meant to be a powerful kick, but strong enough that it let him change his angle of attack on the other guard. He came down on the guard with such force that his augmented hand smashed into his head. He was dead before his body hit the ground. Rounding on the first man he had kicked, Camden followed it up with a second kick to the head that the man did not get up from.

Kail and Camden found themselves surrounded by defeated tower guards. Most were dead, but some still managed to moan or twitch on the ground. "Let's go," Kail said and they went to stand by the elevators again.

"They will probably shut them down once they know we are on them," Camden stated.

"I don't doubt it, but it's the fastest way, even if they do stop them," the elevator door opened and the pair stepped inside. Kail looked at all the buttons and the control lever.

"You have to be kidding me," Camden said when he saw that Kail did not know how to use the elevator.

"What? I've never been on one before," Kail defended himself as he watched Camden push a button and then lock in the choice with the lever.

News of the intruders in the lobby had reached Vincent. There could only be one logical answer as to whom would be so foolish to attack them here. He stopped by his quarters before heading off to the tower. Two Keratin war blades had been wrapped in cloth. He had intended to add them to his collection of trophies, but he now had other plans for them. *One last twist of the knife so to speak.* The meeting when they had returned from Canyamar with Therion had not gone well once the destruction of The Eternal Gateway had come to light. Therion had basically demoted him to what amounted to watching over livestock.

He dismissed the guards outside of the cell where Bastiana had been trying to get the Keratin to talk. He unwrapped the war blades and set them on a nearby table before entering the room.

"Bastiana dear, it is time to leave. Therion has given us our orders."

"No," she told him. "I am going to stay and play. Kail is coming. I saw him earlier. He wants to take her away from me."

"Whatever you wish dear. The Colossus will be near," he said, glancing at the prisoner chained to the floor. "I will not wait forever, be sure you choose before then," he finished and left the room to walk back to his airship.

Kail and Camden stood in silence as the elevator took them higher into the tower. As predicted, the power to the lift was cut, and it shuddered to a stop.

"Guess that's the end of the ride," Camden said.

Kail watched as the big guy placed his hands on the doors to the elevator. His hands changed into the same steel as the doors as he bound them. Camden ducked at the last second as a sword stabbed through the small opening in the elevator door.

"Your turn," he indicated to Kail.

Kail quickly stepped in front of the gap and placed both of his hands in front of him as he had practiced on the Snow Break. He filled the hallway outside of the elevator with a hot bar of magical energy before stepping away for Camden to continue.

Camden pulled open the elevator doors wide enough for them to exit. Six smoking remains of either soldiers or guards, Camden couldn't tell which, lay in the hallway. Small bits of fire sputtered where tables and other items in the hallway had been. On the far side a burned hole showed to the outside. "That made it easy," Camden commented.

"I didn't know how many there would be," Kail said stepping out of the elevator after him. "We need to find some stairs."

Chapter 28

"Here, this floor looks familiar," Kail said stopping Camden from continuing. "I remember this from last time."

Kail and Camden made their way down the hallway. "I don't like this. It feels wrong, too easy," Kail observed.

"It's a government building, not a military base," Camden speculated. "I doubt they posted guards much past the lobby."

Two round metallic balls bounced down the hall towards them. Kail managed to shield them before the clockwork bombs ticked and exploded around them. The deadly shrapnel was not able to penetrate the protection, but the force of the blasts themselves did a good job of knocking them to the floor.

Dust and smoke filled the hallway as Kail got to his feet. "You ok?" he asked Camden as the big man got off the floor coughing.

"Yeah."

"There can't be too many of them. We need to hurry though, or we will never be able to get out of here," he said.

Kail and Camden split up to find Angela faster in the cover of the last attack. He ran down a new hallway and opened doors but found nothing but offices and overnight rooms. He could hear the faint noises of a confrontation as he assumed Camden had found whoever it was that threw the bombs. He tried not to think about the impossible task that escaping was going to be. It seemed like they had been looking forever. The personnel that fled when they started to fight would be telling authorities what they had seen, and they would be sending people after them.

Camden wiped the sweat off his face. Four soldiers lay still on the ground around him. He took a peek around the corner to the next hallway. It was empty of people. Without the kid with him, if he got caught in the open by someone with more of those infernal bombs, he would be in serious trouble. Quietly checking the rooms he did not find anything, that was until he came across a curious sight. A small decorative table stood against the wall in the hallway. Two Keratin war blades sat there as if casually discarded by a child. *This is a surely a trap,* his brain yelled at him as he picked up and inspected each blade. They were defiantly the pair that belonged to Angela.

He could hear someone moving in the room opposite from the war blades. "Kail!" Camden yelled as loud as he could as the door opened to reveal the dark-skinned Bastiana.

"Too big," she said and with a wave of her hand sent Camden flying down the hall away from the door.

Kail heard Camden call his name. Abandoning his search he ran down a side hallway. He skidded to a halt when he saw that Camden was down at the far end of the hallway as Tiana stepped out of a room and advanced on him.

"Tiana!" he yelled. That got her attention as she turned to the call of her name.

"Kail," she smiled. "You're here."

He stood his ground defensively as she approached him but was taken off guard when she wrapped her arms around him in a big hug. "I've missed you so much. Why have you been with these nasty people?"

Kail untangled himself from her hug. "Tiana, I am not here for you, you know that. Where is Angela?"

"What do you mean silly?"

Kail moved down the hallway to the room where Tiana had been. Tiana followed behind slowly. Angela was there in the room. A chain led from the floor to a steel collar attached to her neck. It was the same as he had seen on the train ride to Courduff. "Angela!" he called out.

Angela looked up and saw him standing outside the room calling her name. "Kail?"

Bastiana had been so happy when she saw Kail in the hallway. It made her feel good when he called out her name.

But not now. *He should have been there for her.* Her mind was slowly coming to grips that he was there for the other girl, but she did not want to believe it. Instead he had dismissed and forgotten her and went onto the Keratin instead. *Everything they had done together meant nothing to him.* Rage began to smolder deep inside her. "What are you doing?" she demanded.

"What?" he replied like some stupid puppy.

What. That was his answer, what. "I'll show you what!" she screamed. Tendrils of magic began to gather around her outstretched hand as a blinding blue bar of magical energy shot down the hall at him.

Kail watched as Tiana went from friend to foe in a matter of seconds. He didn't understand how or why, only that she was completely crazy. It was enough warning for him to open himself to his magic and wrap it around him as she let loose with her own. Blocking a full on attack from a mage was completely different than shielding from a more conventional weapon like a blade, or the bombs in the hallway.

He changed the angle of the shield, and her attack bent away from him to cut across the hallway vaporizing what it touched before flashing out of existence. He sent quick successive bursts of magic back down the hallway at her that exploded where she stood.

Bastiana casually walked down the hallway towards him as the dust settled from his counter attack. "Disappointing," she said. She held out her palm and an orb of red energy formed. She tossed it into the air where it split into three smaller versions that shot towards him.

He sidestepped the first, and it buzzed by him to detonate in the hallway. The other two found their mark, and he was battered by the concussive force into the wall. He retaliated by sending a bar of magic back at her. He watched as she simply backhanded his attack away and continued to march towards him. The open hallway was not a good place to be battling her.

Camden got to his feet and could see Kail and Bastiana battling it out in the hallway. Around the corner he saw several more soldiers headed their way to stop them. "Kail! We've got company!" he yelled. Camden moved to block the hallway and stand against the new comers. The war blades felt nice and balanced in his hands when he started to swing at the soldiers.

Bastiana swatted away Kail's attack. *He was weak, but his defensive magic was not*. He had blocked, deflected, or simply absorbed all of her attacks. She was going to have to try something different. Focusing inward she teleported herself down the hall and reformed behind him.

Kail focused his mind as everything began to slow down for him. He saw Tiana turn into magical energy and flash by him. She would have had him easily if he had not manipulated time. He caught her hand as she raised it to blast him. Her attack shot into the floor and followed up the wall to the ceiling as he pivoted her arm away from him. The look of surprise on her face said it all when he back handed her.

Bastiana stumbled backwards a few steps and held her hand to her face where Kail had hit her. "You hit me," she said softly. "I can't believe you would hit me!" she screamed. Power arched from her hands to lash out at the walls around her. She advanced on Kail intending to make him pay. Her first wild attempts to hit him missed. When he brought his arm around to block her, the power sent him stumbling. Their powers fought against each other each time they came to blows.

Bastiana's emotional swings played havoc with her magic. She locked eyes with Kail and said nothing, a shiver of hatred raced up her spine. *He had made his choice when he had chosen the Keratin over me.* There was no way she was going to let him walk away from here with her. She pulled in the opposite direction, and they fell back to the floor with her landing on top of him. She opened herself to more of her magic using the hate and betrayal she felt to drive her. Her magic began to overpower Kail, and she could see it begin to arch across his body. An evil grin emerged as she delighted in the sight of it. *So similar to how I trained the flying woman,* she thought. It was fitting that he would die in same fashion.

This is no good, Kail thought. Tiana had several times the magic experience that he had. It was all he could do to keep her from burning him to a crisp. He tried to swing his leg up or do anything to try and dislodge her, but he wasn't able to as her magic began to assault his body. Her wicked grin scared him into digging deeper into his magical heritage for survival. He could see it in her eyes that there was nothing there but the sole desire to kill him. As she leaned in closer to gloat he slammed his forehead into hers and heard a rewarding crunch of bone. That moment of distraction was all he needed. He slipped his hand free from hers and placed it between them and focused his magic there against her stomach. His magic shot from his hand. The force of it took her off his chest and tossed her backward down the hall. He struggled to sit up, and he could see her smoking body lying on the floor.

"Hurry it up farm boy, or we are not getting out of this mess," he heard Camden yell from out of sight.

He got to his feet and staggered into the room where Angela had been held prisoner. She stood as close to the entrance of the room as her chain would let her. He could tell that she was desperate to be free so she could help them fight and escape. "Angela," was all he said as he reached her. The shift in her eyes from his to the doorway was the only warning he got. Something slammed into his shoulder; it had a lot of magic behind it as it threw him across the room to smash into the far wall.

Tiana stood there, the front of her dress shirt had a smoking hole burned into it. He could see runic tattoos across her flesh. In her hand was a staff with matching runes that she had used to bat him across the room.

"You will never have her!" she screamed and charged.

"You are not worthy of him," a voice said that brought her charge to a halt.

Tiana turned to face where the voice had come. "What did you say?"

"I said you are not worthy. You are a spoiled child, nothing more," Angela taunted.

"You know nothing!" she screamed and advanced on Angela instead.

Kail tried to get up. Angela was no match for the enraged Tiana. Being chained to the floor did not increase her odds at all, but she stood there as the mage approached with loops of slack chain in her hand.

Angela tensed to spring when Bastiana came into range. She shot forward swinging the loose chain with her right hand and caught the loops around the end of the rune staff. At the same time Bastiana brought the staff around to crush Angela. Arcs of magical power raced around the chain when it came in contact with the staff. Angela was already whipping her hips around to launch a side kick. At the same time Bastiana unleashed her own augmented attack. Neither Angela nor Bastiana finished their strike as the charged chain exploded around the staff sending shrapnel and liquefied steel drops around the room. Both women were tossed like leaves in a wind storm.

Kail covered his face and felt the burning bite from the remains of the chain pepper his body. Angela lay on the far side of the room. She was moving, but not much as she was still recovering from the explosion. Tiana on the other hand was already getting to her feet. He sprinted towards her and wrapped his arms around her. He channeled his magic at her and let out a yell as the magic built up. A second scream joined his as Tiana fought against what he was doing. Kail lifted her off the ground as air around them began to distort from the battling magic. Kail felt like he was ready to explode when time started to slow down and come to a stop.

"Never!" he heard Tiana scream as she dissolved into blue energy.

Kail felt dizzy and dropped to his knees after Tiana was defeated. He looked across the room and saw Angela slowly picking herself up off the floor looking back at him. Silent tears started to roll down her cheek. *They had done it,* he thought. He forced himself to get up and walk over to her. He knelt down to pick her up, once again amazed at how deceptively light she was in his arms.

"I pictured this moment differently," he said wincing. "Much more painful than I had planned."

Angela smiled and leaned up to kiss him on the cheek.

Camden came charging into the room with a war blade in each hand. "No time for romantics kid, we need to get out of here now."

Chapter 29

Kail set Angela down when they approached the stairwell of the tower. She insisted that she could move on her own.

"I think these are yours," Camden said to her and handed her the Keratin war blades.

"You two are fools for coming here," she scolded.

"You're welcome," Camden took it as a compliment.

The three of them started down the stairs with Camden in the lead. Kail hoped that they did not run into too much trouble, but he doubted it. There was no way they would let them just walk out the front door. Camden stopped short looking over the edge to the stairwell below.

"We have company," Camden said jerking his head back as an arrow shot past them. "Ideas, dirt farmer?"

"Back to the top, there is an airship mooring there, we might get lucky, but it's a better place than here," Kail said and started to head back up the stairs. The sound of pursuit echoed behind them in the stairwell.

"If we're not lucky, at least you have a way out Red," Camden shouted as they ran through the tower.

"What good is losing two for the escape of one?" Angela countered.

"Come on," Kail called as he bolted down a side hallway that lead to a short flight of stairs to the map room.

Therion lifted his head as the three companions burst into the map room. He watched as they ran across the room to the glass doors that lead to the balcony. *A curious thing they did not seem to notice me,* he thought. So caught up in their minor victory of a rescue, they have no comprehension that the spider of the web has yet to make an appearance.

"Damn it," the brute said stopping at the far door. "So much for that idea."

"Angela might be able to fly and steal one," Kail Falconcrest said.

"Now that sounds like an excellent idea," Therion's voice echoed across the map room. Their utter surprise at his presence was clearly written on their faces. With a wave of his hand he lashed out with a magical attack. Kail was sent sprawling across the map room floor away from his friends. Camden and Angela were both hurled through the glass wall and sent tumbling out onto the balcony.

Therion walked over to where Kail was slowly getting to his feet. "Your friends will be of no help to you." He reached down and lifted Kail to his feet by his throat. "So much like your father. I can see your mother's resemblance as well." A release of power sent Kail through the air to slam hard onto the floor and slide away.

"We tried it Vincent's way the first time, but I grew tired." Therion lashed out and Kail was sent rolling. "And then you had the audacity to spirit yourself away." He raised his hand and Kail was pulled across the floor by tendrils of magical energy. Therion watched as the boy's body was lifted into the air and presented in front of him. "That focusing stone was the last of its kind."

He walked around the floating captive to gaze at the other two sprawled out on the balcony. "The Keratin I can understand. A curiosity from a thousand years ago. Beautiful as she is exotic. I can see why she so captivates Vincent's pet. The brute is nothing. He would have been bound or brought to heel properly." Therion circled back to face Kail. "So pathetic with what little magic he can manipulate."

Kail's joints screamed with pain as he was held in the air by Therion's spell. He tried to summon up any magic of his own, but was unable. He could only listen as the man circled him and ranted. "What do you want," he managed to get out through clenched teeth.

"What do I want?" Therion mused. "That is a list that has grown quite long. You I understand, but these," he indicated to Camden and Angela. "Serve no purpose. Why would The Guardian choose them?"

"Maybe because they care," he forced out.

Therion dismissed the comment. "I assure you Falconcrest. Nothing you can say or do will allow you to sway my emotions into an irrational fit as you did earlier with Bastiana. I find it odd that you, nothing more than a farm hand your whole life would suddenly become so noble. Fighting for a cause you know nothing about because a stranger told you to."

Kail struggled against the magical bonds. He needed to find a way to free himself or else Therion would eventually tire of his debate and kill him while he was helpless. Then he would kill Camden and Angela. He began to feel how Therion had tied the enchantment that held him. It was the same as he had done on the Snow Break earlier. All he had to do was unravel it and he would be free. He needed to keep Therion distracted. "Hair. When did you lose your hair?" he asked.

The question brought Therion up short. "Not the direction a man, who is about to die, I would have expected to take the conversation."

"I saw you. At The Eternal Gateway." Kail continued picking away at the magic that held him. "Mr. Eleazar wanted to know why it showed us the past."

He could see the thoughts churn through Therion's head when he spoke about The Gateway. "Interesting, and what else did you see?"

"You were fighting The Guardian," Kail answered. Almost there, he could feel the enchantment weakening.

"And did I win?" Therion sounded amused.

"I don't know." There he had it. One more tug and he would be free. "The Gateway closed."

"Let me tell you a secret," Therion said coming closer. "I haven't lost my hair," he finished with a smile.

In that moment, Kail pulled the enchantment loose. He slowed time as the magic rushed through him. He could see the surprise on Therion's face when he saw that he was free. Before he had even hit the ground, he shot a bar of blue energy towards Therion's chest. Therion dodged to the side and brought his own magical attack back around. Kail channeled his magic to meet it. The magical energies came together with such impact that it threw them both off balance and away from each other. Kail was on his feet first sending several small fireballs in Therion's direction. Therion rolled away as they detonated on the floor leaving burn marks where he had just been.

Kail wasn't going to give Therion time to recover if he could help it. He hurled another hot bar of magic at the mage. It wasn't a clean hit, Therion had blocked most of it with a shielding barrier and the rest went wide. Kail did not see the attack Therion sent his way, but he felt it slam into his chest and sent him flying backwards. He felt his back slam into the wall half a heart beat before the back of his head did.

Kail wished that he had been knocked out with that attack. The pain caused his head to spin and he felt sick to his stomach as he dropped to the floor. It was all he could do to keep from crying out as he saw Therion get to his feet. Only survival instinct managed to save him in time as Therion's hand shot up and pointed his spread fingers at him and let loose a torrent of magic in his direction.

Therion stepped forward, still channeling his attack. Kail needed to get back on the offensive because he could not last much longer through this assault. He managed to send a slice of his own magic back and saw it catch Therion across the shins. The hit stopped the assault on him for a moment. Kail was instantly on his feet and sprinted towards the mage using his magic to accelerate him faster than normal. He saw Therion channel a ruby swipe of magic towards him. He spun at the last moment and rolled under the attack as he kicked at the same time. Therion cried out as his kick caught him somewhere around the knee.

A clenched fist came swinging around that caught him hard in the side of the head. Spots of light danced in his vision as the blow sent him to the floor.

"Oh, it has been such a long time since anyone has had the ability to fight me," Therion said walking with a slight limp.

This was it, Kail thought as he tried to blink away the buzzing in his head.

Angela had crawled over to where Camden still lay unconscious. She had seen some of the fight between Therion and Kail. She knew that he would not last much longer against the final ruler of the Mage Council. Kail had saved her once before when she had flown too far from the

Snow Break and then again from the torment of the insane mage. The last thing she was going to do was let him die alone if she could help it.

She shook the big man until he started to come around. "Camden," she said and shook him harder. "Get up, we need to help Kail."

Camden slowly came around and suddenly jerked alert at his surroundings. He could see Kail laid out in the other room and Therion limping towards him.

Kail had lost whatever Therion was ranting about. He really didn't care either what the mage had been saying. He caught movement out of the corner of his eye and rolled his head over to get a better look. He saw the dark red hair of Angela near Camden as the big guy suddenly sat. What he saw next did not make any sense. An airship shot past the balcony so close that it nearly blew his friends from it.

Therion halted the killing blow when the vessel shot past the tower. It was not one of his ships that shot past either. His eyes slowly got wider as a second ship lifted and came into view from under the balcony. As soon as its weapons deck cleared the balcony, it fired.

Camden watched stunned as his ship, the Snow Break, rose up from behind them like a savior. He grabbed for Angela and pulled her down a moment before it opened fire above their heads. The cannon blast left him deaf in both ears and everything became a muted buzz.

Kail used the last bit of energy he had to wrap himself with a magical barrier when he saw the Snow Break fire into the map room. The explosion that filled the back of the room washed over him and the force of it sent him tumbling towards the balcony. His magic protected him from the worst of the blast, but it was enough for him to finally succumb to the pain and exhaustion.

Camden was already running to where Kail lay before he even realized it. He hoped the dirt farmer was still alive. He did not see the mage Therion anywhere in the smoke and haze and he wasn't going to spend a second to look for him either. He grabbed Kail and tossed him over his shoulder and made for the balcony where Angela was already securing his ship's ramp for them to board. He did not believe in a higher power, but right now he was thanking everyone that he knew as he ran up into the cargo area of his ship.

He met with Angela and set Kail down on the floor. "Come on kid, hang in there" he said. He could see Kail's eyes begin to flutter open and come into focus.

When he opened his eyes he could see Angela and Camden hovering over him. Their look of relief said it all.

"Help me up," Kail said. With their help he sat up and took a look at his surroundings. "I thought I was seeing things. Why is the ship here?"

"That is a good question," Camden said. "You feeling up to finding out?"

Chapter 30

Vincent walked out on to the deck of the Colossus. The pillar of smoke from the old Mage Council tower rose in the distance. Two airships were darting away. He had no doubt that the Falconcrest boy was responsible, but the boy was not his immediate concern. There would be plenty of time to give chase. Bastiana was his priority. The young girl sat out on the deck with her hands wrapped around and her face buried in her knees. He could hear her small whimpering and the tremor of her shoulders as she cried. He had waited before welcoming her back to allow time for her emotions to settle down. No one understood her better than he did.

"Bastiana my dear. It is time."

"I want them to pay," she said looking up at him with wet cheeks.

"We will make them all pay."

Kail and Camden stormed onto the bridge of the Snow Break. The impossibility of it all still had them reeling. "Bailon? Lieutenant Wilhelm Bailon?" Kail questioned coming up short when he saw who was commanding the helm.

The Lieutenant turned with a serious face. "We're not quite out of this yet, Kail."

"Who was that on the cannon?" Camden demanded.

"That would be Suki," Will answered.

"She is ok?!" Kail and Camden both asked over each other.

"For the most part yes," Will said as he pulled the Snow Break around to fall in beneath the other airship. "I saw her when your aunt and uncle showed up with her at the inn. We were able to patch her up a little better when she came around. I assume you know that she can heal. I insisted that she stay and rest, but when she started to tell her story then I knew," he explained.

"Knew what?" Kail asked.

"That the story your family was telling was a lie. Don't be hard on them, they did not want to give you up, and I respect that. But when I told them that little Ms. Leigh there was my sister they caved."

Camden gave Kail a furtive glance. "Suki is your sister?"

"Half sister to be exact," Will corrected. "Once both sides of the story were out, it all made much more sense."

"What are you talking about?" Camden demanded. Kail felt just as confused.

"That ship we are following, The Odyssey. Her owners, the Masterson's, have been in Aldervale for a week. Nice enough people, but went on about how they were waiting for someone to arrive. Apparently they were waiting for my sister. The weirdest part was when she did show up, the innkeeper's daughter, the little mousy one, Ari backed up their story about a man with blue eyes, a strange accent, and a pocket watch."

Kail and Camden looked at each other and both mouthed the words *Mr. Eleazar.*

"Long story short they convinced me to return to your farm. Once there we commandeered your ship and followed the Masterson's. It was the craziest thing I've ever been talked into, but when we arrived at Courduff and there you all were on the top of the tower I was convinced."

Angela came onto the bridge with Suki right behind her. "Suki has been filling me in with a story as crazy as you two are."

Suki smiled and gave both of them a hug. "Thank you Camden. Thank both of you for saving me."

"I think you returned the favor in spades Suki," Camden returned her affection.

Several hours later both the Snow Break and the Odyssey were on the ground outside of the Kelly Farm.

Lieutenant Bailon was already on his horse and ready to leave for Aldervale. "I told them that I was accompanying the Kelly's back to their home to be sure everything was ok. Just remember, I was here for none of this," he finished pointing at them. "I bid you all well," and he spurred the horse in the direction of the town.

The Masterson's were the next to depart on their ship. Kail was intrigued by the couple. They obviously knew a lot more than they were inclined to share, but he could not complain about their timely rescue. They parted with smiles and the words that they were sure to meet again.

Kail said goodbye to his family once more. This time it was under much better health they joked. It was not safe for them to stay in Aldervale. Courduff and Therion's presence there would put them all in danger. He waved to them from the outer deck of the Snow Break as Camden and Suki lifted the ship into the air.

Angela came to stand next to him and they watched the farm fade into the distance. "What are we going to do now?" she asked leaning her head on his shoulder.

"I don't know. I think Mr. Eleazar had been busy," he said remembering the Masterson's. "But I think this is only the beginning."

CPSIA information can be obtained at www.ICGtesting.com
Printed in the USA
LVOW030331230911

247516LV00005BA/15/P

9 780983 681823